Hallmark
PUBLISHING

✳ *Christmas* ✳
IN EVERGREEN:
Tidings of Joy

Based on the Hallmark Channel Original Movie

NANCY NAIGLE
USA TODAY BESTSELLING AUTHOR

Chapter One

W AY UP NORTH, NESTLED IN the heart of Vermont, there's a little town called Evergreen. Some say it's so far north that on a clear day you might be able to catch a glimpse of Santa's workshop in the North Pole.

Evergreen beckons tourists from all over. Many come just to see its famous magical snow globe that sits in a place of honor in the Chris Kringle Kitchen, owned by Joe and Carol Shaw. People come from far and wide to give that snow globe a good shake and make their wish, then drop a letter to Santa in the big red mailbox in the middle of town square. If they're lucky, they might even catch a glimpse of the old red truck, decorated with garland and bows, delivering Christmas trees to the locals.

A winter wonderland of sorts, most any winter day you'll find Evergreenians skating on the pond as the Evergreen Express, appropriately numbered 1225, brings new visitors from the city to town for a proper dose of holiday cheer.

Only five passenger cars long, the train rides sold out well in advance. And although most of the people boarding the Evergreen Express in New York City this morning were visitors eager to see if all the hype about the small town was for real, Ben Baxter was just trying to get back home.

The bright red Evergreen Express stood out against the other trains in the station.

Ben grasped the shiny brass rail and climbed aboard. As he walked down the aisle to choose a seat, he noticed a pretty blonde in a burgundy sweater taking pictures of the inside of the train so enthusiastically he could almost hear *"Deck the Halls"* playing inside her head.

Thoroughly enjoying herself, she leaned back to get a better angle of one of the wreaths. She clicked off another picture with her smartphone, probably posting it to social media right now. *Tap-taptap-tap-tap.* She looked pleased with herself, and her smile pleased him.

Fresh garland draped the interior of the train from end-to-end above the windows, leaving the scent of fresh pine hanging in the air. Twinkling white lights reflected in the red-and-gold Christmas ornaments. Festive. Beautiful. Every detail had been addressed, right down to a cheery red velvet bow at the end of each aisle of seats in the historic train. The Evergreen Express could probably even tempt Scrooge out of a bad day.

The train, over one hundred years old, had

been restored to its original glory about fifteen years ago. Ben could still remember the weekly news reports about the project. The tongue and groove two-inch wooden plank flooring had been refinished by hand, one board at a time. It'd been a painstaking process, but even today the pine that lined the walls gleamed as if it were brand new. The original bench seats, positioned face-to-face from the days when the train had traveled in both directions on the same track, had been re-installed, but thankfully they'd chosen to update them to add a little cushion for the guests.

For a split second, Ben considered sitting across from the perky blonde, but instead he turned and took a seat a couple of rows forward, facing the direction the train would be running.

Ben glanced across the station at the other trains lined up waiting for passengers. He wondered why someone hadn't taken the initiative to attempt some type of nod to the holiday on any of the other trains. Not a wreath or a bow to be found. They seemed quite bah humbug sitting there, void of colorful decorations.

He considered himself lucky to be aboard the 1225 to Evergreen this morning. He slid a hardcover novel from his briefcase, put on his glasses, and settled in to pass the time on the nearly six-hour ride.

"All Aboard for Evergreen, Vermont!" The announcement boomed with authority across the platform.

And with that, the train whistle blew, and the train lurched and pulled away from Penn Station right on time, headed for the snowy hills of Vermont. Through the city and suburbs there wasn't much to see, but the closer they got to Vermont, the prettier it became.

Ben lowered his book for a moment, letting his imagination wander while enjoying the view. The clickety-clack of the wheels on the tracks changed pitch as they entered the tunnel. In the darkness, the festive lights seemed even more magical.

On the other side, tall pine trees laden with snow seemed to curtsey along both sides of the tracks, a welcome sign of what was ahead. High above the valley, the train chugged over the bridge that crossed the river. Against the icy backdrop, puffs of smoke guaranteed the folks tucked away inside the homes dotting the hillside were warm and safe.

Black cows dotted the bright white fields as the snow continued to fall.

Imagining how hard it must've been for the pioneers working their family farms in this valley during the harsh winters, he was thankful for the modern amenities of today.

Then again, maybe he was more suited to that time. He still couldn't believe how he'd blown that job interview today. Sure, they'd been impressed by his portfolio of work, but they were right. None of his bylines were current. He'd have to prove he still had those journalistic chops if he was going to work in that field again.

He wrestled with the idea of resuming his career at the paper. He'd loved that job, but he loved helping Nan at the library too. And the kids were great. Helping them bond with books, find power in story, it was so satisfying.

Maybe the universe was trying to tell him something.

A photo click from a phone, followed by another and another came from behind him. He was so tempted to turn around to see her again. Self-conscious, he smoothed the back of his hair.

He heard a moan, followed by a grumbling from behind him. "Really? Low battery already?"

The age of technology, he thought with a laugh. He didn't even have to turn around to see who the complainer was. It was a wonder her phone had lasted even this long. She'd been taking pictures the whole ride.

He'd never personally understood why people were so obsessed with taking pictures from their phones. While concentrating on that tiny screen to capture the moment, they missed it real-time and life-sized altogether. Sometimes it was better to just open your eyes and be present. Those memories were the ones that'd last.

A moment later the woman walked down the aisle with her phone charger in hand. Just as he was about to let her know there wasn't a charging station, the train jostled, throwing her off balance right into him.

Ben dropped his book and reached out to break her fall.

"Oh, wow!" She juggled a magazine, her phone and that phone charger, practically plugging it right into his nose.

"Are you okay?" He steadied her by the elbow. Taking off his horn-rimmed glasses, he set down his book and smiled.

She waggled the phone charger in the air. "I'm so sorry. I was just...uh...looking for a plug." The train pitched again.

"Sit," Ben said, motioning to the seat across the aisle from him. "Good luck with that. This train's been running since way before anyone needed to plug anything in."

"Oh, yeah. I guess that makes sense." She studied her surroundings. "This is authentic? It's incredible. Look at all the decorations. It's the Polar Express combined with the Hogwarts Express and ended up the—"

"Evergreen Express. We do a pretty good job of spreading Christmas cheer."

"We?" Excitement danced in her eyes. "Are you from Evergreen?"

Ben couldn't hide his pride. "Born and raised."

"Wow. I've been reading a lot about it. It's been getting a lot of press." She whipped out her copy of *Vermont Traveler* magazine, opening it to a dog-eared page, which she began quoting from. "With a world-renowned Christmas Eve festival, Evergreen, Vermont remains a must-see destination for anyone seeking the magic of the Christmas season."

"All true." His playful side-glance, he offered no apology. Those things were what he loved about his hometown. "People have a hard time believing it, because at first glance, the articles make us all seem like we're wandering around under the spell of some kind of peppermint gas leak and we've lost our Christmas-addled minds."

"Like this?" Katie held up the magazine article. "You have five Christmas tree farms. Not tree lots, but farms?"

"The town is in a pine forest," he explained. "They grow almost as fast as we sell 'em."

"A local coffee shop called the Kringle Kitchen?"

"Yes, but it's not named after Santa Claus."

"Or is it?" She narrowed her eyes.

"No, really, it was originally a bakery that made kringle—"

She raised her hand to stop him mid-sentence. Her voice went up an octave as she went on. "—that *also* has a snow globe said to grant Christmas wishes." She rested the magazine in her lap, then shifted her gaze toward him, eyes narrowed with a crooked smile.

Even he was amused. "Okay. Yes. But. The snow globe draws a lot of tourism. And it—" He paused, unable to hold back a laugh. "I get how it sounds, but that snow globe also sort of works?"

She rolled her eyes. "It grants your wishes?"

"I mean...kind of? Not mine specifically, but people I know. Yeah."

She didn't look the least bit convinced, but she didn't seem offended either, and the bottom line was no matter how cynical she seemed at the moment, she was headed for Evergreen. In a few hours, she'd see and experience it all firsthand.

She pressed her lips together, and he could tell before she even opened her mouth that she was getting ready to come out with a zinger. *Here it comes.*

And she didn't let him down.

Sitting straighter in her seat, she cocked her head and grinned. "So does the town just magically disappear after Christmas, only to reappear at the first snowfall?"

"Like Brigadoon?" Did she really think the musical reference joke would be lost on him?

She responded with a resounding, "Yes!"

"No. They're the next town over." He remained deadpan, enjoying the challenging banter. "We're rivals because we do fewer musical numbers than they do. But our football team is much better."

"Good to know." She pushed her hair back over her shoulder.

Not only pretty, but smart. He was glad to have landed the joke. Not everyone got his sense of humor. "I'm Ben. Baxter." He extended his hand across the aisle.

"Katie Connell." She shook his hand. "Nice to meet you."

"You too." He could feel his cheeks reddening, but he couldn't help it. Her playfulness was fresh, enjoyable. "So, what brings you to Evergreen?"

"Some time off. I had a busy year. I published a novel a few years ago, and since then, I've been working on some freelance assignments, and I've been doing a lot of reading. When I heard about your town, I thought I should come check it out."

She's a writer too. They might actually have something in common, or she could be one of those journalists looking to make fun of Evergreen. It happened all the time. Curious which camp she fell into, he leaned back in his seat. "So, are you also going to be writing about this place?"

"No, you know, I plan on experiencing Evergreen," she answered almost too fast. "At some point I have to start working on my second novel, and I think it might be good for me to take a break. Clear my head. Change of scenery."

As the train rounded the next corner, he pointed out the window. "You're in luck, because scenery is something we do have."

A flicker of excitement played on her lips as she twisted in her seat to get a better view. She lifted her phone, momentarily forgetting she was nearly out of battery. "Oh, wow." She gasped, taking in the view of the evergreens against the mountainside's glistening snow.

"We're almost there." Watching her take it all in was like seeing it again for the first time himself.

"I can't wait." Katie hugged her things to her chest. "It's gorgeous."

The Evergreen Express slowed, its whistle blowing as they inched along to a stop at the train station in Evergreen, Vermont. The depot was small, but with two chimneys puffing white smoke, even with the rooftop covered in snow, it seemed cozy and inviting. Decorated with the same garland and wreaths as the inside of the train, it appeared as if Santa's elves had been hard at work here too.

The train conductor announced, "Last stop, Evergreen, Vermont."

Ben let Katie leave ahead of him.

She rolled her bright blue suitcase to the door, and the porter carried it down the stairs. "Thank you." She grabbed one of the brass rails to steady herself down the steps, extending the handle on her bag. Stepping out of the way, she seemed a little lost as she merged into the throng of locals bundled in their winter coats, hats and scarves, anxiously searching for familiar faces.

Ben exited right behind her with his briefcase, glad to see her slow down and turn back with a smile.

"Wow, would you look at this?" She lifted her

hands out as if she might catch the tiny snow-flakes floating to the ground around them.

He couldn't help but enjoy her excitement. "Can I offer you a ride to town?"

"Oh, thanks, but everything I've read mentions it's a beautiful walk."

"It *is* a nice walk." Surprisingly, he was disappointed she refused. He thought their interaction had been fun. Even borderline flirty. *Wishful thinking.* Shaking it off, he pointed behind him. "So, the center of town is pretty much that way, and that's where all the action takes place."

"All right."

"Okay. See ya." He turned to go to his car, feeling the teensiest bit of rejection.

"I guess, uh..." He turned just in time to see her do a playful jazz hands as she said, "Merry Christmas!"

Everyone around her responded with a rousing *"Merry Christmas!"* that practically knocked her off her feet.

"Oh! My goodness," Katie said. "Wow."

"Welcome to Evergreen," he said. If that surprised her, she would be in for a real eye-opener after spending a little time here.

She was still juggling her big leather tote bag for her ringing phone.

It'd be nice to run into her again. Maybe even over hot chocolate and a fresh kringle at the Kringle Kitchen one morning.

In a small town like Evergreen, it wasn't a

stretch to think they would bump into each other.

And with that, a mental list of ways to improve those odds ticked off in his mind.

Chapter Two

KATIE FINALLY SILENCED HER PHONE as she pulled it out from the depths of her tote bag. With her feet firmly planted in the middle of this overwhelmingly Christmassy town, she answered it. "Hey, Mom."

"Katie, hi. You made it okay?" Mom had probably been tracking the train and knew the second it had arrived here in Evergreen. That woman had a plan for her plans.

"I did. I just got off the train. I'm walking toward town this very minute, in fact." In the distance, a jazzy version of "Rudolph the Red-Nosed Reindeer" played. She sucked in a deep breath of fresh winter air.

"Is it wonderful?"

"The air smells like pine. There's a light snow falling. Not gonna lie, I already feel pretty relaxed. Everything okay there?" She grabbed the handle on her suitcase, her other hand holding her phone to her ear while rolling her bag down Main Street.

Mom gave her a play-by-play of her day so far, which wasn't all that uncommon. They talked all the time, but Katie didn't need all of Mom's aggravations seeping into her vacation-time, and it was already stealing her Christmassy vibe.

Katie half-listened to her mom as she looked at the cute shops and a tiny white church. Potted spruce trees decorated with shiny red bows flanked the tall double-doors. It couldn't hold more than fifty people from the looks of it. The sharp pitch of the roofline over the entrance rose to a point that seemed twice as tall as the church was wide. A bell tower showed off a trio of shiny bells that hung in random positions as if they'd stopped ringing mid-swing.

Who knew places like this—so much like the ones in the miniature Christmas villages that were so popular—actually existed? She made a mental note to visit the church while in town.

"I won't say it's been my best day," her mom went on. "Now, I need to find a writer to help fill the cover story for our next issue."

The cover story? "Oh, dear. Wait." She made herself concentrate on the phone call. "I thought you brought on that sports reporter who was going to do the story about inventing a new extreme sport—"

"I did. He broke both of his hands in the process."

"Yikes. That is extreme. So you're—"

"I'm wondering if you want to throw your hat

in the ring." Mom's words had come across more as a challenge than an opportunity. Mom had made it no secret that she'd much prefer Katie come work at the magazine rather than chase the dream of being a novelist, even though her debut novel had received wonderful reviews. She knew Mom meant well, but it still stung.

"You want me to write a cover story?"

"Well?"

Katie couldn't lie. The cover held appeal, but she needed to focus on what she really wanted, and that was to write her second novel. If she didn't get down to work soon, she might lose the readers she'd already won over with the first book. It was hard to build a good following in such a flooded market. If she was going to succeed in making a living as a novelist, she needed to write.

In the heavy sigh that came across the line, Katie could picture the stress lines pulling across Mom's forehead. It was so hard for Katie to not pitch in to help her, but she'd been putting her own dream aside for so long now.

"I'm really in a jam here."

"But I just started a vacation." With her phone still to her ear, she turned around. There were so many cute shops nestled together on this road. She was itching to explore and enjoy this place.

"I know, but this story possibly could lead to something bigger for you. We're going to be hiring additional full-time staff in the new year, and this would help move you to the front of the line."

Katie pressed her lips together. She didn't want to be short with her mother, but this wasn't how she wanted to spend her vacation. She hadn't even had a chance to unpack her suitcase yet. And working at the magazine was not her end goal. "Mom. We've been over this. Freelancing is one thing, but working at the magazine is not on my radar. I'm excited to write my second novel. I'm here to get in writer mode again."

"I know, but you're really good at this too, and it's still writing. And it'd be nice to get you something, you know, stable."

Katie bit her tongue. There it was. "I know. Mom…" She sighed. *Just say no!* "I don't think I can right now." *Almost a no.*

"Take a few hours and see if an idea occurs to you, and—"

Katie waited, but there was nothing but silence from the other end of the phone. "Mom? Hello, Mom? Are you there?" She jabbed at the buttons on her phone. Her battery was completely exhausted. She grimaced as she rummaged through her bag for her charger, but couldn't put her hands on it.

She'd last had her charger in her hand when she'd been talking to that guy; she must've dropped it. She looked back toward the train depot.

At that moment, the long blast from a horn

sounded. She could hear the train chugging along the track, working to pick up speed to get visitors back to the city.

She lifted her tote back onto her shoulder and rolled her suitcase down the sidewalk in search of a store to buy a new phone charger.

On Main Street, a man and woman hurried past her, carrying a life-size Santa figurine under their arms like a canoe. This part of town was teeming with people. Every storefront and window was in the process of being decorated—absolutely humming with holiday activity. There was almost a sizzle in the air; she felt a rush of the contagious joy while neighbors helped neighbors turn Main Street into a real-life Santa Claus lane.

Maybe she'd read one too many articles about this place. But even that thought couldn't keep her from humming a chorus or two of "Here Comes Santa Claus" as she continued her search for a convenience store.

Townspeople wrapped wide ribbons around the black street lamps, garlands swagged the front of every store, and she'd never seen so many different decorations. Nutcrackers, candy canes, bells, and bows were going up all over town.

A man fastened a big red mailbox for letters to Santa to a platform smack dab in the middle of Town Square. *How fun!* Katie was dazzled by the buzz of activity and beautiful decorations.

Lots of traditional red, green, and gold, but there were jewel tones and pastels too. A kaleidoscope of colors all balanced by the white snow and evergreens covering so much of the area.

She burst into a grin when she recognized the diner mentioned in the magazine article, the Chris Kringle Kitchen. Ben, the guy from the train, had said it wasn't named after Santa, but there was Santa right there on the sign. She raised her chin. All of this had to be a clever marketing advantage.

A man and woman stood in front of the Kringle Kitchen, decorating a live Christmas tree. They took turns hanging colorful ornaments on the limbs. A younger woman joined them with a bright red box in tow, and all three of them huddled around it. Katie wondered what was inside. Maybe it was an early Christmas present.

Katie passed the Letters to Santa mailbox. A father stood nearby as his children dropped brightly colored envelopes into the slot on top. Katie giggled as she read the hand-painted board below the post box. "Drop your letters, *or thank-you cards*, to Santa here." *Wish I'd thought of that. Santa deserves a few thank-yous. I might write him one myself.*

She glanced back across the way toward the Chris Kringle Kitchen again, and her breath caught. The younger woman stood there, shaking a snow globe. That snow globe had to be the one she'd read about in the magazine earlier. Was this all just one big, scripted event?

Tempted to run across the street to check out

the snow globe, she kept herself in check. First order of business: find a phone charger. She forged ahead, walking past a fake snowman that had to be ten feet tall. She raised her hand in the air to give him a friendly high-five. She used to love building snowmen when she was a little girl. Like her Christmas trees, she loved her snowmen as tall as she could possibly make them. With Dad's help, she'd made some real jumbos in the past. So tall that Dad would have to lift her high in the air so she could reach high enough to put the hat and scarf in place.

Each of the shops down Main Street had its own unique look. Some tall and squared off, others more Victorian in style with pretty gingerbread or scrolling trim. The varied styles and colors added to the charm. She must've lifted her phone a dozen times to capture some of this scenery to use as part of her research before remembering the battery was dead. She was dying to take pictures.

Her long white scarf swished nearly to her knees. She lifted one end and wrapped it around her neck to chase the nip in the air.

In the middle of the square, a huge banner was being hoisted across the road. A curly-haired woman stood on the sidewalk in heels and a pretty wool coat, directing two men in an effort to get a giant banner hung straight.

Unfortunately, it hung precariously at an angle.

The woman stood with her head cocked, motioning up and then back down without much luck.

Katie walked over to see if maybe they could help her find a charger. As she stood there, she too found herself leaning—first to the left, then the right—as the men hoisted and lowered the banner.

"Up," the woman said. "Wait. Right there."

The banner hung almost straight for a brief moment before it slipped again.

"No. Back down a smidge."

Finally, Katie and the woman looked at each other and shrugged. "Easier said than done?"

"Apparently."

Chapter Three

MICHELLE TOOK A GIANT STEP back, eyeing the 50th ANNUAL EVERGREEN CHRISTMAS FESTIVAL banner across Main Street.

"Why is it so hard to get this banner straight?" She watched Ezra cling to the lines while perched on the top of the ladder.

Ezra hunched his shoulders as he hung tight to keep the banner from dropping all the way back down to the street. "I don't know."

Joe Shaw, owner of the Chris Kringle Kitchen across the street, steadied the ladder for Ezra.

There had to be a better way. Maybe one of those little bubble levels in the middle of it to help them see where they needed to adjust? It sloped so drastically at the moment that a bird couldn't even perch on it without ending up across the street. That image gave her a brief stress relief.

"Let's try it again," Michelle said. "Up, like, two inches, Ezra."

"Excuse me. Hi."

Michelle spun around. A blonde wearing a deep green coat with a suitcase in tow stood right next to her.

"Sorry to interrupt," she said. "My name is Katie. I just got to town, and I need to find a place I could find a phone charger, and—" She pointed to the sign. "Wow. Fifty years, huh?"

Michelle glanced back up at the banner, wishing it was straight. "Yeah. It's the highlight of the holiday."

"Looks like a lot of work," she remarked.

"That the town has been able to pull it off for that long without missing a single year feels like a miracle sometimes." Michelle hadn't meant to say that out loud. "But no matter what happens, from pipes flooding our venue to snow drifts so high we couldn't get across town, we always manage to make it wonderful."

From up on the ladder, Ezra called down, still pulling on the rope with two hands in a failing attempt to keep the banner taut. "Crooked?"

Michelle gave him the stink-eye. "You say that every year, Ezra."

"And every year, I'm right."

"Which is the most frustrating part." Katie and Michelle both looked at the sign, then tilted their heads. "Yes, the sign *is* crooked."

Ezra shifted his footing. "Well, if Thomas was here, he'd have it up and straight in no time."

Probably true. Thomas was a foot taller and probably outweighed Ezra by more than fifty pounds easy. He'd have no trouble managing that sign. Michelle felt a little pang of loneliness. "I know. Don't remind me. They're racing to close that logging camp before that storm rolls in. I pray he doesn't get stuck there for Christmas."

Ezra studied the sky. A dense bank of clouds hung dark and heavy above.

"So." She took a breath. There was no sense worrying about what she had no control over...although she did it all the time. "For now, we'll just keep with tradition and let the banner hang on a weird angle." She lifted her hands to the side, seesawing them and giving in to a laugh.

Ezra lifted his chin, training his gaze on Michelle. "Ever since you've become mayor, you've somehow relaxed. How is that possible?"

Michelle knew it wasn't becoming mayor that had changed her life. It was Thomas. Him and his son, David. The past year of dating Thomas and the two of them in her life had been a life-changer. She'd gained a new perspective on things, and life sure felt good in this mode. "I guess happiness will do that."

Joe and Ezra smiled at each other, then Ezra turned and came down the ladder.

"You know, Ezra," Joe said as he spotted him down to the ground, "it's not going to be the same around here without you."

Ezra turned to Joe and Katie. "Well, it helps that the new mayor won by a landslide."

Michelle paced her response. "Stop. Saying.

Landslide." He'd said it so many times that it was already getting old.

Katie leaned in. "Wow!"

Ezra propped his arm on the ladder casually with a told-you-so look on his face.

Michelle rolled her eyes. "I was the only one running."

"Well, that's just because nobody wants to run against the woman who had the best plans on how to run a town," Joe spoke matter-of-factly.

Michelle's face flushed. She'd put in a lot of work to pull that town project together. She wanted to earn the trust of the town, and even running unopposed, it had been important to her. She was honored to have been voted as the first woman mayor of Evergreen. Michelle turned to Katie. "She also had the previous mayor's strong endorsement," she said about herself. "That helped. Thank you, Ezra."

"You earned it," he said. "I'm leaving Evergreen in ever-capable hands."

"Thanks." Michelle cocked her head with a playful smile, then pointed her finger toward the banner again. "Okay, you two. Can we take this side up a little bit?"

Ezra started back up the ladder.

Michelle turned to Katie. "I'm sorry. You needed something."

"Oh, I just need a phone charger. But congratulations, Madame Mayor."

"You can call me Michelle. It's fine." She glanced up at the banner, and then back to Katie. "You said your name was—"

"I'm Katie. Nice to meet you."

"Hi, Katie. Phone charger. Right. You'll want to visit Daisy's Country Store. It's located just across the square. They sell everything: phone chargers, wool socks, souvenirs, you name it."

Ezra shouted down from atop the ladder again. "Is it straight enough now?"

Michelle and Katie both tilted their heads up. In unison, they both leaned to one side, slightly off-kilter.

"Well, if it was too perfect," Michelle said with a shrug, "it wouldn't be charming."

Both Joe and Ezra stared at her, puzzled.

"Don't give me that look," Michelle teased. "It's good enough. Ezra, aren't you supposed to be packing?"

"No, but I do have an Evergreen Historical Society meeting at the Kringle." He climbed to the ground. "Got to run. Nice meeting you, Katie. Enjoy your visit."

Katie waved and gave him a thumbs up.

"Thanks, Ezra." Michelle turned back to Katie. "Oh, Katie. The store is right there." She pointed to the flowered sign just up the road. "Lisa can help you with that phone charger."

"Thank you so much." Katie headed for Daisy's Country Store with her luggage still in tow.

Michelle was glad tourists were already starting to arrive. The recent magazine article had the Evergreen Express booked to capacity every day, and she'd seen more day-guests than they usually had too.

The first year Michelle had helped with the Christmas Festival had been back in high school. It'd been part of the Future Business Leaders Association project she'd started, and the school still continued filling that role. Every year, she'd been on the Festival committee, but the last two years she'd chaired the whole thing. Even with having to move locations, they'd been able to have a successful event. But this was her first year as mayor, and she wanted more than anything for it to be the most special Christmas Festival so far.

Across the square, Hannah Tinker stood on the sidewalk out in front of Daisy's Country Store, snuggling a chunky brown-and-white chihuahua mix in her arms. Lisa, the store owner, played with the soft ears of an adorable tricolor Shih Tzu-Yorkie mix.

Allie—or Dr. Shaw, as many people called the local veterinarian—went through a long list of instructions on the care and feeding of the two homeless dogs Lisa had graciously agreed to take care of while Allie went zipping off for the holidays to meet up with her fiancé, Ryan, and his daughter, Zoe.

"A Shorkie? Now, that's just fun to say." Hannah lifted the dog she was holding into the air. "And what are you?" The dog's tongue lolled out of his mouth.

"No designer breed for that guy." Allie pushed her brown hair over her shoulder.

"Well, he's cute anyway. You don't even need a cute breed name." Hannah didn't mind fighting for the little guy's honor.

"I hate to leave these guys." Allie seemed a bit frantic about leaving the two senior dogs behind at Christmas before matching them with forever families. "I thought for sure I'd have them adopted by now, but it's just harder finding homes for older dogs." She reached out and patted the dog's head. "This is a terrible time for me to leave."

"No," Hannah said. "It's not." This wasn't the first time Hannah had seen her childhood friend stress out about leaving Evergreen. The last time, it'd all worked quite perfectly with her meeting Ryan and falling in love, but Allie seemed to have not considered that leaving town might mean another stroke of good luck.

"Fine. You're right. Okay, Lisa, this is Brutus that Hannah's holding." Allie pulled a blue pill bottle from her ski jacket. "Now. Brutus has a touch of arthritis in his front paws, but I brought you a prescription. I'm putting it in your pocket."

Lisa lifted her arm, giving Allie access to the pocket. "The directions are on the bottle."

"Got it." Lisa flashed an over-serious look, followed by a playful glance toward Hannah and Brutus.

"Now this guy..." Allie rubbed the head of the bluish-gray dog snuggled in Lisa's arms. "Max here has a clean bill of health, but he needs a *lot* of snuggles."

Lisa rocked her new furry friend in her arms. "Well, I have lots of cuddles to give you, Max." She kissed the top of the old dog's head, then shifted her attention to Brutus. "I hope both you guys are going to love being with me for the holidays. I've never been a foster mom."

Allie pressed her hands to her hips. "But if you need anything while I'm away, Dr. Myer's in—"

"Montpelier," Hannah and Lisa sang out.

"We know." Lisa said Allie's next sentence for her. "He's looking after all of your patients."

Hannah added, "And if any cows go into labor, he'll handle that too." It was an inside joke from the year all the flights had gotten cancelled. That was when Allie had met Ryan, and they'd both been snowed in, so it hadn't been all that bad. Allie had ended up with a new boyfriend, and Henry had ended up with Allie in town to bring his new calf into the world.

"Ha ha." Allie's lips pulled into a fake pout. "Well? I can't help it if I worry."

"We got this," Hannah and Lisa assured the woman. "Don't you worry one bit."

"And you also have my cell phone number," Allie reminded them.

"We do."

Hannah was almost sorry to have to release Brutus to Lisa, but she had pugs at home waiting on her attention, so she handed the leash to Lisa, who took it in her free hand.

"And when Kevin's back from the logging camp with Thomas, I'll have help." Lisa whispered into Max's ear, "You're going to love Kevin. He's very nice."

"Are you sure you don't mind?" Allie wrung her hands together. "I know this is asking a lot."

"You have got to stop worrying," Lisa said. "You're going to Paris. Come on. Ryan's going to be so excited to see you there when he accepts that award. It's the trip of a lifetime."

Joy twinkled in Allie's eyes. "I know, but I've just never been out of Evergreen for Christmas and it will to be tough to say goodbye to my parents later and—"

"And you always talk about how there's a big world out there and you want to go see it," Hannah reminded her. "Seriously, Allie. Go be with Ryan and Zoey. I've got the truck keys." She jingled the keys to the famous red truck from her fingertips. "And I'll feed your fish."

"That's right," Lisa said. "And I've got these

two little boys. We're going to have so much fun." She dropped a kiss on the dog's nose.

Hannah stage-whispered to Allie. "You know she's going to end up adopting them."

"Oh, yeah. A thousand percent." The three of them laughed and although they were giving Allie a hard time, Hannah knew she'd miss her while she was gone.

"Excuse me, I'm sorry to interrupt."

All three of them spun around to see a blonde with a suitcase at her side, trying to get into the store, which they'd unknowingly blocked in their dog detail huddle.

"Not at all." Allie stepped aside.

"Hi." Lisa set Max down on the ground and handed his leash off to Allie. "Sorry. Welcome to Daisy's Country Store."

"Thanks. Are you Daisy?"

"Ah, no, that's a whole other story. Daisy was the original owner. I'm Lisa. I own the place now. I kept the name to keep the spirit of what she built here."

"That's really nice." She placed a hand against her heart. "I'm actually just looking for a phone charger—"

"Just a charger?" Lisa asked. "You sure? Nothing else? Because we are just filled with all kinds of cute little quaint things made right here in Evergreen. Wonderful gift ideas, too."

Hannah held back a laugh as the stranger

flashed her a look, locking eyes as if to say, *Is she always like this?*

"See those hats over there? They're really great. Right? Hannah, right here, made those hats!"

"I did." Still holding Brutus, Hannah offered up a finger wave.

"For real, those hats are so cute," Katie said, "but I, um—"

Lisa pouted. "But like everyone else who comes into a general store, you're looking for something practical and general."

"Lisa, don't worry." Hannah reassured her. "Tourist season is just around the corner."

"She's right." Katie lifted her left hand. "Actual tourist here."

"Be careful now," Allie said. "A lot of people come here as tourists and end up as residents." She thumbed toward Lisa.

"It's true." Lisa raised her hand. "Actual resident. Let me go get you that charger."

"Thank you." Katie watched Lisa skip off into the store, then turned to Allie and Hannah. "Do you guys happen to have directions to Barbara's Country Inn?"

"Yeah," Hannah said. "I'm dropping off decorations over there in just a minute. Do you want a lift?"

Katie's eyes widened. "Wh—Are you sure?"

"Of course. No problem at all." Hannah jingled the keys to the red truck in her pocket.

Allie offered Katie a knowing smile. "Welcome to Evergreen. People are a lot friendlier than you could ever imagine around here."

"I can see that." Katie couldn't help but shake her head.

Lisa came back, carrying a few things. "All right, here's your charger," she said to Katie, then handed a box to Hannah. "And here are the decorations." Then back to Katie again, she lifted a pretty striped toboggan in shades of pink and blue and handed it to her. "And the hat is on me. It gets cold in Evergreen. You'll need it."

"Wow." Katie held the hat. "Thanks. You guys really are nice. Thank you." It was too warm for a hat today, Hannah thought, but it sure was a nice gesture.

"That's a terrible way to run a business," Allie said to Lisa in a low voice.

"Whatever. Be nice." Lisa slapped at her. "It's Christmas."

Allie's giggle made it abundantly clear that she enjoyed poking fun at the newest business owner in town.

"Come on." Hannah carried the decorations over to Allie's red truck with Katie dragging her suitcase behind her.

"Very cool truck." Katie stood there for a moment, checking it out. "Can I just set my bag on the floorboard here?"

"Yep. Should slide right in." Hannah slipped

behind the wheel while Katie got situated, then slammed the door closed.

Katie stood there, looking amazed, as Hannah climbed into the red pickup truck. "You even decorated the truck?"

"Oh, yeah. It's tradition," Hannah said. "But it's not my truck. It's Allie's."

"My brother would have gone crazy over this truck." Katie stroked the metal dashboard. "He and my dad were always working on old cars. What year is this? A 1956?"

Hannah shrugged. "I have no idea. It's just part of Evergreen. It was Allie's grandpa's truck. Allie and I went to high school together. We used to beg her grandfather to let us drive this truck. Allie loves it, even if the truck is finicky sometimes."

"Sentimental reasons." Her voice softened. "I get it."

"Whenever anyone needs a truck, she lets us use it."

"That's really nice of her." Katie laughed. "I feel like I've said that like a hundred times already. Everyone really is nice."

"Guilty as charged," Hannah said with a wrinkle of her nose. "And proud of it."

The truck rumbled along, vibrating under their feet. It took less than two minutes to make a loop around the square and one turn to arrive in front of Barbara's Country Inn. Hannah parked right in front, noticing the inn had transformed into a Christmas paradise since yesterday. A pretty wreath hung on the door, and even the garden trellis now seemed festive decorated with ribbon and decorations.

"I feel like a dope," Katie said. "I could have definitely walked this far."

"No way. I was coming here, anyway. It's my pleasure." She got out and came around to the other side of the truck to help the new guest. "You're going to love this place."

Hannah watched as Katie got out of the truck and saw Barbara's Country Inn for the first time. Katie shook her head. "I honestly think I already do."

Hannah wasn't sure if Katie meant Evergreen or the inn, but both were equally wonderful.

Chapter Four

K ATIE SLID HER SUITCASE OUT carefully to be sure she didn't scrape the paint on the old truck. She knew how much effort went into the restoration of these old vehicles. Hopefully she'd see the truck around town again while she was here so she could snag a picture to send home to her brother. He'd be so jealous to have missed out on the ride.

Hannah had already skipped around to the passenger's side of the truck. "Got it?"

"Yeah. Thanks." Katie set the bag down and lifted the handle, but it wasn't very easy to roll on the snow along the edge of the driveway, so she lifted it and carried it to the sidewalk, which had been cleared.

A wooden sign painted in forest green hung from two slight chains on a tall wrought iron bracket with Barbara's Country Inn in fancy white scripted letters.

On the porch, two people passed garland back and forth around the tapered white columns on the front of the Craftsman-style house. Gray stacked stone covered the bottom of each post to the handrail, which offset the deep burgundy house paint. The inn had welcoming curb appeal.

"Hey! Hannah!" A good-looking guy stepped from around one of the porch columns. His close-cropped curly hair accentuated his big brown eyes. "You're just in time for the lights." His smile was playful, and he couldn't take his eyes off Hannah.

"Great. I brought some more snowflakes for you, and a couple of other things you can use inside or out." She walked up the sidewalk, stopping just short of the front steps. With her chin tipped up toward the man in a big smile, she introduced her. "Katie, this is Elliott. He runs the arts center in town."

"Hey, Katie." He ran down the steps toward her. "Hannah, I told you, I'd like to keep calling it The Turner Tinker Shop."

"And that's sweet of you, but it's an arts center too." She turned to Katie. "The Turner Tinker Shop used to be my parents' store, where everyone in town used to go to get things repaired."

"I reopened it." Elliott chimed in. "And I still like fixing things. Plus, there's so much history in the name." He turned his focus to Katie. "You should stop by and see it, Katie. I just set up a new area for crafts, and a glassblowing studio."

"Wow," Katie said. "There's a lot going on in this town." People thought New York was busy, but this place had more action per capita hands down, and she hadn't even unpacked yet.

Hannah's gaze never left him. Katie could feel Hannah's appreciation for what Elliott was building. They were so cute together.

"Plus, the rumor around town is the place has something to do with a secret Christmas time capsule." Elliott winked.

"A Christmas time capsule?" Katie wondered when the amazement would end. "Really?"

"Really," Hannah said with a sheepish grin. "Actually, I think that's the town's longest-running rumor. I used to hear my parents talk about it when I was a kid, but it's one of those things that people really aren't sure actually exists."

Katie liked Hannah's honesty. "Well, as rumors go, I'm sure that one is pretty good for tourism. Like the snow globe or that mailbox."

"Those aren't rumors. The snow globe and mailbox...they exist," Hannah said with all seriousness.

"You mean to tell me you believe in the snow globe granting wishes?" How gullible did these people think she was?

"Oh, I most certainly do. I've seen it in action," Hannah said.

Katie wasn't about to argue with yet another Evergreen resident who seemed to believe in Christmas magic, but someone was crazy, and she was pretty sure it wasn't her. Then again, if she did run across that snow globe, it couldn't hurt to make a wish just in case. *If that snow globe grants wishes, that would make one best-selling novel!*

From up on the porch, a woman called out, "A little help?" She struggled with an armful of garland already adorned with silver ornaments. Definitely a two-person job.

"Oh! Excuse me. I'm helping Megan." Elliott touched Hannah's arm before acknowledging Katie. "Welcome to Evergreen." He took the stairs two at a time to the rescue.

Katie wished someone looked at her the way Elliott had just looked at Hannah. "You two are the cutest couple."

"Huh?" Hannah stepped back as if what Katie had just said made no sense at all.

"You two." She pointed toward Elliott up on the porch.

"Oh. Us? A couple? No. We're just friends," Hannah insisted. "That's it."

"Oh. Sorry. The smiling and the banter and the back and forth...y'know, just the overall demeanor. I thought—"

Hannah gave an insistent, "No."

"Okay." She wasn't buying that at all.

"Common mistake, but we've been friends since we were little. He runs the arts center, and he's way too handso—Busy. We're both very busy. Let's get Megan to check you in. Shall we?"

Katie caught the stumble over Hannah's words. That girl was more interested than she was letting on. From here, it was more than obvious. She watched Hannah trip over herself trying to deny it all the way to the steps, where Elliott stood smiling at her. This was adorable. "Sure. Let's get me checked in."

"Megan," Hannah called up to the porch. "You have a guest. Who needs—you need to check her in."

Katie wasn't buying Hannah's act that she was completely unaware of a little something between her and Elliott for one second. She followed her onto the porch, and before they got inside, all the lights in the garland and on the house came on at once.

Elliott stood there proudly with the cord in his hand, smiling.

Hannah lit up as bright as all of those lights. "Ahhh. It's so pretty."

His smile broad, he nodded, clearly pleased with himself.

Katie was pretty sure by the look on Elliott's face that he was thinking something like, *And so are you, Hannah.*

Friends? Sure.

"Come in." Megan opened the door.

Katie followed her inside.

Inside, the warmth from the brick fireplace in the living room washed over them. It felt so good after being in the cold damp air, and the room smelled good, too—like fresh-baked goods and Christmas. Tiny white lights blinked on the tree in the corner of the room, the light dancing off of dozens of clear glass ornaments. Fluffy white hydrangea and deep red poinsettias, almost the color of the exterior of the house, peeked from between the branches. Gorgeous golden ribbons swept in and out of the limbs from bottom to top in a flourish beneath a beautiful white feather-winged angel.

Megan pulled a card with Katie's name on it from the card file on the desk. She handed her a barrel key on a ring in the shape of the sign out front.

Katie admired the old key. "How pretty."

"Thank you. We're so glad to have you here at Barbara's Country Inn. You're in the Holly room. It's one of my favorites. I think you'll be very comfortable in there. The light is wonderful in the afternoon. I'm Megan. My sister owns the place. Welcome again."

"Nice to meet you," Katie said. "I'm looking forward to my visit."

"It wouldn't be a B&B without breakfast. You'll find everything you need to know about that on the desk in your room. If you'll just leave the slip on your doorknob before you go to bed tonight, or bring it down and drop it off here any-time, we'll take care of that. We host a gathering every night here at the inn with hors d'oeuvres and desserts. I call it Meet and Mingle, because it's not just for the guests—locals stop in too." Megan's face was animated as she spoke. "I love how people always find common ground. It's so lovely. I hope you'll be able to squeeze in at least one night with us, but I understand with so much going on."

"It sounds wonderful."

"Good. There's a complete calendar in your room of things to do in Evergreen during your stay. It's right next to the complimentary basket of goodies."

"You've really thought of everything."

"We try." Megan stepped around the desk. "Can I help you with your bag?"

"No, thank you. I can manage."

"Upstairs. First door on the right."

Katie climbed the wooden staircase to the second floor. Just as Megan had said, the Holly room was right at the top of the stairs. Evergreen, Spruce, Poinsettia and Mistletoe were the names of the other rooms she could see from here. She rolled her bag on the wooden floor. The door to the room was propped open, so she brought her bag inside and closed the door behind her.

It was much bigger than she'd expected. She had plenty of room to work. Delighted, she left her bag sitting where it was and toured through the room. Chairs in front of the windows and a desk against the wall offered two great options to nestle in for writing, should inspiration strike. The bed was covered in layers of fluffy linens of red and white. Two pillows were wrapped like presents in front of the heaping pile of fancy pillows. A huge poinsettia took up the better part of a round table in front of the window. The king-size bed looked so comfortable with the pillows piled on top that she was half tempted to forego unpacking and stretch out for a long nap. Maybe even until tomorrow.

She laid on the bed face down and let the quiet hang around her for a moment before turning over and staring at the ceiling.

As much as she wanted to just lie there in the pretty room and absorb the joyful environment, it nagged at her that she'd kind of left Mom hanging when her phone had died. Mom was probably wondering what the heck was going on. She got up and plugged her phone in, and set up her notebooks, pens and laptop on the desk. A tiny red glass vase held a single sprig of holly. She tapped the edge of her finger against one of its bright-green pointed leaves. The berries were so glossy they didn't look real. Just like the rest of the town, it seemed too perfect to be true. Yet it was. She shifted the tiny bud vase, letting the sprig lean as if pouring inspiration toward her workspace.

Since the battery on her phone was now at least charging, she made a quick call to her mom, but it went straight to her voice mail. Because living out of a suitcase was too distracting, she unpacked her clothes and hung most of her things in the pretty mahogany glass front armoire on the padded silk hangers provided, then slid the empty suitcase into the closet. She liked being settled in for the long haul, even if it was only for a week. That was certainly long enough to come up with some good ideas for the next book, and even get some plotting done.

Excited to check out the rest of the B&B, Katie took her charger, phone and laptop downstairs. A few people chatted in the living room, but the den was empty except for the warm fire blazing an inviting orange. She closed her eyes and wrote whatever came to her mind, and the ideas were flowing. She'd never even considered writing a story set at Christmas, but it was beginning to feel like there was something to be told here.

She was in the zone, her fingers hitting the keys as fast as she could to keep up with the thoughts rolling through her mind. Her phone rang, breaking her concentration. Mom? She took the call. "Hi, Mom. Sorry. My phone ran out of battery."

"I figured. I don't mean to rush you, but I've reached out to just about everyone I normally rely on and—"

"You know," Katie cut her off, glancing down at her scribbles in her notebook, "I was thinking there might actually be a story here."

"In Vermont?"

"Well, it's this town. You should see this place. This inn is gorgeous. I'm feeling very spoiled at the moment, and kind of liking it, I'll admit. Every business here in Evergreen has some kind of

Christmas theme. There's even this Christmas time capsule—"

"You're hired!" Mom's voice was as certain as if an auctioneer had just banged a gavel to punctuate the sale.

"Okay, Mom? Slow down." Katie paused, allowing herself to absorb it, too. "At least let me send you a pitch or something. We'll see if you like it."

"I already like it," her mom said. "Christmas town turns Christmas profit."

Not what I had in mind...at all! But the assignment was for a business magazine, so of course, that's what would pop into Mom's head. "I don't know if that's the angle entirely, but I can try to—"

"Honey, just send me something as soon as you can. And oh, Katie, thank you. You really are helping me out of a bind."

A touch of longing filled her. Mom had always been there to help her no matter what came up, but this was different. This time Katie could help her, and maybe writing this article might be a little consolation prize for Mom at the holidays, even though Katie had no intention of working at the magazine long-term. Could it possibly be a win for them all? "You're welcome, Mom," she answered softly.

"Just do your best."

"Okay, bye." She lowered her phone and scrolled through the comments already piling up about her trip to Evergreen. And that was just in response to the pictures she'd posted from the train.

Wait until folks saw all of this.

Huge letters spelling JOY had been hung from the staircase, and the fact that the letters rose up, left to right, wasn't lost on her. The reason for the season. *Joy to the World!*

She stepped to the middle of the den, squatted to get the fireplace right behind her, and took a smiling selfie to post too. Then one with the Christmas tree, this one adorned head to toe in an assortment of little red truck ornaments made of glass, resin, painted, origami, popsicle sticks and even carved ones. She'd never seen so many different red-truck-themed ornaments in one place, and it was all tied together with a playful buffalo-plaid garland ribbon. How fun was that?

She uploaded the rest of her pictures from her phone to her laptop, then pulled her feet crossed beneath her on the couch, recalling the people she'd met throughout the day.

Ben from the train. Handsome, witty.

The mayor. A woman, at that. Along with Ezra and Joe, short and tall, who were helping with the sign. Ezra had mentioned a historical society meeting. What would they be discussing? Was there some kind of history here that would make a good story?

And the three gals at Daisy's, which Lisa owned. There had to be a story to that. Allie, the veterinarian, and Hannah, whom she'd instantly felt a connection with. Allie hadn't been kidding when she'd said people were nicer than she could even imagine.

If she were writing a romance, she was quite certain there'd be a winner in the story of Hannah and Elliott. She could almost see the hearts dancing above their heads, popping into smaller heart confetti with each bashful glance between the two.

She glanced down at her notebook. She'd doodled hearts, Christmas trees, a red truck and snowflakes. It wasn't an idea, or a story, but it sure was pretty. Her first novel had been more of a family saga, but everything her muse was sending her way since she'd arrived was romantic and magical. Totally different from what she'd anticipated writing.

She sat back. There were no rules. No expectations. She wasn't under contract, so she could absolutely write whatever moved her. That freedom tempted her to at least consider a different kind of story this time. Romantic, even. The thought made her heart race a little.

Her first impression of Evergreen was almost too good to be true. How had these people kept this town such a secret? Maybe that had to do with the Evergreen Historical Society she'd overheard Ezra mention yesterday.

She connected to the WiFi and typed Evergreen Historical Society in the search bar.

The next time she looked up, there was laughter coming from the living room, and the sky out the window had turned to dusk. She closed the top on her computer. Suddenly hungry, she got up to join the other guests for a cup of tea and a few hors d'oeuvres before calling it an early night. Only, time slipped away as she met and mingled with the other guests and was introduced to a few of the locals who'd dropped in. People hadn't solely come from the north, like she had on the Evergreen Express. There were guests from Virginia, North Carolina, and Texas too. From all walks of life, from farmers to financial advisors, they all found common ground here at the inn. Conversation was easy, and she even learned about a club for people who wanted to travel across the country and stay in inns like this one.

"I'm writing the names of those two places in my notebook right now," Katie said to the other guest. "Those sound amazing." Maybe she should consider nonfiction. She could see herself flitting from inn to inn across the country and comparing them to the nicest big-city hotels.

When she finally called it a night and climbed into bed that night, she had so many ideas floating through her head she could barely sleep.

Chapter Five

KATIE HAD FINALLY FALLEN ASLEEP while reading about the long line of Greens who'd been mayors of this town, the most recent being Ezra, whom she'd just met yesterday. It was an even bigger deal than she'd realized for someone new to step into that role, not just because she was the first woman. *Good for Michelle.*

When she woke up, she realized she'd dreamt she was the mayor of Evergreen herself. That made her laugh. The last thing she wanted was to be mayor. And crazier than that was the thought of living in a small town like this one. Maybe the dream had been more of a call to action to settle on an idea for this book now, or else! Hopefully the day would hold something equally as exciting that screamed for a book of its own. She bounded out of bed, ready to explore.

Intrigued by the amount of tradition here, she was eager to see what else she could learn about Evergreen. She quickly showered, got dressed and raced down the stairs toward the aroma of fresh coffee and bacon.

Megan greeted her with a pot of coffee. This time she was wearing a cheerful apron with snowmen on each pocket. "I hope you got a good night's rest."

"I did." Katie sat down at the dining table with another couple. "I'd love some of that coffee." Katie turned the generous-sized mug in front of her upright.

Megan filled it, saying, "This morning I'm serving a puffy apple omelet. I know you marked the pastry and fruit on your menu, but if you've changed your mind, I've got plenty."

The lady to her left placed her hand on top of Katie's. "You've got to try it." She raised her hands to the heavens. "Absolutely the best breakfast I've ever had. And I'm no spring chicken."

"How can I say no to that?"

"I'll be right back then. It's really popular around here. Some people say it's the reason they come back to stay here." Megan gave her an appreciative nod and turned toward the kitchen.

"Do I smell bacon?" Katie asked, hopeful.

"Is it breakfast without it?"

"I like the way you think." Katie sipped her coffee.

Megan came out with three plates lined up her arm. Without even a wiggle, she moved the plates from her arm to the table.

Katie lifted her fork and dove right in. The

puffy apple omelet was not only beautiful, with the red skin of the apples peeking out from the omelet, but it was tasty. "Is it rude for me to beg for this recipe?" she asked.

"Not at all. I'm happy to share."

The woman seated across from Katie raised her hand. "Don't you dare share that recipe with me, else he"—she thumbed toward her husband, who was already munching—"will expect me to make this. I prefer to come back and let you make it for us. What a treat. Plus, it gives my dear husband a way to give me something he knows I'll love."

"Good plan." Megan patted the man on the shoulder as she fussed with the empty cups and plates and then disappeared back into the kitchen.

Katie and the couple shared pleasantries, and it was hard not to break out a pen and paper as the couple went on and on about their previous visits to Evergreen and all their favorite memories.

"Well, we are off to the general store, and to the Christmas tree farm for a wreath-making class." Her husband stood and held his wife's chair for her to get up, then the two of them grabbed their coats and left.

"Can I freshen up your coffee?" Megan asked.

"No. Thank you, I think I'm ready to start my day too." Katie handed Megan her plate. "I was wondering, is the library walking distance from here?"

"It sure is. I have a map of the town. You can walk just about anywhere. The Christmas tree farms are all a little further out on the edge of town, but if you need a ride, just let me know. I'd be happy to give you a quick lift."

"I'm a city girl. I don't mind a walk."

Megan pointed her in the right direction to the library and then showed her the path from town square back to the B&B on the map.

It'd been a brief truck ride from Daisy's Country Store to the B&B, but that shortcut made it practically in the backyard.

With the map tucked into her back pocket, off Katie went, and it wasn't long before she was strolling down Main Street. The decorations that had been a work in progress yesterday now filled the streets with the sounds and excitement of Christmas. Everyone she passed said good morning or waved from across the way, leaving her feeling more at home here than she did in her own apartment building.

Two blocks up and one turn ahead, Katie recognized the building Megan had described as the library.

She walked up the walkway to the green turn-of-the-century house with the blue-green trim. The covered porch stretched across the front of the house. Stars cut from old stamped due date cards hung from lengths of silver-and-gold cord from fresh garland from end-to-end. The idea of all the hands those well-loved books had passed through made her tingle.

An Evergreen Historical Society marker consisting of a bronzed plaque was posted next to the door to show the significance of this building. Originally the home of Nan's family, later it had been donated to the town as its first library.

The porch had a gentle slope to the right, but comfy chairs lined the porch for comfortable reading, and she could picture herself in one of them with a copy of one of the old classics—preferably in hardcover.

The invigorating scent from the pine garland that hung along the eaves seemed to clarify her mind, instantly giving her a lift, or maybe that was just the caffeine finally kicking in. Either way, she could barely contain her happiness today. She twisted the old brass knob on the door and let herself in the nine-window-paned door.

Someone had done a wonderful job transforming the big three-story house into a tastefully decorated library. Just inside the door, a beautiful desk was stacked with books someone had just dropped off. The smell of old books teased her senses, drawing her further inside.

Katie wandered past bookcases overflowing with titles, lined up by genre. Different niche books were set up on tabletops and dressers. Knitting and quilting books here. Architecture and design books over there. It was well appointed and well-stocked. Voices from the adjacent room caught her attention.

Light shone through the large double windows. At least a dozen children sat on the floor, enthralled by the storyteller sitting on the stool in the middle of the room. His convincing character voices and appropriate inflection held the children's attention. She used to love story hour at the library when she was a kid.

She let herself fall into the story. When she noticed the narrator, she did a double take. The man wearing glasses was Ben, whom she'd met on the train. She hadn't recognized him at first, but it was most definitely the same guy. She looked on, enjoying his authentic connection with the children and the way he imitated all the voices. He was very animated, emphasizing each part of the story. The kids hung from his every word. And she couldn't take her eyes off him as he read on.

"'A Merry Christmas, Bob,' said Ebenezer Scrooge with an earnestness that could not be mistaken as he clapped him on the back.'" Ben did a good Ebenezer. He then read in another voice, "'And a merrier Christmas, Bob, my good fellow. Now Ebenezer Scrooge...'"

A hand on her shoulder startled Katie. Her hand flew to her chest as she turned to see a tiny older woman smiling up at her. She wore a whi' blouse and a steel-blue sweater that matc her eyes, looking every bit the part of small-town librarian.

"Story hour." She spoke in a low whisper, and Katie leaned in. "Not my favorite Christmas story," the woman continued. "But it's a crowd-pleaser. Louisa May Alcott's is better. Can I help you find anything in particular?"

Embarrassed for being caught seemingly peeping at the handsome storyteller, Katie tore herself away from watching Ben. "Yes, actually. I'm looking for some local history."

"Oh, yes. Come here." She led the way to the front room away from the story hour. "I'm Nan. I'm the librarian here. We have a whole section of Vermonters. From Rudy Vallee to Allison Bechdel. Robert Frost—"

"Ben and Jerry," Katie joked.

Nan laughed politely. "Them too."

"What about Evergreen, specifically?"

"Oh, well, we do have a lot of newspapers." She opened the front of a glass case and handed Katie a pile of yellowed papers tied with a rib-bon. "These are some of the most historically significant papers in Evergreen's history contain-ing information about the people who started this town. Look at that. So old and beautiful."

Katie took the delicate bundle into her hands. The size was small, so unlike the papers of today, and the paper brittle with age. She cradled them in her palms, afraid to damage them.

"The local paper has never been digitized, but

we've got everything on microfiche. You could go through those archives if you don't find what you're looking for."

"Okay."

"And then we have things like this." Nan pulled a black top hat from the curio cabinet. It had to be at least fourteen inches tall, decorated with holly along the band, and on top, a bright red cardinal rose from a snowy branch. "A hat from the very famous Evergreen Hat Factory." She gently placed the hat upon her head and posed. "It was our first industry. Which changed, of course." She lifted the hat as if a hundred memories flooded her mind. With a sigh she placed it back into the case.

The thrill of story angles filled Katie's head. "You know, I think there might be a good article here."

"You *are* a reporter." The voice came from the doorway. Ben stood with his arms folded. Story hour had ended, and by the way the vein in his neck was pulsing, he didn't look particularly pleased.

"Oh, well, um—" She handed the papers back to Nan and went over to him. "It's sort of hard to say."

He shook his head. "Except for on the train, you said you *weren't* writing about Evergreen. So?"

"Because on the train, I wasn't."

His expression didn't soften, and that big sigh

he just let out could've blown out thirty candles in a heartbeat.

Is he mad? Do I really need to defend myself on this? He's got to be teasing. "But with all the Christmas goings-on, and this rumored time capsule—"

"You should see our choir," Nan said with excitement.

Ben flashed Nan a bit of a glower, and proceeded slowly. "It's just that these reporters, they show up in town and then they write these articles that make us all look like we're—"

"Here we go again." Nan placed a hand on Katie's arm. "My grandson is very protective of Evergreen. And I keep telling him, Evergreen is a town that takes pride in what it is."

Ben dropped his chin to his chest, shaking his head. Just as he took in a breath to speak, the front door flung open.

A teenage boy rushed inside. "Hi, Ben! Hi, Mrs. Baxter!"

"David. You're early."

"I came to tell you something. Carol wanted to know if you were okay to have today's meeting at the Kringle Kitchen so she can see Allie off?"

Ben didn't seem to really like the idea of the change. "It depends. I don't know if Nan can spare me."

"Of course I can," Nan said. "Go off to your stuffy old historical society meeting."

Katie's ears perked at that comment. *This might be just the break I need.*

"Bring back pie too." Nan rubbed her hands together. "Would you? Please and thank you?" There was mischief in the tiny woman's eyes.

"Of course," Ben said as his grandmother headed back around to sit at her desk.

"Historical society, huh?" Katie moved closer to David and Ben. "Can I come along?"

"It's pretty much members only," Ben interjected.

What was so secret about Evergreen that they couldn't let her listen in? "I see." But not one to give up so quickly, she turned to David. "Do you know how one becomes a member of the Evergreen Historical Society?"

"Yeah!" With no hesitation, he spilled the beans. "Just go to the meeting."

"Ah-ha!" Katie beamed, giving Ben a two-can-play-at-this-game look.

"We've been trying to get more people to participate all year," David said.

"Great." She walked toward the exit. "Lead the way."

David held the door for her.

"Great," she heard Ben say with a lot less enthusiasm from behind her.

She stopped and took two quick steps back inside the library. David waited for Ben to move, but he just stood there. "Are you coming?" Before giving him half a chance to answer, she poked at him a little saying, "I don't want to be late. I hear there's pie!" She hurried out the door, hoping he'd follow, which he did. When Katie glanced back, Nan waved with a knowing smirk.

Chapter Six

B EN, DAVID AND KATIE MADE the short walk
from the library to the Chris Kringle Kitch-
en without much conversation.

Ben wasn't really sure if this woman flustered
or fascinated him. And what was she really up
to, anyway? He didn't take kindly to people mini-
mizing the good life here in Evergreen. It might
seem old-fashioned to some, but it was a wonderful way to live. Each year, some reporter would
show up to write some story about the town, and
each time it ended up being a slap in the face.
He knew writers were paid to write stories that
sold papers, but making fun of people was not
his idea of good journalism.

He looked over at Katie. Her fair coloring and
blond hair made her seem almost angelic. He'd
been fooled by beautiful women before, though.
Was it possible she was different?

When they got to the diner, Ben held the door
for Katie and David. He watched Katie eye the

huge portrait of Santa that covered the wall on the right.

She turned his way, an eyebrow arching slightly.

He knew exactly what was going through her mind. Not named after Chris Kringle, huh? The larger than life-size painting had to be the size of the portraits of the presidents on display at the National Portrait Gallery in Washington, D.C. Maybe the name was a little bit after the jolly old fellow too, but everyone around here knew it was a play on words because of the pastry they were known for.

He saw Katie staring across the way.

Okay, from her perspective, it might seem over the top. She was watching Nick, who looked just like Santa Claus, sitting at his usual table with the local artist who was freehand sketching a holiday scene.

If he put himself in Katie's place, he could see how it might look to an outsider. Maybe a little too perfect. His case for the town that this was legit and not some marketing scheme seemed a bit wobbly.

Hannah rushed over to Katie. "Hey. Are you settling in okay at the inn?"

"Yes. I am. Less than twenty-four hours in Evergreen, and I'm already joining societies."

"David has a way of getting people involved," Hannah admitted. "This is great. We can always use a fresh point of view."

"I was willing," Katie said with a laugh. She turned, and moved straight for the counter where the snow globe sat on a bed of fake snow. "Is this the famous snow globe?"

Ben watched with amusement.

"It is." Hannah picked it up. "Do you want to make a wish?"

"I do! Thank you." Katie took the snow globe between her hands. She blew out a breath, then drew in another so deep, so hopeful. Eyeing Ben and then Hannah before concentrating on the snow globe itself. "I know there's a second book in me, snow globe. Please don't let me down." She stared into the snow globe, closed her eyes and gave it a shake, holding it until the snow finally settled again. When she opened her eyes, she gave Hannah a resolute look. When she turned to Ben, he gave her a hopeful nod.

"Magic," he whispered playfully, hoping she was sincere in her excitement and at the same time that the snow globe granted her wish so she'd believe in it too.

"I hope so." She set the snow globe back down in its place of honor.

Carol, owner of the Kringle Kitchen, walked over, carrying a tray of fresh-from-the-oven cookies. "I see we have a new face."

"We do. This is Katie," Ben said. "She just arrived on the Evergreen Express yesterday from the city."

"Hi, I'm Carol," the pretty blonde wearing a

Christmassy red sweater said, "and that's my husband Joe." She waved to him to respond. He was much taller than Carol, and his glasses were just as red as her sweater.

"Hello," Joe called out from the table in the back as he waved.

"Thanks for letting me crash your meeting." Katie followed the others.

Ben let the ladies finish their introductions, heading over to the table with the others for the meeting.

"She a friend of yours?" Ezra asked him quietly.

"No. Don't know her, really. I bumped into her on the train yesterday. Turns out she's a reporter of some kind writing a story about the town."

"Oh?" Ezra perked up, as he was known to do when a hint of publicity was in the air.

Carol carried the tray of cookies over to the table, and Hannah sat down next to her nephew, David.

"Come on. Sit." Carol was still talking to Katie. "Join us."

"Glad to have you aboard." Ezra motioned Katie to an empty seat at the long table. "Ben was just telling me that you're writing about Evergreen."

Ben could feel his face go red. He hadn't meant for Ezra to share that. *Why didn't I keep that comment to myself?* He pulled out the chairs for Carol and Katie.

She looked into his eyes, as if the gesture had been unexpected, but took the seat. Her eyes seemed even bluer up close.

"Thank you." Katie sat down and directed her response to Ezra. "Well, to be fair, I'm not entirely sure I'm writing about anything yet. But I'm collecting a few notes. I've been reading about this time capsule..."

Ben sat down next to her. It hadn't taken her two seconds to stir up old Evergreen lore.

"Oh—whoa. We haven't talked about that for a while." Carol placed her palms on the table. "That one's a mystery. Has been for years. Maybe some fresh eyes can help us figure it out."

Looking excited about the possibility, Joe's glasses lifted on his face as his eyebrows rose. "And now we have two journalists for the price of one."

"Two?" Katie looked puzzled. "Who?"

Ben pressed his lips together, trying to make it look like he wasn't regretting Joe's comment. He avoided Katie's gaze, but he could feel it without even turning her way.

"Well, you and Ben," Ezra explained. "He has a journalism degree. He wrote for a paper in Chicago before coming back to—"

"Okay." Ben leaned his forearm on the table wishing he'd thought to ask Ezra not to mention that. "Okay. It's not a—"

"He failed to mention a journalism background." Katie turned in her chair, her back to him. "All right, bring me up to speed on this time capsule."

"Well," Carol said. "My parents used to run this diner when it was just a bakery. And they were best friends with—"

"My parents," Hannah continued, "who, of course as I already told you, ran the town Tinker Shop."

"Which is also the town arts center." Katie remembered from Elliott and Hannah's discussion at the inn.

"Yes," Hannah confirmed.

"When we were kids," Carol said, "we'd always hear this talk about a Christmas time capsule, but then every time we'd ask our parents about it, they just kind of smiled and said 'oh, you'll know one day,' but that day never seemed to come."

"Then a few years ago, we found this archive of newspapers and found this article." Hannah flipped through papers in a folder on the table in front of David. "David's been tracking it since he could read. We love puzzles."

"We do, and we're good at them. We'll have to tell you about the key to the bells."

"Later," Hannah said. "That's a whole other story. So, this time capsule…" She passed the old copy of the Evergreen Mirror across the table.

The paper had only been a quarter back then. The headline in bold black ink read: "Evergreen Hit By Record Snow!" Below it, a picture of snow piled high along the power lines and fallen trees filled half the page. The article was titled, "Blizzard Blankets Evergreen."

Ben watched as Katie scanned the article. He knew the content by heart. As a kid, he'd once tried to solve that mystery too. There probably wasn't anyone in town who hadn't spent at least a little bit of time over the years trying to piece together if it was fact or fiction.

"Yes," Joe said. "The Christmas blizzard. Fifty years ago, a blizzard kept everyone in town for almost the whole month of December. And if you read right there. Down at the bottom..." Joe pointed out something in the article. "Read that, David."

"Some residents of Evergreen also passed the time by making a surprise time capsule to be opened in fifty years."

Katie put her hand on the date of the newspaper in the top right corner. A little quick math in her head, and her eyes widened. "Meaning this year?"

"Uh-huh," Hannah remarked.

"The problem is, there haven't been any other articles written," said Ben. "No new clues uncovered."

"And our parents have passed," Carol said with a shrug. "There's really nobody who remembers anything."

"Nobody?" Katie looked skeptical to him, but then, he was a little too. He tried to squelch his mixed feelings about her. Since the divorce, she was the first woman to catch his attention. Then again, he had no plans to repeat that mistake. There was never a good reason to start something up with someone just passing through town, either. He knew better.

"Well," David added, "Nan said there might be another box to go through at the library."

"Keep at it, buddy." Ben loved how tenacious David was about these mysteries. He'd solved the key to the clock in the church tower last year. If anyone could figure this one out, it would probably be him. "Is there anything else you'd like to discuss before the meeting?"

"Oh yes, let's start the meeting." Carol jumped at the sound of a horn from out on the street. She glanced at her watch. "It's Allie." She turned to Katie. "She's our daughter. Michelle is driving her to the..." She fanned her face, trying to stop the tears already puddling at the rims of her eyes.

"Now, honey." Joe lifted his chin. "We can be brave about this." He stood from his chair. "Probably," he said with a wiggle of his brows.

Ben held the door as Joe jogged to catch up with Carol, who was already out at the curb calling Allie's name.

Allie's red truck was parked out front. Michelle and Allie were hugging when Joe and Carol got there.

Ben was excited for Allie. She and Ryan had really found something special.

Allie spread her arms wide and announced. "The great world awaits." She saw her mom and dad standing there. "Mom!" Allie hugged her tight.

Joe patted her shoulder. "You tell Ryan and Zoey Merry Christmas."

"I will, and I'll be back after New Year's." Her lips quivered at the edges of her smile. "Everything's going to be fine. I promise. I mean...I hope."

"Oh, Allie. I love you." Carol wrapped her arms around her. Joe joined in the group hug, as did Hannah.

"Merry Christmas," Allie said to Hannah. "I'll bring you some croissants."

"Yes, please!" Hannah hung close with the rest, wishing Allie a good trip and heartfelt goodbyes.

Michelle climbed behind the wheel of the truck, and Allie walked around curbside to get in. Everyone had joined there on the sidewalk, including Nick, who stopped Allie before she got to the truck.

"Have a splendid adventure. I'm sure you'll have safe travels and all kinds of Christmas surprises." He opened the door for her with a twinkle in his eyes.

"Thank you, Nick."

Nick closed her door, and Allie rolled down the window. "Okay, the moment of truth."

Michelle squeezed her eyes closed and twisted the key in the ignition.

Ben knew the truck would start. Allie belonged with Ryan. That finicky truck had enabled the whole relationship from the get-go. Today would be no different.

Joe stood behind Carol with his hands placed sweetly on her shoulders as she crossed her fingers on both hands.

Everyone sort of held their breath, except for Katie, who wasn't aware of the local lore and this truck...yet.

The truck started, and everyone cheered. "I guess the truck says we're a go." Allie waved.

"Bon voyage!" Hannah yelled.

Ben raised his arm above his head and waved. They cheered as Michelle pulled away from the curb with Allie grinning ear to ear. "*Joyeux Noël!* Merry Christmas! *Au revoir!*"

Chapter Seven

*L*ATER, AFTER THEY'D ALL GONE back into the Kringle Kitchen and worked through the Evergreen Historical Society agenda, everyone packed up to go about their day.

Ben still couldn't help but wonder what Katie's intentions were. An anxious swirl in his gut made him pause, though. It wasn't like he hadn't experienced nosy journalists before, but this reaction was different—more personal.

He walked outside with her, stopping her before she crossed the street. "So, did you learn everything you needed about Evergreen?"

She cocked her head to the side. "If I'm being totally honest, it all feels a little too good to be true."

There it was again. Her doubt agitated him. "Which part? I'm just curious."

"Well, first off, you have a guy who looks exactly like Santa Claus on vacation." She pointed inside, where Nick was still sharing coffee and pie with the artist.

"Yeah. Nick." Ben knew how that looked. "He splits his time between Evergreen and—"

"The North Pole?" she teased.

"No." The joke bothered him more than it should. "Burlington. He comes from Burlington for the month of December."

"Look. Fine. But come on, even your alleys are decorated for Christmas. I get it. I'm all for it. I mean, you have to put on a good Christmas show. It's for the tourists." She was being playful about it, even raising her hands into the air and spinning as she spoke.

"No. It's not that." His jaw pulsed. "It's not like that at all. We truly love the holidays, and it's wonderful that people like to get out of the city and come here to Evergreen to enjoy a real Christmas."

"Wait-wait-wait." She held her hand up, increasing the space between them. "Are you saying that city Christmases aren't real?"

"No. I'm not saying that." Or am I? This isn't going well. "I mean we're not cynical here."

"Who says we are?" She tempted him with those pretty eyes, although right now they were carrying a bit of challenge too.

Honestly, he hadn't meant to accuse her or the city of being cynical. He dropped his hands to his side. What could he say that wouldn't just dig him in even deeper?

They'd gotten as far as the gazebo before he stopped her. He made an effort to keep his voice level and calm. "If you're truly interested in Evergreen, it's important to understand that we embrace this for real. I want you to experience the real Evergreen if you're going to write about it."

Their eyes held for a long moment.

Her smile softened, open to giving it a try.

He relaxed a little, excited to experience it with her.

A shrill scream, followed by the sound of something breaking, came from inside the Kringle Kitchen. Ben and Katie turned and raced for the diner. He entered first, with Katie on his heels.

As the door shut behind them, they both came to a full stop just inside and gasped.

You could've heard a pin drop in the Kringle Kitchen at that moment. All eyes were trained on the wooden floor at the entrance.

Shattered glass and water had splattered across the floor in front of Hannah. Chunks of the heavy wooden base were strewn too. An evergreen tree lay on its side next to the horse drawn carriage, as if there'd been a terrible traffic accident. Even the church had been flung off to the side, lying near the counter in a precarious position, its steeple off to the side.

Hannah stood there, frozen in place with her mouth hanging wide.

Nick stood just behind her with Carol, Ezra and Joe looking on, all in a state of shock.

David clutched his folder, tears in his eyes.

With her hands straight out to her sides, fingers splayed wide, Hannah slowly raised her head. "I was just trying to make a wish." She could barely get the words out.

Ben's muscles involuntarily tensed as he watched the woman process what had just happened.

On the floor, the town's most treasured holiday attraction, the snow globe, lay in a hundred messy pieces. Had the magical snow globe tradition just come to a tragic end?

Chapter Eight

KATIE STOOD SILENTLY AS THE locals rushed to rescue the fragments of the famous snow globe from the floor of the Kringle Kitchen. Carol scurried behind the counter and came back with a box.

Hannah's hands shook as she picked up one of the trees.

Carol handed the box to Joe, who began scooping the augmented fractions of the snow globe into the box. "Maybe it can be fixed." Joe's words were promising, but there wasn't much hope in his tone.

Nick walked over. "I'm partially to blame myself. I bumped into Hannah and—"

She swallowed back a tear and shook her head. "No. I should have had a better grip on it. I'm so sorry, guys." Her voice cracked, and tears fell to her cheeks.

"Accidents happen." Carol watched Joe pick up the pieces.

"This globe has been an Evergreen tradition for years, and now—"

Joe placed the last pieces in a box. A waitress rushed over with a mop to clean up the area and keep anyone from sliding as they came inside.

Joe stood. "Let's focus on having it fixed, Hannah? Okay?"

Nick and Carol guided Hannah over to a table, trying to reassure her.

Hannah nodded. "Do you think Elliott might be able to do something about it?"

"It's worth a try," Carol said.

Katie felt horrible for Hannah, and everyone else too. They were all genuinely upset. Anxiety filled the air. Even if that snow globe brought in a lot of customers, who else would know if they just replaced it with another one? No. Something was up with this one, which only made her curious to hear some of those stories about the wishes this particular snow globe had supposedly granted.

Ben went over to the glass bakery case and picked out a pie for Nan.

Katie had almost forgotten about the pie. Especially after Carol had filled them up on cookies and her famous apple dumplings. Right now, all the sweets were twisting in her gut. She could only imagine how Hannah felt.

With the boxed pie in hand, Ben met up with her. "I guess I'd better get back to the library and check on Nan," he said to Katie. "She's probably already heard about what happened with the snow globe."

"I've heard word travels fast in small towns." Which had already been proven by how fast people found out she was a writer and thinking about doing an article on the town. She hadn't even really decided.

"Oh, yes. News will beat you home if you're not careful. Makes it tough when you're a kid testing boundaries. Everyone knows everyone, and they aren't shy about making a phone call or taking it upon themselves to set you straight."

She could imagine him as being one of those kids who was always into mischief. The class clown, even. That quick wit didn't happen overnight. It wasn't hard to picture him as a pre-teen giving his teachers a challenge. "I never had that problem living in the city." She thought about it a second. "Then again, it might have been a good thing if I had on a couple of occasions. I got away with so much after Mom and Dad got divorced."

"Were you young?"

"Twelve, I think. My older brother moved out west with my father. I stayed in New York with Mom."

"Must've been hard being separated from your brother."

"It was at first, but you know, you get new routines. We were at that age where we didn't want to be around each other anymore. He was driving. After a while, you just get used to phone calls and cards to keep up. He got married last year. I talk to him more now than I ever have."

"I always thought it would be nice to have a brother or sister."

"We were really close when we were little. Yeah, if I ever have children, I'd definitely want two." She made a goofy face. "I have no idea why I just told you that. Too much information?"

"No. Not at all."

"So, tell me about you. You're masquerading as a mild-mannered librarian, when underneath it all—the glasses and button-down shirt—you're actually a mild-mannered reporter?"

He rubbed the nape of his neck. He knew this would come back up. "Okay, yes, I was a journalist. But it's not what I do now."

"Why not? You can't possibly think all reporters are that bad, can you?" She noticed something that flashed across his face as he paused. "What? Too nosy?"

"Yes." But then he loosened up. "No. Not too nosy. Curiosity's important. It means you're good at your job."

"Thank you."

"Journalism was what I thought I wanted when I was younger. And I was pretty good at it. But then, I came back here to help out for a little bit and..."

Katie waited for him to finish, but he didn't go on. "And?"

He shifted his weight, lowering his gaze to the

ground. "The library is...sort of like my family. After my parents died, Nan raised me." He said nothing else, but he lifted his gaze from his feet to her face as if searching for something.

There was pain in his eyes, an emptiness that was almost tangible. "I'm sorry. Follow-up questions. Occupational hazard." She resisted the urge to reach out and touch him.

"Nan's great. The best parent a kid could ask for, and as for the library, it started as a private collection from Nan's family. It was her lifelong dream. I grew up around books, and so it's no surprise I love them so much. Anyway, it's a long story."

She'd love to sit down and hear the whole thing. "So, if I need help with town history—"

"That would be David," said Ben.

That wasn't exactly the answer she'd expected, or had wanted to hear. Had her prying questions made him want to pawn her off on David? How could a middle-schooler be the go-to on town history over a librarian?

Ben continued with all sincerity, "That kid is the eyes and ears of this place."

"I'll keep that in mind." She wished she'd kept her mouth shut earlier.

"He's always in the library though, so, I probably will see you around."

Good. So, maybe he does want to see me again.

But Ben smiled and turned away before she

could get a good read on him. She watched him walk through town square all the way until he turned the corner toward the library.

She didn't mind getting pawned off to David for research as long as Ben was still going to be in the wings to brighten the way. She looked forward to the next excuse to go to the library and maybe bump into him once more.

The door to the Kringle Kitchen opened behind her. Katie turned to see Hannah walking out, carrying the red-and-white Christmas box Joe had scooped all the broken snow globe pieces into earlier.

"So what were you wishing for?" Katie asked.

"I have a complicated relationship with this snow globe." Her hands shook as she held the box, almost as if she was afraid she'd drop it and make things worse. "Even more so now."

Katie wanted to ask if Hannah considered this the "breakup" from the snow globe, but was pretty sure it was a little too soon for that joke. Trying to be supportive, but also just dying to know more, she asked, "It hasn't granted your wishes?"

"Sometimes I think I'm not specific enough. Sometimes I think I'm too specific. Honestly? I don't know."

"Yeah." Katie felt a little silly for making a wish on the famed snow globe now. Sure, it was a town tradition, but it wasn't like her to let fantasy woo her like that. Besides, she didn't need a snow globe to tell her she had a second book inside her. She'd known that for a while. She just needed to come up with an idea and start writing. Which was the whole reason she was here in the first place. "But do you really think it grants wishes?"

"I know it does." Hannah pulled the box closer to her. "I know it sounds crazy, but it's worked. More than once, and even though I haven't gotten exactly what I've wished for, it has opened some doors."

"Like how?"

"Well, a couple of years ago I wished for a special someone to spend the holidays with."

"That sounds like a perfect wish."

"Well, technically I got that wish. I met this great guy at the festival. We were wearing the same exact Christmas sweater. I mean, seriously, what are the odds?"

"I don't know. Was it a white cable-knit sweater?"

"No. It had scotty dogs with little ribbons around their necks on it. And he was awesome. We had so much fun, but we weren't right for each other. We enjoyed the holidays, and we're good friends now, but that's not what I was really looking for."

"That's what you mean about not being specific enough."

"Yeah. It's hard to explain."

Katie couldn't resist the opportunity. "But others' wishes have come true?"

"Yes. Lots. I had a friend who wished her parents would stay together, and no one thought after what they'd been through it could ever happen. But it did. And when the town was in dire need of a preacher, one wish, and Rev. Zach showed up on vacation and never left. He's been here six years now. And get this, the only reason he stopped in Evergreen was because he blew out a tire at our exit."

"That does sound serendipitous."

"Call it what you will. Michelle wished for someone to come into her life, and wham, she and Thomas met and it was kismet."

"I've seen them together. They make a great couple."

Hannah shook the box in front of her. "And now I've ruined it for everyone. I'm sick over this."

Katie placed her hand on the woman's arm, wishing she could help. "What are you going to do with all those broken pieces?"

"I'm going to take this over to Elliott and see if there's anything he can do to help repair it."

"At the arts center?"

"Yeah. It's worth a shot. I have to at least try."

"I'm actually a little curious about the arts center after hearing you and Elliott talk about it. Mind if I come with you?"

"Not at all. It's just up here around the corner." Hannah seemed to welcome the company.

The Turner Tinker Shop, in great big red letters on the sign across the front of the building, was just ahead.

An old forest green pickup was parked at the curb, which was pretty much the only color in front of the gray building.

Even their choice of transportation in this town was kind of magical. The Evergreen Express train number 1225 that dated back so many years. Allie's red antique truck with the garland and wreath decorating it, and now this one—just as unique, even if it wasn't wearing holiday attire. Somehow, all of it seemed perfectly normal here in Evergreen.

She followed Hannah up the steps toward the door to the shop. Big glass front windows on each side of the door were filled with artwork and antiques that had been restored to their original beauty.

The building was narrow, but deceiving, because when they walked inside, it looked like the place went on forever.

A fan kept the warm air circulating in the old building. It smelled of craftsmanship. Oil, turpentine, and paint. People gathered shoulder-to-shoulder around a table on the right side of the shop, working on Christmas ornaments. The table was filled with paint, glue, glitter and beads, and in the back of the shop she could see artists working in other mediums. The chatter among the artists was melodic, and the sound of the heavier tools back in the glassblowing area only added interest. She'd never seen anything like it.

Who's to say what normal is, anyway?

Maybe this was the article she was meant to write about Evergreen.

Chapter Nine

MICHELLE WAS SEATED AT THE craft table in the Turner Tinker Shop, now also known as the arts center, making a Christmas ornament. David sat next to her, his attention intent on the work in front of him. With Thomas out of town, she and David had been taking advantage of some of the new classes here at the arts center, and they weren't the only ones.

Every chair at the table was filled.

Michelle was glad to see town residents taking part in the offerings. As new mayor, she hoped to get neighbors engaged as much as possible, keeping the heartbeat of this town alive and prospering. Entrepreneurs, like Lisa reopening Daisy's Country Store, and Elliott here at the Turner Tinker Shop, were already breathing fresh life into Evergreen.

Michelle knew Elliott had always been good at fixing things, but his skill as a craftsman really shined on this renovation. The outside was still as Plain Jane as could be, but inside the place dazzled, just waiting for inspired artists and craftspeople to put their hands to good works.

What had once been a space full of wooden shelves, dark and dusty, had been transformed with just a few coats of bright white paint. It'd been such an easy fix and had done wonders on the old dusty building, but Elliott hadn't stopped there.

He'd updated the old workroom, tearing out a wall and adding a work-height counter and shelving along the entire back wall. A series of cabinets, drawers and shelves, even diamond-shaped bins perfect for storing the hand-spun wool being made here, since they rebranded it an arts center. Henry had added a herd of Angora goats to his farm to improve the petting zoo, and Elliott had immediately seen the win-win to buy the angora from Henry to teach folks how to spin their own yarn on the drop needle spindle that'd been in the storage room unused for who knew how long.

Michelle couldn't wait to have the team update the city website with the recent additions in the new year and find ways to connect more activities to the calendar to grow tourism for the town.

Elliott came from the glassblowing room carrying ornaments. "Remember. A good Christmas ornament has color, evokes a feeling of nostalgia and is made with care." He placed the ornaments in the middle of the table for them to decorate.

He leaned over David's shoulder. "What are you making there?"

"Oh, this?" David held up the ornament he'd just finished, painted gold. "It's a key ornament for my Aunt Hannah. I really want her to know how much fun I think she is."

Elliott set the palms of his hands on his knees, to David's level at the table. "She definitely is that." The words were simple, but Michelle caught a hint of something more in the statement.

Michelle leaned over to see David's project. "I see, like the key that started the church bells. I still can't believe you and Hannah figured that out last year. It was absolutely amazing. I can still remember hearing those bells come out of nowhere that night." She placed a hand on his arm. "Still gives me chills. That's a really good ornament. She's going to love it."

"Yep. What's yours?" he asked.

She held her ornament so he could get a better look. "It's a candle for your dad. See, last year we were searching for candles in the storeroom at Daisy's Country Store for the midnight candlelight processional, and that's when I knew I—" She caught herself. The moment she'd known she was interested in Thomas wasn't exactly the conversation she needed to be having with his son. She corrected the course of the conversation. "I really love candles."

"Cool," he said. "Then, he'll probably like that too."

Elliott was walking back to get more ornaments when Hannah and Katie walked in. Hannah was carrying a box. "Elliott?" His name came out high-pitched, nearly frantic.

Michelle set down the candle ornament, worried by the sound in Hannah's voice.

"Hannah. Hey, I was just leading a workshop on ornament making," he said. "You should join us. There's a seat next to David."

Hannah glanced over, but looked back to Elliott with pleading eyes.

Michelle watched David quickly tuck his ornament under art supplies so Hannah wouldn't see her present, then grab one of the glass ornaments from the center of the table and start dabbing paint on it.

"You can joi—Whoa." His voice shook.

That was all Michelle had to hear Elliott say to be on her feet and at his side to see what was going on.

Elliott lifted pieces from the box, one by one, examining the condition.

Michelle clapped her hands over her mouth. "The snow globe! Oh, no." She hadn't meant to remark out loud. She scooched closer to Hannah. "What happened?"

Hannah shook her head, placing her hand over her heart. "Michelle, I'm so sorry. I know it's an important part of the Christmas Festival, and—"

"It's okay, Hannah." She offered a hug. Poor Hannah was so upset. "We've withstood broken pipes and flooded venues, even blizzards during the Christmas Festival. Really, it's okay." She smiled, hoping to ease her friend's concerns. But this wasn't good. Not good at all. There were so many pieces in that box. Not even the best puzzle maker could put that back together.

Hannah's lips quivered. "Really? You're not mad?"

"Of course I'm not mad. It's not ideal," Michelle admitted with an obvious nod. "But we can't change the past. Now, we just focus on fixing it."

Hannah turned her attention to Elliott. "Do you think you can fix it?" Her eyes were glossy with tears.

It appeared to be a lost cause to Michelle.

"Uh…" Elliott looked like he was going to say no, but when his eyes met Hannah's, he said, "Absolutely."

Michelle stood there in disbelief.

Elliott scrambled over to the counter and started spreading out the pieces. "Let's see. The two pine trees are intact."

"That's good," Hannah said.

"The horse is…fine." He turned it in his hand then pulled up the magnifying lamp attached to the wooden counter to evaluate the piece closer. "There's something?"

"What do you see?" Hannah asked.

"It looks like…"

David got up and joined them at the counter. He eased in closer to Hannah.

Elliott held the horse carriage at an angle for Hannah to see. "There's a little key carved underneath the sleigh."

"But…why?" Elliott and Hannah said at the same time. They both slowly lifted their gaze from the broken fragments of the snow globe to each other.

Close enough that Michelle thought for a moment Hannah might bump right into Elliott when she lifted her head. But they didn't collide; they simply stood there, staring. Hoping mostly, if Michelle had to guess, that they could scrounge up a miracle and fix one of the town's most famous residents—the snow globe.

The intensity of Elliott and Hannah's eye contact clearly showed a new level of awareness between them.

Hannah licked her lips, biting down on her lower lip. Katie glanced over at Michelle with a smile. She'd noticed it too. Hannah cleared her throat and took a step back, pushing her hair from her face.

Elliott hesitated, but only for a moment. "I'll get to work on this right away."

"Great." She nodded.

"If you'd like to help..." He glanced back her way. "You could come by tomorrow?"

"Yes, it's a date," Hannah blurted out.

Michelle almost laughed out loud at the blunder.

Hannah looked like she wished she could slurp the words back up, but they were already out there. "I'll see you tomorrow," she said, as if that would erase the earlier comment.

"Tomorrow." His voice came out like a song.

Michelle and Katie laughed quietly together, sharing a nudge, while those two tried to downplay the very obvious attraction between them. Even David noticed, which Michelle found quite charming.

Michelle watched Elliott lower the ceramic piece he still held in his hand to the counter, while his eyes followed Hannah until she was out of sight.

Love is in the air.

Having found love herself just last Christmas, Michelle couldn't be happier to see Hannah finally finding the same. If it took a broken snow globe for those two to realize there was something between them, it was worth it.

Chapter Ten

A T BARBARA'S COUNTRY INN THAT evening, the Meet and Mingle was in full swing. Katie had been so inspired by her day in town that she'd taken over the desk in the den to set up her laptop and get all of her thoughts down while they were still fresh. She didn't want to lose a single moment or emotion.

In the other room, guests were visiting, and Ezra had stopped by. He was talking with a couple visiting from Boston, and since that was where Ezra was getting ready to move, they were in full-out sharing mode. They'd even already set up a night out in Boston next month. Ezra was putting notes into his phone on people to look up and places to see.

Megan hadn't been kidding when she said she'd be serving heavy hors d'oeuvres. Katie didn't need a meal after all of the delicious appetizers. Holiday music played from the speakers above, making the conversations seem even more festive.

So many things floated through Katie's head. This town, and its kindhearted and talented people, had inspired her with everything from tradition, history, mystery and blooming love. For the last hour, she'd sat here at the writing desk in the den, pouring her heart onto the page, afraid that if she didn't, she might lose something. She wasn't sure what all of it would amount to, but just the act of typing words on the page had her creative juices flowing.

Megan swept through the room with a small tray of homemade marshmallows, dropping them into the cocoa mugs from little silver tongs like some kind of marshmallow fairy princess.

Katie reached for her mug, taking a sip, then licking a melty marshmallow from the edge. The ooey-gooey sweetness reminded her of so many childhood Christmases in the city.

"Thank you," Katie said, lifting her cup in a toast to her in appreciation.

"You're welcome," Megan sang out as she worked her way across the rest of the room.

"Hello, everyone!" Nan called out the greeting as she walked through the front door. She unwrapped her long scarf from around her neck and peeled out of her coat. "Oh, Megan," Nan called out. "I've got something for you."

"For me?" Megan turned, placing the tray of marshmallows down on an end table.

Katie turned, curious to see what it was too.

"Look at this." Nan held something in her

hands, her back still to Katie, but she could see the way Megan's face lit up.

Nan turned to Katie, flashing a copy of Katie's debut novel, *Wooden Fishes*—the hardcover edition. Megan grinned ear to ear as Nan turned the book to the back of the book jacket with Katie's picture on it. "We don't often have published authors in town."

Katie's heart nearly skipped a beat at their excitement. "You have my book?" She could barely swallow. It'd been a long time since someone had shown up with a copy of her book in their hands, and even then, it'd been a planned book signing event.

Megan danced. "When I heard you were a writer, I looked it up and asked Nan for it."

"I run a library, so I have a lot of books." Nan made light of it. "And Megan's wasn't the only request I've gotten for it since you've arrived. I special ordered this one for her."

"Oh my goodness. Thank you both." Katie felt like this happening at the moment she was pouring thoughts onto her laptop was a sign that she did have a second novel inside her. Maybe that snow globe did have some magic. She quickly dismissed the silly idea. There was no magic in writing a book. It was hard work. Every single word of it.

Nan handed the book to Megan. "Here you go, sweetie."

"Thank you." Megan immediately turned to

Katie. "I hope this isn't overstepping with you being a guest and all, but would you? Sign it?"

"Of course!"

"Oh my gosh. This is so exciting. I'm going to keep it right out here where guests can enjoy it. They'll love that you've been a guest here. You wait right here. Let me get a pen."

Katie giggled. What a surprise. Megan was back with the book and the pen in a jiffy.

"May I personalize it to you?" Katie asked.

"I'd love that." Megan clapped her hands, and she and Nan held hands as Katie bowed her head to autograph the book.

"Here you go." Katie handed her the book. "This is more exciting for me than it is for you."

"Somehow we doubt that," Nan said.

Megan placed the book, face out, on her bookshelf. "The perfect spot."

"I like it, and it does go with the decor," Katie assessed.

"Even more so when it's not all red and green for the holidays. I love my book. Thank you both. I've got to tend to the other guests. Enjoy." Megan took off to the kitchen, reappearing in an instant with a tray of cheese puffs.

Katie had almost forgotten the thrill of seeing her book in a reader's hand. Her heart pounded wildly.

Nan glanced down at Katie's laptop. "How is the article going?"

"Tricky, actually. You know, my mom works

for a business magazine, but honestly I'd rather write about the Christmas time capsule."

Nan sat down in the chair next to the desk. "Don't give up hope on being able to write that. The time capsule was intended to be a surprise," she explained. "And this town loves a mystery as much as they love—"

"Wait a minute," Katie said. "I thought nobody remembered anything about the time capsule."

Nan froze, her cheeks filling with air as she sucked in a breath and averted her eyes. There was something going on in that look on her face. "Well, yes…" Nan tripped over her words. "I guess—"

A rambunctious ho-ho-ho came from the doorway as Hannah, David and Michelle all entered in high spirits, shedding their coats and piling them on the bannister.

Katie's thoughts were still on Nan's reaction to her comment about the time capsule. Her writer instincts twitched. *She knows something.*

"I was beginning to think you weren't coming." Megan had just walked back into the living room with more coffee for the guests.

"We wouldn't miss this," Michelle said.

"This is one of my favorite traditions." Hannah draped her coat on top of the others on the bannister, making herself at home.

"With more guests coming next weekend, it's time to make more cookies." She turned to the guests standing by the fire. "Everyone is welcome to help."

They gave Megan a nod. Katie turned back to her laptop, pecking at the keyboard on her notes, trying still to come up with the right angle for that article for the magazine.

Megan leaned close. "I know you're writing, but if you'd like to help, we always need more hands."

"Oh, I—" She waved her hand, almost ready to tell Megan she was going to pass, when Ben came through the front door, looking handsome in a blue half-zip sweater that really set off his blue eyes. On second thought, spending time doing some holiday baking sounded like fun... especially if Ben was going to be involved.

"Hey, everybody." He closed the door behind him.

"Yeah. Sure." Katie changed her response to Megan, then bounced right out of her seat. "I'd love to help." Her pulse accelerated. Rushing to get to the kitchen before Ben realized he'd influenced her decision to join, she tried to look calm while waiting for more directions from Megan.

Ben tossed his scarf over the handrail, rubbing his hands together as he headed into the kitchen. "Yeah! Cookie time."

His enthusiasm tickled Katie. From the doorway of the kitchen, she overheard Nan talking to David. "I found a few more news clippings in the archives, and I know you're on another search. I didn't find anything explicitly about the key you mentioned, but maybe this will be helpful." She handed him the blue folder, and Katie couldn't help but wish Nan had given that folder to her.

"Wow." David flipped through the pages. "Thank you, Mrs. Baxter."

"You're very welcome, David. I just know if anyone can figure this out, it's going to be you."

Katie ducked back into the kitchen, convinced Nan was up to something.

Everyone was claiming workspace around the vast kitchen island, and Megan was moving another batch of cookies into the oven. There were cookies everywhere. She must've been at it for hours. No wonder the inn smelled so good. It was like a factory in here.

Gooey frosting and perfectly browned fresh-baked cookies were already cooling on racks on the table and the long counter, ready to be decorated once they got these next batches all rolled out and onto trays ready for baking.

David was stamping out snowmen like an old pro.

"You've done that before," Katie remarked.

"Yes, I have. I love helping Megan with the baking any time of year."

"Good for you." She watched as he spaced the snowman shapes on the baking sheet then carried it over to Megan, who'd just closed the oven door. "There's no more room?"

"No problem." Megan took the tray from him and slid into the convection oven on the counter.

"All right." He smacked a high-five with her. "Can I get started decorating while those bake?"

"It looks like we have plenty of people making the cookies. You can start decorating."

Delighted, David hopped up on a stool in front of a stack of truck-shaped cookies and began spreading colored icing across them.

"Hey, is there room for me?" Henry, from the tree farm, tied a green apron around his waist as he walked into the kitchen.

"Always," Megan said. "Guests, this is Henry Miller from Miller's Christmas Tree Farm. He has the very best trees in town. That's where the wreath-making class is held too."

"Hey everyone." Henry walked over to Ben. "Hey Nan, I picked out the perfect tree for out in front of the library."

"Wonderful."

Ben tugged the dish towel from his shoulder. "I'm late getting started on that."

"You want to come by tomorrow to pick it up?" Henry asked.

"Yeah. Sure. That would be great. I'll ask Hannah for the truck, and I'll pop by sometime tomorrow."

"That would be good. We're getting real busy out there." Henry sprinkled flour across the space in front of him and rolled out cookie dough.

"I put aside a nice, tall one for you. Just like you like them."

Ben, apparently happy over the news of the tree, did a celebratory fist-pump. "Awesome."

Katie held back a laugh at the youthful antic. Yes, it was easy to imagine Ben as a kid growing up in Evergreen.

He made his way around the island and rolled chilled dough with a fancy ceramic rolling pin that looked almost too pretty for real work.

She leaned in close enough to get a whiff of his aftershave, which was nice. Using her best newscaster voice-over cadence, she said, "People come from miles around to witness the sweet folksy charm of Henry Miller's Christmas Tree Farm."

He stopped and gave her an approving glance. "You're just writing that article right in front of me, aren't you?"

She nodded with playful confidence and continued pushing the copper cookie cutter into the dough. "I'm just that good." She'd never met someone quite like him. The banter was so easy, like they'd known each other forever.

"Why doesn't that surprise me?" He grabbed a silver dragées and pushed it into the raw cookie at the top like a star. "You're welcome."

She hoped the article would be as easy to write as it was fitting in to the day-to-day here in Evergreen.

Chapter Eleven

THE KITCHEN AT BARBARA'S COUNTRY Inn was elbow-to-elbow with help. Megan, wearing a red apron decorated with snowflakes across the bib, handed out aprons to Henry and Ezra, who'd just joined in to help. Megan insisted everyone working in the kitchen wear an apron while decorating.

The guys moaned and groaned about the frilly patterns of the full over-the-head style aprons, but Ben finally folded one down to only wrap around his waist, and the rest of the guys followed suit.

Katie liked the pretty apron she'd been given to wear. She lifted it over her head and struck a pose.

"Very nice." Ben's cheeks pinked as if he hadn't meant to say it out loud, and hers did too.

Ben wore his apron like a tool belt, and it wasn't a bad look on him at all. He seemed to know his way around the kitchen too. She liked that.

The song playing over the speakers started with a long orchestral lead-in that everyone recognized. "Twelve Days of Christmas," Hannah shouted, throwing her hands in the air.

"Our favorite," David said.

And with that, everyone sang along, someone different picking up each of the days.

"On the seventh day of Christmas, my true love gave to me," they all sang. Then Hannah pointed to Katie to fill in the blank.

"Ack! I'm not sure."

"Swans-a-swimming," David hinted over her shoulder.

"Seven swans-a-swimming," she shouted out in a hurry.

"Six geese-a-laying," Henry sang, followed by Hannah in perfect pitch singing, "Five golden rings."

"Four calling birds," Megan sang.

"Three French hens," Henry belted out in an accent, something close to French.

Ben hooked his thumbs together and waved his hands as he sang, "Two turtle doves," then everyone joined in, "...and a partridge in a pear tree."

Each progressive round started with nervous laughter as someone was picked to start. And so it went for all twelve days of the song. At the end, they all cheered and clapped. The mingling aromas of sugar, lemon, ginger, peanut butter, and chocolate floated around them.

Megan slid out the last three trays of cookies. "That's all the baking!"

"Hooray!"

"Now on to decorating."

"I got a head start," David said, standing up and holding a big red truck cookie for everyone to see. A shiny glaze of red icing flooded the top of the cookie like a high-dollar custom paint job. David had outlined the details in black and even added green garland and a wreath to it. "It's just like Allie's truck."

"It sure is."

"I made one like Elliott's truck too, Hannah." He showed her the green truck, and Katie watched Hannah for a reaction.

Hannah pulled her lips together. "I like it." Her smile suggested more.

Elliott joined them in the kitchen. "Did I just hear my name?"

Hannah looked like she'd been caught with her hand in the cookie jar. Her mouth opened and closed before any words started coming out. "You did. David made a cookie for you."

"Aw, man. That's awesome. It's just like my truck." Elliott slapped his arm around David. "Great job, man."

"Thanks!" David raced over to his stool and went back to work.

Nan was painstakingly decorating small ornament-shaped cookies with a fine tip, while Megan worked on 3-D tree cookies that were basically two stacked cookies, then she used a fringe tip to dab lifelike pine needles on them.

Ben lifted a pastry bag and snipped the tip like a pro. Katie was quite impressed when he started dabbing the tip against the cookie with all the skill of those television pastry chefs. She struggled with her Christmas tree in an effort to make it a little prettier, or at least presentable. She dropped a few more sprinkles across it. "More sprinkles is always good, right?"

"Definitely." Nan lifted two exact duplicate ornament cookies and held them up to the sides of her face like earrings. "What do you think?"

"Those are too pretty to eat," Katie said.

"No such thing," Michelle corrected her. "I never met a cookie I couldn't eat."

"Me neither," Henry said. "But if you have any you don't think are worthy, send them my way so I can prove you wrong. I'll consider it my favor to you."

"You're just too generous," Michelle said.

Katie placed another chocolate-coated candy on her Christmas tree cookie, finally satisfied that it was pretty enough to consider complete. She glanced down at Ben's. "Whoa, wow, I am not as good as you are at this." His cookie, a star shape, was a work of art.

"I know my way around a cookie." He held up his star. Edged in white, the pretty sky-blue star was piped in a filigree pattern. "Plus, this one is extra special."

"Really? Are you gloating?"

"Not at all. Watch this." He raised the cookie above his head and lowered it slowly back to the table. "It's a falling star. That's why it's extra special."

"Of course it is."

"Hope you made a wish."

"I wish I could compete with that," she teased. Katie held up her less-than-amazing cookie. The only cookies she'd ever made were of the slice-and-bake variety, and she wasn't sure she could remember the last time she'd done that. Perhaps before her parents' divorce, when she and her brother had surprised them with homemade cookies. "Mine's not amazing."

"You'll be happy to know there's no such thing as a bad Christmas cookie."

She did feel better for that. At least it would taste good. Katie washed her hands and came back to the table. "I think if I'm going to help, I need a lesson. I guess it's obvious I'm a beginner," she said to Ben.

"Like, absolutely first-time beginner or—"

"I mean...my mom and I didn't do a lot of baking or cookie decorating. She was busy. We bought our holiday baked goods at the bakery down on the corner."

"That's still good."

Katie pulled her lips to the side and scanned the table. She brushed flour from the front of her apron. "Not as fun, though, I have to admit."

"There's all different types of fun. What kind of traditions do you have?"

"On Christmas Day, Mom and I go to the movies. We volunteer. It's been just the two of us since my parents' divorce." She lifted her shoulders. "It's nice, though."

"I'm sure it is." His smile was gentle.

"I'm seriously considering boxing a few of these up to send to my brother, though. Especially those red truck cookies David decorated. My brother is a total car nut. He'd love them," Katie said.

"Do it," Megan said. "Didn't mean to eavesdrop, but we have plenty. I even have a little priority mailer you can ship them in. Such a good idea."

"Thanks. I will." Katie looked around at the room full of people, laughing. *I've never had a holiday gathering anything like this.* She felt like these people were her family tonight. "What about you?" she asked Ben. "It was all—"

"It was all Evergreen. Caroling, sledding, wreath-making."

"So you grew up in a Christmas movie?" she teased.

Laughing, Ben had to admit, "It felt that way sometimes."

"Did your parents love Christmas too?"

"Ah, I really don't even know. They died before I could even talk."

"I'm sorry." How many times was she going to stick her foot into her mouth?

"Nan was the best parent figure I could have ever wished for." He motioned to where she was showing off another ornament cookie. "She clearly adores the holidays. Not just Christmas, either. All of them."

Katie nodded; that made sense.

Megan carried another batch of cookies over. "Okay. We need to taste test these. What do we think? Enough cardamom?"

Ben handed Katie a cookie and they tried them at the same time.

Katie's eyes popped open wide. "Oh, wow. Of all human inventions: the wheel, the printing press…"

"Cookies are right up there, yeah."

Ben and Katie went back to decorating the cookies. "Let me help you decorate this one."

She stepped in closer, his breath tickling her neck as he reached around her and assisted her with the pastry bag. She held back a nervous giggle.

"I'll get you started. Hold the bag like this, and you're going to gently squeeze." His arms were warm against hers. His moves were light and adept. "You try it." He let go of her hands but didn't move from behind her.

"Like this?" She moved the icing across the cookie. It wasn't perfect, but it was better. She turned her head to the side to see his reaction.

"Yeah. See? You're a natural. You just needed a little Evergreen magic."

The private lesson felt like magic, too.

Nan scooted a bowl of translucent glasslike sugar in front of Katie. "This is my secret weapon. Anything with these sprinkles always looks pretty. Plus I love the crunch of it."

"I see." Katie dipped her spoon into the sprinkles and dribbled some across the still-damp icing. "Wow, that does jazz it up."

"Mm-hmm. Who do you think taught Ben?" Nan winked.

"Truth comes out." Katie wondered how she'd gone this many years and had never decorated Christmas cookies.

Megan held up a decorated gingerbread man with gumdrop buttons. "Isn't he cute?"

Michelle held one up she'd decorated in a Christmas apron. "Look at mine! They can be friends."

"We are flying through these," Megan said. "Thank you so much. I would've been working on these all week long to get them done."

A round of you're welcomes bounced through the room.

"Ben, will you help me? I made something for us to reward ourselves with."

"Sounds like food. Count me in." He raced to her side, and she whispered instructions to him. Ben left and then came back carrying a white milk glass pedestal cake plate. A tall three-layer cake frosted in white had 3-D Christmas trees made from ice cream cones turned upside down and green frosting tips. On the side, perfectly spaced, were more trees.

Ben set the cake in the center of the table. Megan carried the sifter over to the table and bumped it a few times to add a few real snow-like flakes from confectioners' sugar across it for that final touch.

"Who wants a piece?" Megan carried a stack of red plates to the table.

Everyone raised their hand in the air.

"Cake for everyone." She began cutting the cake while people cleared off their little work-space.

"Hey, Hannah," Ben said from across the table. "Can I borrow Allie's truck to pick up the tree from Henry's lot for the library tomorrow?"

"Yeah, sure." She reached into her pocket and pulled out the key. "Catch!" She tossed it with no further warning.

Ben snagged the key out of the air. "I'll give you a lift home when you're ready to go."

Hannah shook her head. "No way. I'll walk home. It's a perfect night to walk off all the cookies I sampled, not to mention the hunk of cake I'm getting ready to devour."

Katie felt like she was going to have to walk all day to work off the snacking she'd done tonight.

Megan clapped her hands. "Thank you all for your help. We have more than enough cookies to do the job." Megan's eyes sparkled as she handed out the cake. "Is there nothing we can't do when we come together? My biggest heartfelt thank-yous to you all."

"We haven't bumped into anything we couldn't get done yet," said Hannah as she took a bite from her piece of cake.

"And we won't on my watch," Michelle teased in regard to her new role as mayor. "Y'all better be careful—I'll be tapping you all for new committees I'm going to put in place for Evergreen."

"Works for me," Megan said. She handed a "something special" wrapped in paper towels to Ben. "For a little late snack. I know they're your favorite."

Ben peeked inside and grinned. "Thank you, Megan."

"Count me in on your committee," Carol said as she washed up, and Joe nodded in agreement.

Katie cleared the red paper plates from the counter. "Looks like we filled up an entire trash bag." She pulled it out and tied it up. Ben swooped in and took it from her. "I'll take that out."

Everyone else began getting their coats and hugging out goodbyes.

It was like a cookie-scented parade out of Barbara's Country Inn as everyone went their separate ways. Katie was glad she didn't have anywhere she had to go. She went to the door to see off her new friends.

"Nan, wait. I can drive you home." Ben hurried to catch her as she and Hannah walked down the steps.

Nan turned and looked at him as if she were ready to argue. "No. I'm fine. I'm going to walk."

Katie appreciated the way Ben watched over Nan. It was really sweet.

"You shouldn't walk alone." He stepped onto the front porch.

"Benjamin, I am perfectly capable of walking home. It's not that far, and it's good for me."

Hannah tried to hold back a laugh. "I can walk her down a ways." She placed a hand on Nan's arm. Nan gave Ben a victorious smile as she took Hannah's arm and started walking down the sidewalk. Over her shoulder, Hannah said, "Nan always has the best stories."

"Okay," he conceded. "I appreciate that, Hannah." Ben waved, and Nan rolled her eyes.

Katie wished she'd offered to walk Nan home now. She did enjoy a good story. But she was staying here, and saying goodbye to all of her new friends was a little bittersweet. Besides, offering to walk Nan home would've meant shortening her time with Ben. She looked up at him. One of the good guys. She hated for the night to end. She could've hung out in that kitchen all night with him. A million novel-worthy thoughts raced through her mind.

Ben was the last one out the door. As he descended the steps, he stopped and turned to her. "It was fun tonight."

"It was. So, tomorrow," Katie said. "When you go to get the tree. I should come along. Yes?" She twisted her hands in front of her, hoping he'd say yes, but he was hesitating, and that felt like a looming no. Was he not feeling the spark like she was? Not one to give up so easily, she said, "Do you mind if I tag along?"

He shoved a hand into his pocket. "Why would you want to do that?"

You're fun. I want to spend more time with you. Can't you see that? But she couldn't say that. "What better place to prove this isn't all some kind of Christmas hallucination than to see it for myself? Right? You say it's all authentic. I say prove it."

His response to the playful banter was exactly as she'd hoped. That playful smile turned her insides out. "Okay. Fine. Tomorrow morning. Right here." He pointed to the steps.

"Right here." That was the answer she'd been hoping for. "Okay."

He pulled the key to the truck out of his pocket to leave, and if she wasn't mistaken, there was a lift to his step. If she weren't afraid he might turn and catch her in mid-bravado, she'd do a little leap in the air right now.

He stopped and waved before sliding behind the wheel.

"Oh, wait." She leaped off the porch, and ran

to the truck. "Let me give you my number. You know, in case you decide you want to get an earlier start." She held her hand out, palm up.

His lips pressed together. He gladly placed the phone in her hand.

She typed in her number and her phone rang. "Now we're all set."

"Yes, we are. I'll see you in the morning."

"Yeah." She clung to her phone. "I'll see you then." She turned and ran back to the porch.

The red truck with the wreath and fresh garland down the sides started with a throaty rumble, then slowly made its way down the road.

She waved from the porch, tightening her charcoal-gray sweater around her and glancing at the sky as tiny dry snowflakes started to fall. Another perfect evening in Evergreen. She couldn't wait to see what tomorrow would bring.

Chapter Twelve

WHEN BEN DROVE UP TO Barbara's Country Inn, Katie was sitting on the front porch, writing in her notebook. There'd been a time when he'd scribbled like that in one. Seeing her made him envy that a bit. He wasn't even quite sure when he'd gotten out of that habit. From here, the sun glistened in Katie's hair, like an angel among all the gold ornaments and ribbons that decorated the porch.

The truck puttered to a stop in the driveway. The way she smiled when she looked up captivated him, making him happy he'd agreed to take her along for the ride. He stepped out of the truck, feeling young and inexperienced, which he wasn't, but it'd been a long time since a woman had made him so nervous.

He stepped out onto the running board, stretching tall above the door. "You ready?"

"Waiting on you." She leaped to her feet and ran down the stairs toward him.

Her enthusiasm was addictive. He couldn't

get enough of it. Once she experienced Evergreen for herself, he was certain the story she wrote wouldn't be like those fluff-pieces of the past. "Well, come on. Let's get a tree, but first let's start by having peppermint hot cocoa. Sound good?"

"Well, yeah! That sounds really good." She climbed into the truck. "Is this another one of those Evergreen traditions? Peppermint hot cocoa?"

"I guess it will be if you agree to do it with me again tomorrow."

She smiled wide, nodding slowly. "So that's how it starts."

"It's just the beginning." Ben started up the truck and made the short drive around the block to Kringle Kitchen. "Just a short pitstop, then we'll be on our way."

"Fine by me."

She hopped out of the truck, and the two of them went inside. Before the door even closed behind them and Ben got the words, "Morning, everyone," out of his mouth, David was out of his chair and across the room in front of them.

"I was just at the library looking for you. I've been going though these things Nan found, and look! Do you know where this picture was taken?"

Ben waved to Carol. "We need two peppermint cocoas to go, please."

"Coming right up."

Ben took the picture from David and examined it closely. The old photo was grainy and had faded over time. The Turners, Hannah and Thomas's parents stood smiling in front of a building with a winter mural painted on it. In the background, he could make out a red truck. "That has to be Allie's grandfather's truck in the background, but I don't recall ever seeing a mural like that in this town. Are you sure it was taken here?"

Hannah walked across the room to see what the fuss was about. Peering over David's shoulder, she said, "I've never seen this photo before." Her smile was an exact replica of her dad's in the picture. "I miss them so much." She reached for the picture. "Where'd you get that?"

Ben showed Katie, then handed the photograph to Hannah, who marveled at it.

"It was in the stack of papers Nan brought me," David said.

Joe motioned over their shoulder. "That's Kringle Alley. Right outside. You can see the old bakery sign in the photo." He pointed to the edge of the photo. "See? It's where I park the cocoa cart."

"I wonder what happened to the mural," David said.

"Uh-oh, looks like someone's wheels are turning," Katie teased.

"Oh, he does love a puzzle," Hannah said. "Just like me."

"Yes," David quipped. "I promise to tell you all

about the key and the mystery of the silent bells in the church last year."

"Sounds like a Nancy Drew mystery." Katie's eyes lit up. "Put me down for that story time."

"No time for that this morning," Ben said. "We're off to pick up the tree for the front of the library. Henry's waiting on us."

"Soon," Katie said to David.

"Deal!" David was more focused on the picture than his conversation with her, though.

Carol carried two large cups of cocoa to go for them. "You two have fun."

"We will." She took one of the cups and headed for the door. Ben held the door for her as she skipped outside and playfully raced him to the truck.

She climbed into the passenger seat and announced her victory, but it was clearly a tie.

"Here we go." Ben turned the key, and they set off for Henry's Christmas Tree Farm.

Katie sipped her hot cocoa, and he liked that she didn't feel like she had to fill every quiet moment with words. Instead, she watched thoughtfully out the window. He pointed out a couple of landmarks, including the old grist mill. "It's still a working mill in the spring and summer. Very primitive, but productive. It's really pretty too that time of year. And over there is where Allie's grandfather used to live and practice. Like Allie, he was a veterinarian. A lot of people would bring their animals to the big barn for his care. Allie focuses more on pets in her clinic in town, but she still does large animals too."

"And this was his truck?"

"It was. He used it for his house calls, and Allie does too."

"This truck really gets around."

"He may not look it, or always act like it, but he's one of the more reliable things in town."

"I'm sorry. But, *he*?" Katie's brow lifted.

"Yeah. He. You're really an Evergreen somebody if you've driven the red truck. And we all know he's a he."

"And let's be honest, what's more picturesque and appealing to tourists than a big red truck hauling Christmas trees?"

There she went again, assuming everything was part of a big marketing master plan. "Yes. I suppose that's one way of looking at it," Ben said.

"What's the other?"

He sucked in an exaggerated breath. "A truck is a good way to haul a tree."

"You've got me there."

"I hate to even say this when we're having so much fun, but why do you keep making this all about tourism?"

"If you were me, writing an article about Evergreen, what's the angle you'd take to translate the monumental amount of 'Christmas magic' here?"

"I don't know." He really hoped she'd see the town for what it really was. "This town is genuinely filled with good hardworking people who enjoy sharing their love of the holiday and the true meaning of the season."

"Not just the commercial side? I mean, there are ten-foot blow-up snowmen, the magic snow globe. Oh, and we wouldn't want to forget that every single store-front, without exception, is decorated. And those people wishing Merry Christmas at the train station. You really think I should believe that was a coincidence?"

"Why is that so hard to believe?"

She pressed her lips together and lifted her shoulders. "It's my experience that when a situation seems too good to be true, it probably is."

He waited, hoping she might elaborate. It was kind of sad that she couldn't just enjoy the joyful mood around here for what it was.

"Okay, so once, before Mom and Dad split up, Dad took my brother and me to see Santa at this little place outside of the city. It seemed like we'd been transported to the North Pole. There were even elves with pointy shoes and ears serving hot chocolate. We got our picture taken with Santa. I was so excited. I still remember what I asked Santa for that night."

"So you've been around people who love Christmas for what it is."

"Not exactly. You see, later that night when we got back, Dad realized my brother had left the picture behind. We heard Dad telling Mom about how he'd wasted two hundred bucks on the charade, and we weren't even appreciative enough to keep track of the picture. Then he told Mom what I'd asked for. Santa couldn't even keep a secret? Not only did I figure out Santa wasn't real, but it was pretty clear the whole experience was just one more way to turn a buck."

Ben could see why she might be a little sour on the idea, but then, why had she come in the first place? He looked into her eyes. He could see that childhood memory hanging like a dark curtain over her mood, but she was here now. She really wants to believe in Christmas magic. "I guess you just need to see for yourself." He turned down the gravel lane that led to the tree lot.

"Fair enough," she said quietly.

So many other vehicles had already driven down this path today that the snow was packed down into two vertical strips, making it like steering a slot car to the barn.

A couple of goats played King of the Mountain on a snowdrift next to the fence, and cows dotted the snow-laden pastures as they lazed in the sun.

"This is so pretty." Katie sat forward in her seat to get a better look. "Business must be really good. That new barn is huge."

Ben hadn't really thought of it that way. Henry worked long and hard to afford that new building. He could see her point though. The shiny red metal barn highlighted how faded the old wooden one right next to it was. The old barn looked almost a muddy pink in comparison now.

He pulled the truck in front of the old two-story shed that housed all the wreath-and-garland-making supplies and put the truck in park.

Henry waved as a family drove off with a tree tied to their roof.

Carol came from around the building, carrying a wooden crate of pine limbs toward the wreath shed.

Ben and Katie got out of the truck. The sun was shining, and even though everything was still covered in snow, it was warm enough that Katie didn't even have to button up her coat.

Henry recognized the red truck immediately. "There you are." He met them halfway, then waved them over. "Come on. Follow me. It's that big tree in the back. I picked out a real winner for ya."

Ben saw it, much taller than the others. "It's perfect."

"I knew you'd like it." Henry motioned for the lot boys to bring it on over to the truck.

"Looks like you've got a good operation out here," Katie said.

"Thanks. Customers are pretty faithful to us." Henry nodded toward Ben. "You can just ask this guy. He worked here three winters when he was in high school."

Ben snickered. "Everybody works here in high school."

"My high school job involved a lot more filing. I'm sure yours was probably more fun."

"It was a good place to work." Ben watched three teens muscle the tree over to the red truck. He jogged over to help them put it into the bed so they didn't scratch the sides.

Katie and Henry watched from nearby. "It smells amazing out here," she said.

Ben shook his head. He knew what was coming next. Poor Katie. She had no idea what she'd just stepped right into.

"Terpenes," Henry blurted out.

Ben laughed. He should've warned her.

Katie looked completely confused. Henry was always happy to share his knowledge about Christmas trees. Ben had heard this speech a million times over the years.

"Each year, someone asks me why Christmas trees smell so nice," Henry went on. "So I went to the library, and guess what. Terpenes. The trees give off the scent to protect themselves from bugs, and some people believe the scent floats up and seeds the clouds and brings the snowfall."

"Wait, is that true?" She turned to Ben for confirmation. "Trees helping the clouds rain and snow? He's pulling my leg. Right?"

Henry interjected. "No. It's true. It's not just a nice smell. They call it cloud-seeding. Do a little of that journalist research. You'll see."

"I will. Thanks for the tip." She pulled out her notebook and jotted it down. "Terpenes."

Henry shrugged; clearly, he'd never been challenged on the trivia before. "I leave the science to scientists. They're doing more tests, but all of it working in a circle like that. Just imagine. It's amazing. I've got trees. I've got snow. Who am I to argue?"

"Wow. Christmas trees," Katie said. "Who knew?"

"Henry knew." Ben tried to hide his amusement.

"Hey, Ben, would you mind?" Henry raised a hand in the air. "I have a library book I need to return."

"No problem. We'll walk up with you."

Just then, Katie's phone rang. She looked at the screen. "I've got to take this. I'll catch up."

She laid her notebook down on the hood of the truck and answered the call, then walked toward the building, talking the whole way.

Ben couldn't help but slow down to take a glance at what she'd written.

Down a snowy lane, you leave the road for a place that's a hive of activity. On the side of the new barn, a cheerful red-and-green sign hangs above the sliding doors—the kind with the white X's on them. Henry's Christmas Tree Farm painted in fun red lettering with snowflakes that look to be hand-lettered on the sign, with a big Christmas tree and red-and-green presents underneath. From the trees and the mistletoe, to the wreath-making barn, not one thing is out of place. Rows and rows of trees line up like toy soldiers, ready to do their part for the holiday. There is a feeling of order, but more so of joy that hangs over the place in an inviting way.

Nice. Maybe she understood more than he gave her credit for.

Chapter Thirteen

KATIE LEFT THE GUYS TO take the phone call. She knew Mom was probably getting antsy about that article. She'd been hoping she could buy a little more time before talking to her, but she couldn't ignore the call, either. "Hi, Mom."

"How's the article coming?"

"Pretty good, actually. I'm at a Christmas tree lot. You should see this place. All red, green and terpenes."

"Ter-what?"

"Never mind. Good to hear from you."

"Great! Because I'm very excited about your article, and so is the editorial board. But more importantly, I'm calling to invite you to our Christmas party at the magazine."

"Mom." Katie found it hard to hide her aggravation. Mom was worse than a matchmaker, only instead of setting her up on dates, she was always trying to get her a job...and she knew Katie wanted to write that second novel.

Katie meandered along the wooden fence. Fresh garland in different lengths hung like decorations until someone bought them. Even all these terpenes couldn't keep her from getting a little tired of the same old discussion about Mom's office party.

"I know. I know I invite you every year. And every year you say the same thing. I also asked your brother if he could make it to the city, but with the new baby on the way, they aren't going to leave Seattle. I told him I'd come out when the little one is born. Maybe you can come with me."

"That would be great. I still can't picture him as a father."

"Hopefully, he'll be more involved than your father was."

She didn't engage on that comment. Dad had been a dutiful father. He always told her he loved her, and supported every activity she was involved in, and there had been many. Sure, he'd worked a lot, but she'd never felt neglected. It'd been hard when they'd split up, though, because neither parent had anything nice to say about the other. Probably exactly why she was so careful about her relationships.

"It'll just be me and you this year again, honey."

"I'm okay with that. I like our Christmas traditions. I like that we keep them small. I like ordering in on Christmas day. Keeping it just us is nice." The thought of sharing Mom with not only her brother but with a grandchild suddenly made her more eager to spend Christmas alone with Mom this year.

"And we will do all of those things. But it's not so bad to share the holiday with more people. And it could open some doors for your future—business and personal. It's a great place to mingle."

"Okay, Mom. I hear you. Listen, I'm not here to ruin your fun. I like that you enjoy big parties. I just like quieter gatherings." She watched the families selecting their trees. They were making memories. "You'd love Evergreen too, Mom."

"But you're RSVPing no."

"I am."

"I suspected as much. Okay, so when am I going to see something about this article?"

"You can expect an email with some story ideas within the next day or so, okay?"

"I appreciate that. Thank you, honey."

"You're welcome, Mom."

A family across the way was having a heck of a time deciding on the perfect tree. Apparently harder than it sounded. Something she'd never done. Living in the city, her apartment building didn't allow live trees, so it was only a matter of putting up an artificial one when she even bothered. If she had to pick one out today, she didn't know where she'd begin. It seemed nearly impossible to pick between them all, standing tied to the posts like that. Fat ones, skinny ones, tall and short. Long needles, short needles, prickly or soft.

Doing her own little test, she checked each of the different species Henry had on the lot. There were firs, pines, and spruce trees, and there were two or three varieties of each of those. Even between some of the same species, the firs for instance, there were subtle differences. The subtle smell of the Douglas Fir was different than the Fraser or the Balsam Fir, which smelled more like her favorite candles; even the needles and colors were slightly different.

Grazing her fingers across the needles, she gave them the sniff test, trying to imagine them decorated. She could imagine for a moment that she was alone in the forest. A calm came over her, so relaxing she wondered if it might wash away her every worry. It was as if Christmas angels on the terpene clouds had rescued her and whisked her away to this magical Christmas place.

She looked around, having lost track of Ben and Henry while on the phone with Mom and this little research side trip. Finally, she caught a glimpse of the back of Ben's green jacket as he entered the barn, carrying a huge box.

"Ben. Wait." She caught up with him. "What's all that?"

"Henry upcycles all the scraps from the trees so others can make wreaths." He set down the wooden box of scraps, similar to the one Carol had been carrying earlier.

"Oh, I see." She followed him over to where Carol and David were crafting a couple of door-sized wreaths out of the pieces. Across the way, others gathered, wrapping bows, live holly sprigs with berries and ribbons into their wreaths. "This just never stops."

"Why does mine always turn out lopsided?" Carol lifted her egg-shaped wreath for them to see. "That's why Allie always hangs mine up at the vet's office."

"The cats don't seem to mind," David teased.

Carol laughed. "So cute. Thank you, David."

Katie found the whole thing quite charming. Her eye caught something off to the side: a sleigh. "Wow. Would you look at this?" She wandered closer. "That sleigh is beautiful."

Henry followed her with a nostalgic twinkle in his eye. "It's been years, but we used to hitch up a horse or two and take this sleigh right through the town square."

Carol joined them. "I used to love that. You know, all these years looking at the sleigh in the snow globe, I always sort of wondered if it was based on this one," she admitted.

"You should see if this one has a key under it like the one in the snow globe," Katie said, half joking.

"What key?" A puzzled look crossed Carol's expression, and Henry seemed none the wiser, either.

"Oh, well, when we took the broken snow

globe over to the tinker shop, Elliott discovered underneath the miniature sleigh in the snow globe, there's a key." Katie ran her hands over the blue velvet seat of the sleigh.

David jogged over. "I heard you talking about the key. Yeah, there's a tiny golden key engraved underneath the sleigh from the snow globe. If there's one there, maybe... Do you think I could..." He pointed to the sleigh, dying to take a peek.

"Go for it," Carol said.

David didn't waste a moment. He scrambled beneath the sleigh, searching the undercarriage. "I don't see a..." He pressed on something, his feet kicking out as he tried to get a better angle. "Wait! Hold on." A clunk and a clang followed and something hit the floor.

David grabbed the key, and Henry gave him a hand from underneath the sleigh.

Astounded, Henry said, "I can't believe it. After all these years."

"No way." Katie reached out and took the key from David. "What?"

Carol spoke up. "It's sort of like the key that David was searching all around town to find a lock for last year."

David eyed the key. "No. This key looks different than the one we found last year."

"The one that got the church bells ringing again?" Ben asked.

"But what does this one go to?" David asked.

Katie shrugged. Henry, Carol, David and Ben surveyed one another. The energy from their imaginations going into overdrive clicked in the air around them.

"And why would someone hide it so well? Were we meant to ever find it?"

Old keys won't open new doors.

It had been fun spending the day with Ben and being a part of finding that key. She was going back and forth with herself about just how real and spontaneous all of this was. They knew she had that article to write. Was she only part of this one big, scripted act to trick her into believing all this Evergreen stuff? And if so, why would they go to all this trouble? That just seemed crazy.

Later that evening, Katie had gone over to the library to work. She was sitting at Nan's desk with books and papers all around her. She scribbled another note on the pad next to her laptop, then began typing like a fiend.

Footsteps caught her attention. When she looked up, Ben was standing in the doorway. "Calvin Coolidge."

Okay. That was the last thing she'd expected to hear. Where had that come from? She tried to make a connection. "Was from Evergreen?"

"No. He was actually born in Plymouth, Vermont. But he was also the first American President to light the National Christmas tree in 1923. He ordered a Balsam fir—"

"I don't believe for one second that Henry is that old."

"No, you're right. Henry isn't that old, but Calvin Coolidge did buy a tree not too far from here. Just a fun little fact."

Katie reached over to a piece of paper and wrote it down. "Calvin Coolidge. Super into Christmas trees. Got it."

"Is that your article?"

"Yeah."

He reached for it, lifting the red folder sitting in front of her to check it out.

"Oh, it will be, yeah." She snagged it back from him. "I like to get it down on paper first." She tucked the folder back under a book and tapped it with a protective hand. She wasn't quite ready to share this with the world yet, and especially not with Ben.

"I'm the same way. Paper. Pen. Old-school. I just like the feel of it."

"Yeah. Me too, but as I'm typing it all in now so I can send to the magazine, something just isn't quite working. Do you mind if I print it again? See if I can figure it out?"

"Be my guest."

"Thank you." Katie sent the file to the printer, and started packing up her things. "So, that tree we picked up today. Did you get it all set up?"

She walked into the other room to grab the print-out from the tray.

"Yes. Now all that's left is to decorate it."

"And when will you be doing that?"

"Tomorrow sometime, if you'd like to help. And also, they're clearing off the ice-skating pond tomorrow if you want to—"

"Oh, no. No, no, no."

"What do you mean, no? Before I even finished asking?"

"People say, 'come do this charming super-cute winter thing. Ice skating.' And then your feet are freezing and—"

"What happened to the 'getting to experience everything in town so you can write about it' girl?"

Katie thought for a moment, then stacked her things. "Using my own words against me is low. But effective. I can't promise winter sports, but decorating, I can. Yes."

Ben smiled and handed Katie her bag. "Don't forget this."

She took it, absolutely charmed. "Thank you. Decorating. Tomorrow. You and me."

"Yes, ma'am."

Chapter Fourteen

THE NEXT MORNING, HANNAH CHANGED clothes three times before finally settling on a red sweater with a wide black-and-white plaid. Not too dressy, but not like she hadn't tried at all. Plus, she always received compliments when she wore red.

I've known Elliott for years. Why is today any different? Relax.

But it was different. Something had changed, or was it just that Katie had made that suggestion the other day at the inn?

And then there was that awkward slip-up. *It's a date!*

She still couldn't believe she'd said that. How awkward. Part of her wished she could avoid him forever, but she really didn't want to do that. She liked spending time with him, and she hoped he could fix the snow globe.

They hadn't exactly set a time, he'd simply said morning, but she knew he was an early bird. She'd hung around the house as long as she possibly could, then made her way down to the shop. Since Elliott had bought the old building and reopened, she'd missed Mom and Dad more than ever.

Elliott's truck was parked out front. She hesitated at the front door. He was working on the snow globe. The only one in the shop. She opened the door and stepped inside.

"Good morning," she said.

He lowered the piece and smiled. "Hi. I'm glad you came."

"Me too." She moved closer to the counter. "I mean, I want to help if I can. You know."

"I was up late working on it last night." He scooted the somewhat-repaired snow globe into view.

"Oh my gosh. It's looking good." She reached for it and turned it carefully. "So good." Overcome with relief, she took in a deep breath. "Thank you so much, Elliott. I know this was a nearly impossible task."

"I wanted to help you." His words were soft, kind. Comforting.

"You are so wonderful."

"Let's see if we can get it back to a hundred percent."

"Okay."

Elliott held the miniature church in front of him, the tiny steeple between a pair of hemostats. With the steady hand of a surgeon, he positioned it back into place and let the glue take hold. "What do you think?"

She clapped, smiling. "I can't believe it."

"One step closer." Elliott didn't breathe a sigh of relief until he'd glued the church back into its place of honor in the center of the decorative base. Still missing the glass globe, at least the trees and the horse-drawn sleigh were back in place too.

"Oh." It came out more of a sound than a word. Hannah swept her sweating hands together and let out the breath she hadn't even realized she was holding. "I can't tell you how much I appreciate this, Elliott."

"It's my pleasure." Without pause, he looked into her eyes.

The warmth of his gaze made her heart leap.

"Now all that's left is to let the glue dry," he said. "Megan said she'd help us get the glass blown to the exact measurement."

"You're a lifesaver." Giddiness from being so near him left her a little wobbly. "It's nice being back in the shop." She meandered through the space, remembering how much time she and Thomas had spent here as kids. She ached for those childhood days when her parents had filled this space with their hard work—where she'd learned that singing made any task more fun. She and Momma would sing through every single project.

"I love this place. Fixing things. Giving broken things a new purpose."

"You did a nice job on the remodel. My parents loved it here. Said it was like a second home. I took my first steps right over there, apparently." She walked over to that spot and stood. She could hear her mom telling the story, like she had a hundred times.

"I'm excited to carry on the tradition that they'd built, even if it is after more than a ten-year pause."

"The years just flew by. This building just sitting here empty. I don't know why we never thought to do anything with it."

Elliott shook his head. "Sometimes we're too close to the memories to think of a place in any other way. Sometimes it's like that with people too."

Was he trying to tell her something? "Maybe." Or maybe it'd been too hard to face those old memories. Out of sight meant out of mind, and what you didn't think about couldn't weigh on your heart. "Thomas and I spent so much time here. Chasing, playing and fighting like siblings as close in age as we are have a habit of doing."

Elliott came around the counter to stand next to her.

"We used to go on all kinds of treasure hunts around this place." She spun the handle on an old hand-crank vise that was still on the counter.

"Treasure hunts?"

"Sometimes like scavenger hunts. Mom would give us a list, but mostly we were looking for Mom's wedding ring. She lost it in the store one day. My brother and I spent weeks searching for it."

"Where did you find it?"

"Never did."

"No." He looked sincerely sorry about that.

"She ended up finally replacing it, but she said the ring would be here somewhere in the store." She let her arms fall to her side. "But we never came across it. Being in here makes me feel close to my parents again. Like we're all home for Christmas again after all these years. That probably sounds crazy."

"No. It doesn't. You know, they're working on opening the pond. Once they do, if you'd like to—"

"I'd love to," she said before he could finish. She shook off the blunder. "We should definitely go ice skating together."

"I've improved enough since high school and can keep up."

"Keep up?" Hannah smirked. "With me?"

"You were the best skater in the high school. And the valedictorian, and the drum major. Keeping up with you took a lot, but I can still remember trying to get you to ice skate with me. You'd always speed away."

"I don't remember it being that way at all. I remember it as being so much fun."

"Really? Well, then I wish I hadn't mentioned it." He shook his head, as if trying to stir up the memory. "I was so embarrassed I couldn't catch up to you. That's why I quit skating and started piano lessons."

"Oh, gosh. I'm sorry. I didn't mean to—"

"No. It's fine. You were still the best friend anyone could have had."

She'd really hurt him. Her heart sank. "Had?"

"Could have. Still are. You know what I mean."

She chose her words carefully. "Well, you're... also still a good friend." She wanted to tell him she thought they could be more, but she was struggling for the words.

Elliott smiled, gazing at her for a long moment that made her insides zing. She lowered her lashes.

"Should I call you when we're ready to take the next step?" he asked.

Those words, *next step*, caught in her brain. She jerked her head up.

Their eyes locked. Hannah couldn't think of anything except him saying *the next step*. Was he feeling this too? But they'd been friends for so long. Wouldn't she have noticed before now?

Hannah touched her face. "What? Umm, what do you mean? Next step?"

"Yeah." He turned back to the counter, pointing to the nearly repaired snow globe.

"Oh? Right. Yes." She recovered quickly, now

realizing he was talking about the snow globe project—not the two of them. *Did I really just do that?* "Great! Please do that. Yes." She fumbled a little, finally escaping before saying something else embarrassing.

She raced down the steps feeling like a fool, but when she looked over his shoulder, he was standing there with a half smile and his head cocked in amusement...or something. Hopefully something good.

Hannah walked straight out of the store to town square without so much as a pause. Her heart was still racing. She was so relieved the snow globe could be repaired, but even more than that, her heart was doing back flips, and those were for the man behind those repairs.

She touched her brow, damp with sweat even in the cool air. *Oh Elliott, I hope I'm not the only one feeling this way.*

When she came around the corner, David stood there in the alley with his hands in front of him like a movie director. As she got closer, she noticed the picture of her parents in his hands. "Do you think that's where the picture was taken?"

David turned and nodded. "I do. I mean, I can almost line up the whole thing. I just don't understand why someone would remove that mural. And why?"

"Maybe it got damaged in the Christmas blizzard?" Hannah said. "I guess that picture would've been about the time of the blizzard."

A tsk came from behind them. Joe had walked up. "It's a shame. The mural really would have been nice to keep up."

David stared up at the wall, still puzzling through this. "I was really hoping I would find it before my dad got back to town. I wanted to show him that I'd solved another puzzle."

Hannah placed a hand on his shoulder. "Think of it this way. You found something about both Evergreen town history and our family history. He's going to be excited to see you either way."

"I can't wait to see him. It's been a couple of weeks this time." David stood there mesmerized by the wall that had once had the mural on it. Maybe what made it more interesting to him was that the picture had his grandparents in it. He'd never gotten the chance to know them. They'd have loved him so much.

It was such a gift that she and Thomas had stayed so close over the years, and when he and his first wife had had David, she'd been the proudest aunt on the planet—like he was her own.

Carol walked around the corner from the Kringle. "Good morning. You're here early."

"David's still trying to figure out that picture," Hannah said.

"And now the key too." David lifted the photograph of his grandparents again. "Two mysteries at once."

"When I was a little girl, my dad would take breaks from the bakery out here," Carol said. "And sometimes I'd come out with my chalks, and I would write all over this wall. He would put a milk crate down, and I would stand on it...right about here."

"You'd have thought he'd mention there'd once been a mural there."

"He never did." Carol walked to the center, and then turned to face the wall. With imaginary chalk in her hand, she swept her arm through the air. "I would design plans for my own diner. The windows were up there. The counter over there, and I'd always put the door here, because see..." She pointed to a spot about eye level now. "There's a little knot in the wood here somewhere that's shaped like a keyhole. See, it's right there." She pointed playfully, as if enjoying the memory, then jumped back, startled. "Wait!" Carol put her hand on the wall, then tapped it. "Is it an actual...?"

Hannah raced over to see.

David clocked in to what was going on. "It's a real keyhole? Do you think the key from the sleigh fits it?"

"I don't know, but this could be something wonderful...or nothing at all."

"We should try it." He was so anxious that he was jumping like a kangaroo on coffee.

"Let's gather everyone. If it's nothing, no big deal, but if it's something, don't you think the gang would like to be a part of it?"

"You're right," David said. "I'll run down the Historical Society phone tree and get everyone to come over."

Chapter Fifteen

KATIE STOOD IN THE INN'S kitchen, refreshing her cup of coffee. She popped a tiny quiche into her mouth. Megan provided such a wonderful spread of delicious nibbles that Katie was afraid she wouldn't fit into her holiday dress if she wasn't careful.

I'm sure going to miss Barbara's County Inn when it's time to leave.

A few pounds was a small price to pay for the new friends and memories she'd made here.

The days were clicking off much quicker than she'd like. Her phone rang. With coffee in hand, she hugged the phone to her shoulder as she doctored it up with a sugar cube and creamer as she answered.

"Did I wake you?" her mom asked.

"No, I've been up for a while. I'm dressed and ready to go."

"Does that mean I'm going to see that story soon?"

"I just have a few more tweaks to make. But I

wanted to start fresh this morning." Katie slid the copy she'd reprinted at the library last night from her notebook.

"Well, I can't wait to read it," Pam said with all the excitement of someone who'd had four cups of coffee already that morning.

"Mm-hmm." Katie picked up the print out, glad this last bit of work would be done and she could get back to what she'd come for—vacation-mode. Only, it wasn't her article. It was a readers group discussion guide. She groaned. "Oh, no. Except I grabbed the wrong paper off the printer last night and—"

"Sorry, what?"

Her breath caught when she realized what had happened. "Oh, no. Mom, I'm going to have to call you back." She slugged back a sip of her coffee and put the mug in the sink, then grabbed her coat as she race-walked out the door to get to the library before someone else found her notes.

She knew the walk to the library by heart now. Her boots clicked on the wooden walk in front of Daisy's Country Store. A pretty gold-dipped snowflake ornament caught her eye in the window, but there was no time to stop and shop now.

As she walked past Allie's red truck parked along the street, she heard someone call out her name. Across the way, a crowd was gathering in the alley next to Kringle Kitchen.

"Katie." She spotted Ben in the crowd. "Katie, come over here."

Hannah, David and Michelle were all staring down Kringle Alley too. Nan and Nick stood off to the side chatting, their faces beaming.

"What is going on?" Katie went up on tiptoe so she could see.

"I honestly don't know," Ben said. "David called me to come down. He said they'd found something. He called everyone in the historical society." He looked around. "As usual, word travels far and fast around here."

Another woman chimed in. "I just saw the crowd gathering and stopped. I don't know, but it's exciting."

Carol came out of the diner, and with a dramatic shrug, she gestured to Hannah and David to join her. "I don't know about all this." She balled her hands into fists then crossed fingers on both of her hands, excited about something. "It's a long shot, but...I don't know, I just have a feeling." She took David by the hand. "Come on."

The two of them marched right past that huge growing group of locals up to the wood slat wall of the building.

David took the key from his pocket, and together he and Carol twisted it into the keyhole that'd been long hidden-in-plain-sight behind the stained wooden siding.

It took a little wiggle. To the left. To the right. Followed by a click that caught Carol and David so off guard that they leaped out of the way. The trim pieces on each side of the building pulled back, and then every horizontally stacked board plummeted into a well-planned stack in a trough below.

The sound of over two dozen boards slapping to the ground in a heap was a little dizzying, but as the racket subsided, a collective gasp replaced it.

Every single person standing there looked up in awe. The only stained boards of the facade that remained were those along the peak of the gable roofline. From the point at the tippity-top all the way to the bottom was one massive masterpiece embedded into a larger-than-life shadow box painting of an Evergreen winter.

"That's the painting from the picture of my grandparents," David shouted.

But it was so much more than just that.

The opening around the painting held carved wooden pieces—snowflakes, evergreens at the base with a single snowman, top hat and all. Twenty-four wooden boxes, each one numbered, framed the shadow box from knee high all the way to the top.

Katie stumbled back, but Ben caught her by the arm. "Is this the, uh…"

"What in the—" He looked to the others. "Is this the time capsule?"

"Wow." Ezra still stared above. "So it's…"

Michelle covered her mouth with her hands. "I can't believe this."

"Is this…is it the time capsule?"

"Yes! Finally!" Nan threw her gloved hands in the air as she spoke. "I cannot tell you how many hints we had to drop. And how perfectly we had to time all of this."

Carol's jaw dropped. "You knew about this?"

"Oh ho." Nick grabbed his belly as he laughed. "We've been dropping hints for three years!"

Nick and Nan were busting at the seams with joy.

"Wow," said David.

"What? For years?" Hannah's eyes popped open wide. "You've known all these years?"

Nan explained with dramatic flair. "The timing had to be just right so you'd all be curious—"

"But not too curious." Nick added, joining Nan in front of the time capsule.

"Until December first of this year," Nan announced, throwing her arms wide. "Today!"

"Sorry. What's happening?" Katie pulled out her notebook and started taking notes. She'd suspected Nan was up to something, but this? No, this exceeded her expectations completely.

Nick stepped closer to Nan. "Carol. Hannah. This was built by your parents fifty years ago during the Christmas blizzard."

"But…how?" Carol's jaw slacked.

Hannah leaned in too, trying to make sense of it all.

Nick went into story mode. "Fifty years ago, Nan and I were much younger then."

"You got that right," she inserted.

"We were all at the Tinker Shop. Hannah, your parents were always hosting something or other, and between it and the bakery just over here, we all were forced to make do through the terrible snowstorm. No supplies, except for what was on hand, but luckily both places were well-stocked and surprisingly everyone was at such peace about it."

"It was like a planned campout."

"With a lot of craft projects."

Nick explained. "That storm lasted for weeks, and since there's only one road in and out of town—"

"We were for most of the month of December hunkered down together," Nan said. "We started a system to share food, share firewood."

Nick said, "And...after a while, it surprised us to find we were really enjoying ourselves. It was more like Christmas than it ever had been before."

"It was wonderful," Nan said. "It was so rare that an entire town would get to come together like that. The twins taught piano lessons. We had embroidery lessons, and there was a lot of music. We read books aloud, we talked, we laughed, and since we had so much time on our hands..."

"It was decided that we'd all work together to build the time capsule," Nick said. "Using everyone's unique skills and talents, we went to work." He pointed to Hannah and Carol. "You kids were so small; you had no idea what we were working on. It was all hands on deck, though, as we created the mural and boxes."

"It was such a huge project, but no one minded," Nan said.

"And that picture of your grandparents, David. That was taken here in front of this wall after the mural was painted and before we assembled the time capsule that spring."

"Wow! It really is a special photograph." He clutched the photo in his hand.

"All of the wooden boxes were made and painted and stenciled during the storm, as were the contents for each of the boxes right there in the tinker shop."

"My friend, you see me having coffee with him often, he was a young artist back then. He designed the mural. The original drawing was just on an eight by ten canvas. In the spring, it was transferred to the wall, and a group of us from school helped fill in the colors like a giant paint-by-number."

Katie could almost picture them huddled together during that storm and the bonds that had to have been made through that experience. It must've been amazing to have all that creativity happening at once. She looked at the mural again. To be a part of something like that, a beautiful mural that would stand the test of time? Truly a gift.

"But why keep the secret?" Carol's brows pulled together, the look of disbelief still in her eyes. "Why didn't you just tell us?"

Joe placed a loving hand on her shoulder.

Nan laughed. "That was your father's idea, Carol. He loved surprises."

"Don't I know it." Carol placed a hand on her heart. "It's a little overwhelming to know Dad had a hand in all of this."

"He wanted us to lead you all to it," Nan continued, "but have you find it on your own."

Carol sniffled back a tear. "Dad always said, 'What's a Christmas present without a little surprise?'"

Nan was enjoying this. "And look! It's not just a time capsule. It's twenty-four boxes. A new surprise every day all month."

"It's an advent calendar." Michelle began making sense of it all. "A Christmas countdown."

David elaborated. "One box for each day between now and Christmas." He about bounced out of his boots at the prospect.

There was an awful lot of head-nodding going on. Katie could hardly take it all in. Was there any way this could even be true? She wrote feverishly in her notebook.

She caught Ben watching her. *Am I being silly? Is this all some big annual Evergreen prank that every out-of-towner is just a pawn in? Like one of those murder mystery dinner shows, only on super-holiday steroids?*

But Ben looked as surprised as everyone else.

"I'm not sure I've ever used the phrase 'Christmas magic' unironically in my entire life, but this..." Katie shook her head. "When's the last time you saw anything like this?"

"Should we open the first box?" Hannah asked.

A resounding yes came from the crowd that'd grown even bigger since they'd first gathered.

Ezra got into the action. "Michelle, care to do the honors?"

Carol urged her on. "Come on, Mayor."

"Sure." With a big smile, Michelle marched right over to the newly found town treasure.

Ben touched Katie's arm. She sucked in a breath, then turned to him with a smile. "I'm going to go help them." He went over to help Ezra steady the tall wooden ladder Joe had just brought around from the back of the building.

Katie rubbed her fingers across her arm where Ben had touched her.

Everyone pushed in as Michelle carefully climbed the ladder in her high heels, up to the top, where she could reach the box marked with a one. Michelle placed her hand in the half moon at the top of the box and slid it forward, kind of like a filing cabinet drawer. She lifted a red envelope from the box.

"Okay, here we go." In a strong and commanding voice, she read the letter so all could hear. "To the people of Evergreen. Now that you've found this calendar, it's our great hope that you will enjoy the gifts inside. The first being—" Michelle stopped. She was reading ahead silently.

The crowd below sensed her hesitation.

Michelle's voice softened. "Carol, this is from your mom and dad."

"Really?" Carol patted her heart, tears streaming down her face. Joe stayed close to her.

Michelle tucked the note back into the envelope and emptied the rest of the contents from the box, then closed it before climbing down the ladder to hand the note and a red book over to Carol.

Joe stood at Carol's side, and Ben walked over and gave Nan a hug with Nick standing close by.

Now that Katie could get a better look, she could see they'd crafted the numbered boxes from old wooden milk crates that had decorative fronts on them. The pin-striping and numbers on each drawer appeared to be hand-painted. She wanted to touch the carved snowflakes in the scene's corner. Done with such precision, it was hard to imagine a group of townsfolk in the middle of a blizzard constructed this all by hand fifty years ago.

This wasn't even her town, and she was emotional about it; she could only imagine what Carol and Hannah were feeling today.

Carol opened the letter and continued to read it to the others, who'd all moved in even closer now. "The first being the original Kringle recipes." Joe tossed his head back with a smile.

Carol read on. "We've placed them here for our daughter Carol so she'll always have a part of us close. May the Christmas surprises in the next twenty-four boxes of this calendar inspire the whole town. Merry Christmas. With love, Mark and Sue Fenwick." A tear in her eye, Carol clung to Joe. "Mom and Dad. I just can't believe it."

Touched, Katie stopped taking notes.

"This is so special, honey." Joe hugged her close. "And exciting."

Before she even realized it, Katie had leaned against Ben, mirroring Carol and Joe. Praying he hadn't noticed the emotional moment, she pulled away. But even that tiny moment left a spark inside her that still tingled in her fingertips. Did he feel that too?

"Well, everyone, it looks like now we have some new recipes to try," Joe said. "So stop by the cafe for some Christmas kringles!"

The town applauded, and people began moving in different directions to get their day started.

"Ready?" Ben asked.

But Katie was too inspired—in awe, really—by what had just happened that she was afraid to forget even one teensy detail. "You know what?

I'm just going to hang back here for just a few minutes and get down a few more notes."

"I should get to the library." Ben hesitated, but then explained, "I'm the one who puts the lights on the tree." He pivoted, walking back toward her. "I've got to get the lights up. I'm the light guy. Stop by later?"

"I will." She watched him walk down the street, right past Ezra, who stood in front of the time capsule still staring up at it. But her focus was on Ben. The confidence in his stride held her attention.

There was so much energy coursing through town square at this moment: smiling faces of the people who'd just witnessed the time capsule reveal, and delight of others as the gossip whipped like a wildfire in a windstorm through town.

She was so thankful she'd been walking by when this had happened.

Suddenly she remembered she'd been heading to the library to rescue her article from the printer. "Ben, wait!"

But he was pretty far ahead. Hopefully, he'd be busy putting up lights until she got there. She couldn't risk missing out on this. She stooped to the ground, placing her notebook on one knee, and scribbled as fast as she could before walking over to Ezra and asking for a few comments from his perspective as the former mayor of this town.

It was no surprise to Katie that Ezra was astounded he hadn't been part of the secret and maybe even had hurt feelings, but with all the seriousness of a politician, he'd responded, "I'm not surprised at all. Evergreen has always held a certain amount of magic and excitement. This is just par for the course."

Chapter Sixteen

KATIE WAS RELIEVED THE TREE in the front of the library was still bare. Hopefully, that meant she'd beaten Ben back to the library. She raced up the steps and inside. Nobody was at the front desk.

She let out a breath. Thank goodness luck was on her side this morning. She walked toward the back room, where the printer was.

Ben stepped around the corner from Nan's office.

"Ben. Hi." Katie froze. From the strained look on his face, she had the sick feeling he'd already found what she'd come to retrieve. "There was a paper that I left on the printer that—"

He moved to the center of the room, where he normally read to the children, and lifted a piece of paper in front of him. The low children's bookshelves made him look larger than life.

Her breath caught.

Without a hint of a smile, Ben began reading from her outline. His voice was clear, and he projected as if performing. The deep crease between his eyebrows further accentuated the tension that already came through in his tone. "Despite the warmth and honest connection these people feel, it's hard not to wonder how much of Evergreen is an act."

Katie hoped her knees wouldn't buckle beneath her. "Okay, first of all, that's just the notes I was taking to send to my mother. Who is also my editor, but—"

He looked so disappointed in her, and that hung heavy in her heart. "I get it. I get how easy it is to say, 'what a bunch of Christmas weirdos,' or 'look at those oddballs running around their Christmas Village.'"

His words stung.

He twisted the paper between his hands into a scroll. "But you've met these people. You've become their friend. Why would you make so light of their feelings? Of who they truly are?"

The words on that page were harsh. It was a story—not the one she wanted to write, the one she should write. "Oh, Ben, that's not what I was doing." She'd never have submitted that draft. She knew it wasn't right yet. She hadn't meant for anyone else to see it.

"Do you really think this is all for show? You can't imagine for a minute we're doing what makes us happy?"

It had been her first impression. She couldn't deny that. "I think a lot of people would come here and find it all a little too good to be true, yes."

"And what about you?" His gaze was laser-steady. He wanted an answer.

Feeling under attack, she didn't know how to respond. "I just watched your mayor open up a wall that has Christmas presents from fifty years ago. I gotta be honest, I'm not sure what to believe."

The twinkle that usually danced in Ben's eyes was nowhere to be found. It was as if a heavy cloud hung over him. His words came slow and steady. "Some places, some people are just...earnest and want what's best for each other. Small towns are—"

She clenched her teeth. "That again? Small towns don't have a monopoly on people caring about each other. I know plenty of hard-working city-dwelling people who make sure everyone around them is cared for."

"You're oversimplifying my point," Ben said.

"And so are you. You're going to have to trust me that I'm not here to write a hit piece about your town."

Ben frowned. "Right." Before he could say anything else, a triple knock at the front door broke his train of thought. "That's the fourth-grade class coming over. I have to get that." He walked past her and opened the door. "Ah! Welcome to story hour, everyone." He masked the situation by imitating a funny inflection. "Get settled. I promise to do my most hilarious voices."

The kids giggled at his Transylvania-vampire accent and gathered around the empty stool where he'd soon sit and whisk them away into a fairytale or holiday story.

Ben corralled them into the room, casting a look of irritation in her direction. He sucked in a breath, then played to his audience like there was nothing wrong.

Most of the kids greeted him by name as they marched inside in what seemed to be an endless parade of kids.

"Ben, I—" She didn't want it to be like this between them.

"I should get in there," he said.

"Ben, wait. I really have enjoyed my time here. Despite my vacation turning into a work trip, I really like the peppermint hot cocoa and the way the whole town rallies to put up Christmas decorations. And I really like..." She caught herself. Surprised that what was getting ready to come out of her mouth was *I really like you.* She stood there, shocked by that realization.

He handed the outline back to her. "Write the article you want to write."

She took it, unable to speak a word.

Quietly, he said, "I hope it turns out." Taking his place on the stool at the front of the room, he poured all of his focus on his audience. "Okay.

Gather around." He spoke with contagious enthusiasm.

Katie watched the children lean in anxiously with their chins tipped up, already enthralled in the story yet to be told.

"On Christmas Eve, on the long, long day that was the twenty-fourth of December..." It was as if Ben's voice had already lulled them into a trance.

Unsure if it was his storytelling or the man himself that had her feet so firmly planted there in that spot in the library, she didn't move. The children's laughter and joy made it hard to pull in another breath.

She lowered her head, hoping he'd forgive her and feeling more conflicted than ever over what to write, or why she was even doing it in the first place. She may have just blown a potentially special friendship with Ben, maybe even more.

A Christmas tree made from books all stacked in a pyramid stood in the corner. Instead of a star on top, there was Louisa May Alcott's A Christmas Dream and How It Came to Be True. Nan had mentioned it was her favorite. It'd be just like Ben to have put that together for her.

Katie slowly backed out of the library with regret and walked through Town Square. Shoppers came in and out of Daisy's Country Store with bags full of gifts for loved ones, and the smell of sausage and bacon, mixed with something sweet, drifted from the Kringle Kitchen. A few people sat outside. Filled to capacity, no doubt. She knew why. Not only was the food good, but the family-owned business truly cared about their role in these people's day. She walked past the Letters to Santa box and went directly to the inn.

Maybe she should just head home now. Had she worn out her welcome in Evergreen?

When she got to the inn, she didn't stop to talk to Megan, who was in the kitchen. Instead, she went straight to her room and closed the door behind her. She stared at her suitcase, wondering what she should do.

She crawled across the bed and closed her eyes. Her intentions had been good. There was something about Evergreen, that was for sure. It might be Christmas magic, it might just be a bunch of kind people with good hearts, but whatever it was, it had had a profound effect on her. Her life wouldn't be the same after this. There'd always be a little sparkle of joy from what she'd experienced here.

She knew what terpenes were, for goodness sake. You couldn't unknow that.

Ben's recitation of that one sentence from her outline hung over her. Was that what her visit here was meant to be? No. No it was not.

Great clarity came over her. She'd come here to work on a new novel. A story that would touch hearts and uplift readers. That assignment wasn't what she was really here to do at all. In no way did it get her closer to her goal of finishing a second book.

She opened her laptop and started perusing the novel notes she had so far. There were a few good ideas here. She could spend the next day or two shaping the outline, getting the plot points down and putting together a plan.

But the appreciation in Mom's voice when they'd been on the phone came back to her. Mom was in a bind. Would it really kill her to write one quick article? It wasn't like she hadn't done so dozens of times before. If she stayed focused, she could probably get the article completed in two days, and then still have time to work on the novel too.

She turned to a clean page in her notebook and picked up her pen. Pacing the room, she jotted down interesting things she'd already seen in town. Things that hadn't been mentioned in the other articles she'd read.

An hour later, she was taking a self-guided tour of Evergreen. She toured that adorable little church and learned that last year David had been the one to figure out the mystery about why the church bells had no longer rung. At the noon hour, the bells rang. They swung inside the tower independently, sending three distinct sounds out across the town.

Katie learned the church was quite the attraction during the summer. People came from all over to get married here. She could see why. With its original handcrafted stained-glass windows, bell tower and history of lasting marriages, the church was like a storybook place.

She spent time at the railroad depot too. The renovated train really had once been the main source of transportation into this town, and still all these years later, there was only one paved road that led in and out of Evergreen.

That night she shuffled through her notes, looking for connecting points that might make an interesting story. She fell asleep in a puddle of papers, but her dreams had been vivid, a mixed-up conglomeration of her childhood and all the things she'd seen and learned today. At one point, she was hand-painting pews in the church. Funny how dreams could be such a mishmash that made total sense while you're in the dream and none once you woke up.

And that's where she was right now. By morning light, all those dreams that had seemed like a fairy tale now seemed like a Picasso. Something was there, but it sure was hard to make sense of it.

She sat up and scooted to the edge of the bed.

A soft tap came at the door, followed by Megan's voice. "Excuse me, Katie?"

Katie slid off the bed and opened the door. "Hi. Good morning."

"I'm heading over to watch them open the second box on the advent calendar. Would you like to walk over with me?"

"Yes. I would love that. Can I take a quick minute to change into something warmer?"

"Absolutely. I'll meet you downstairs," Megan said.

With her hand on the edge of the door, Katie leaned out. "Megan. Thank you so much for checking on me. I'll be right down."

"No worries. Who would want to miss this?"

Indeed.

Chapter Seventeen

KATIE AND MEGAN ARRIVED AT the mural just in time to find everyone already gathered around in anticipation of the second box being opened.

It was eye-opening to realize how many of the people standing around her she could name, aside from Megan. Hannah and Elliott. Michelle and David. Nick and Nan. Carol and Joe. Ezra. Lisa. Even Henry had driven in for the big moment. And Ben. She hated where things had landed between them. There'd been something special happening. A physical, emotional tug of something promising like she'd never experienced before.

She noticed Elliott edge closer to Hannah. "It's chilly out here," he said to the woman.

"I was just thinking the same thing. But I'm so excited to see what's in the next box, it's keeping me warm." Hannah pressed her lips together, not putting any more space between her and Elliott. Katie hoped they'd admit their feelings.

I'm a hopeless romantic. They'd be so good together. If she found herself standing in front of a man who looked into her eyes the way Elliott looked into Hannah's, she wouldn't ignore it for even a second. Her mind drifted, her heart doing a *grand jeté* as she imagined herself in that situation.

Elliott cleared his throat. "After this, do you want to come over to the shop? Megan said she could help us get the snow globe glass done."

Hannah's long lashes lifted. "Oh, yeah. Count me in."

Katie watched the two of them, wishing Elliott would be brave enough to reach down and take Hannah's hand in his. For a moment, she thought he might, but Michelle, dressed in a pretty cashmere coat, chose that second to get things going, and the Evergreenians broke into applause for her.

"All right. Good morning, everyone," Michelle said. "Thanks for coming out to see what is in our second box."

Ezra leaned over to Katie. "She's doing an excellent job of Mayor-ing, don't you think?"

Katie noticed David smiling as he overheard Ezra's compliment. "Like she was born for it," Katie answered. Unable to keep her focus on the advent calendar, she snuck a glance over to where she'd seen Ben standing. He was looking right at her too. She made eye contact with a sheepish and apologetic smile. Ben acknowledged her, but only with a half smile back. It was more of a polite smile, not playful like when he'd seen her yesterday morning. Her heart sank, regretting the misunderstanding and missing the fun he'd added to her time here.

Michelle had everyone else's attention. "Now, I know it will be tough to choose who gets to open these boxes every day, but I have a plan for that."

Ezra folded his arms across his chest. It appeared difficult for him to let go of some of these activities. "Voting system. That's what I'd do."

Michelle lifted a stovepipe hat into the air.

Ezra looked baffled.

"Nan has been kind enough to lend us this beautiful hat. The last original from the Evergreen Hat Factory. It seems quite fitting for such a historical moment as this. After all, how often does a town uncover a fifty-year-old time capsule?" She placed the tall hat on her head, then curtseyed. "So if you're interested in participating, write your name down on a slip of paper and drop it into the hat sometime today. Every morning, we'll meet here, and I'll draw a different name from it." She took off the hat and set it aside. "For now, I think we can all agree that the second box should be opened by the two people who kept the secret the longest. Nick and Nan."

By the applause, it seemed everyone in the crowd agreed.

The two guilty secret-keepers joined Michelle in front of the time capsule. Nan placed a gentle hand on Nick's Christmas tree tie. Applause rose, and Ben ran over to help them. He climbed the ladder all the way to the top to reach the box with the big red number two painted on it for them.

Steadying himself by the frame, Ben carefully slid the box open and reached inside. He withdrew another red envelope and displayed it to everyone, the number two on the front in gold. Like a playful elf standing up on that ladder with his scarf hanging around his neck and that sprightly grin, he seemed to enjoy adding a little dramatic suspense to the process. He bent down, handing the envelope over to Nick and Nan. "Here you go. Number two."

Nan didn't waste a second. She ripped opened the envelope and pulled out the letter. "Ah, I remember this one." She read, "Dear Evergreen, usually by this time of year, the pond has frozen over and it's time for skating. We know there won't be enough for everyone, but may you all enjoy the skating. Inside this box are some Evergreen scarves to keep you all warm. Love, Mike and Marsha Strall."

Ben tossed a stack of scarves tied in a red ribbon down from the ladder, then modeled a long hand-knitted one. "There's a pair of skates in here too."

Michelle interjected. "The Stralls owned the sporting goods store, but they've moved to Ohio."

Nan glanced up as she took the stack of scarves from Ben and began lifting the corner of each one, admiring the stack. "Yes. That was before you could buy everything online. They had all of their things made here locally."

A man stepped forward from the crowd and raised his hand. "I think I can explain this one. Oddly enough." He was dressed in a fancy ski jacket with at least ten ski tags hanging from the zipper. "The Stralls were my grandparents, on my mom's side. Years ago they sent me several boxes of skates and scarves to hang on to until someone from town asked for them. I thought it was a surprise donation or something. I guess it actually kind of is."

"You've got to be kidding."

"Nope. They're stacked up in my shed."

"A lot of planning went into this," Michelle remarked.

"Glad I was here when you opened the time capsule. I remember Grandpa talking about it when I was a kid. Do you think I can borrow Allie's truck? I can take all the boxes down to the pond, and you can distribute them there."

"Absolutely," Carol said. "I can make that happen."

Nan said, "I used to be quite the skater. I still have my skates too. They're quite fancy, in fact. Blue with silver stars on them. Hannah blinged them for me when she was just about David's age. She's always been so artistic in every way." Nan searched the crowd for Hannah. "Do you remember doing that for me, Hannah?"

"I do!"

"Katie, you should borrow them," Nan said.

"Oh, no. I'm not a skater."

"Just in case you change your mind then," she said with a wink.

Michelle clapped her hands. "Everyone, remember that the volunteer fire department is still clearing off the skating pond and making sure everything's safe, so we'll see everybody down there a little later on."

As the crowd dispersed, Katie was hoping to grab Ben and apologize about this morning, but he'd already taken off.

"Hello, Katie. How are you enjoying Evergreen?" Nick stood there, his round cheeks slightly pink from the cold.

She forced herself to turn her attention away from Ben. "Oh, hi, Nick. I can honestly say I've never seen anything like this."

"Wait until you see the skating pond all set up. One of the most fun traditions we have in Evergreen. You really must give it a whirl. I just know Nan's skates would be perfect for you." Nick sailed off as Katie watched Ben walk away without another word.

She'd never been much of a skater, but then, she'd never been anywhere like Evergreen. It'd been a long time since she'd even tried. Nick's words danced in her mind. This time capsule advent calendar made the twelve days of Christmas look like slacker duty. And she was no slacker.

An idea hit her, and it was better than a partridge in a pear tree.

She rushed across the street and entered Daisy's Country Store.

"Hi, Katie," Lisa said from behind the counter. "Good to see you again. Are you looking for something fun, or need something practical again?" She pretended to pout.

"Nothing practical at all. I saw something the other day that would be just perfect for someone." She turned and walked over to the decorated Christmas tree in the center of the store. "I see it from here."

"Great. Let me know if I can help." Lisa turned to help a man who'd just approached the counter with his arm full of gift items.

"I hope you can help me by wrapping these," he said to Lisa.

"Are you kidding? I am the best gift wrapper around. Wait until you see the fancy bows from wire ribbon that I'm going to make for you."

Katie loved how Lisa was so into her store and customers. She browsed through each of the decorated spaces in the store. Lisa had created the most inviting nooks filled with similar items to help customers match items to the people on their shopping list.

Beside a robin-egg blue upholstered chair was a table covered in a rich brown satin tablecloth. Somehow that spring-colored combination felt so homey among all the Christmas decorations. The hand-lettered sign on the table read "Gifts for Mom." Katie took her time, enjoying the chance to perhaps find something special for her mom. She was so hard to buy for. She had everything, and she was funny about certain things like clothes, so there was no sense in trying to buy her anything like that. But there were unusual items here. She picked up three small things. Together they'd be a wonderful gift.

She paid for her purchases, then walked over to the arts center. She'd been meaning to check out the glassblowing ever since Elliott had mentioned it that day at the inn. Today would be the perfect time, since they'd be making the dome for the snow globe. Maybe she'd stumble into more details for her story too.

The air nipped at her nose as she entered the arts center. She raced up the stairs, glad to rush inside and get warm. Near the door, a group of people were whip-stitching felt stockings together. A stack of completed ones were piled high at the end of the table. Two women sat behind fancy sewing machines, embroidering names on them one at a time.

Katie passed by, wishing she'd thought to have one made with her name on it. She hadn't ever hung a stocking by the fireplace in her apartment. Mom probably had the ones they'd used back when she was a kid. She could remember what they looked like—all four of them hung up from left to right: Dad, Mom, Bill, Katie.

Red stockings with white cuffs and plaid toes and heels. Hers had a snowman juggling snowflakes on it. She wondered if she'd loved snowmen before the stocking or the stocking had made her love snowmen.

The room warmed dramatically the closer she got to the fiery furnace, where the glassblowing was taking place. For some reason, she'd pictured the furnace being about the size of a grill, but this was more like a massive full-service brick pizza oven. Long metal tables filled with a plethora of odd tools made up workstations in front of it.

"Hey, Katie," Elliott said as he pushed a long pipe into the furnace. "We're just getting started."

She wandered a little closer while staying out of the way of the equipment. "I hope you don't mind if I just hang out and watch."

"Not at all. Just grab some protective goggles and enjoy."

Katie got a pair of goggles and put them on. They were so big on her face she felt a little like a ladybug. She walked over to admire a towering rack of red-and-green sparkle-laden glass ornaments that'd just come from the annealer and hung to finish the process.

Everyone in this part of the center wore the big safety glasses that, combined with the furnace and all the strange tools, made her feel a little like she was in some kind of sci-fi movie.

Katie took notes as Elliott explained each step to Hannah.

"The furnace heats the glass to two thousand degrees, making it malleable." He dipped one end of the blowpipe into the furnace and rolled it over the molten glass until a gob attached to it. "We call this gathering."

"It's kind of intimidating," Hannah said.

"From here we move to the marver."

It looked like an old metal table to Katie, but apparently whatever it was made out of helped keep the temperature and shape of the glass. She walked over to where Megan was working on something else. "These decorations you've made, Megan. They're so beautiful." Katie opened her blue notebook.

"Thank you." Megan looked up but never stopped working. "Hot glass is like honey." She rolled a metal pipe with a blazing gob of molten glass on the end across a steel worktable. "Co-ordination is key." In a wide-legged stance, she shifted her weight almost like a lunge. "It's like a dance between heat, gravity and centrifugal force." Megan lifted the blowpipe, the gob of glass no longer a small gob but already taking on a distinct shape.

"Where did you learn how to do this?"

"My mother taught me. Also my sister, Barbara. She actually owns the inn. We've been making glass ornaments for years. I sell them down at Daisy's."

"Okay," Elliott said as he pulled a blowpipe out of the glory hole with Hannah standing by.

Katie stepped out of the way, still jotting notes. This was absolutely fascinating. A hero glassblower would have to make it into one of her books someday.

"Let's do this." Elliott placed the gob on the table just as Megan had done with hers. Hannah hovered close, one hand on his back as he shaped the glass. "Time to put the globe—"

"—back in snow globe," he and Hannah said at the same time.

"Thank you for fixing this."

"See, it's still sort of a tinker shop as much as it's an arts center," Elliott said. "I like the name." His eyes were wide, hopeful.

"I know. Thanks for keeping the name. It's just so much more now. The more time I spend time here, the more I fall in love with all it has become. I admire what you've done. Thanks for carrying on our legacy along with it."

"It's part of this town. It should always be." Elliott guided Hannah as she spun the glass on the end of the stick. From behind her, his muscles gave her a steady place to rest as they moved the pipe and formed the shape.

Katie wasn't sure what Hannah was feeling at the moment, but to Katie it looked like a very physical process. "I've never seen this before. It's absolutely mesmerizing," she said to Megan.

"Yeah. It is." Megan walked over to help Elliott and Hannah.

Both wearing protective glasses, they looked like two love bugs. Elliott helped Hannah take over, him guiding her diligent attempt to roll the pipe shaping the form.

She leaned against him, and Elliott snuck a glance from over her shoulder. "Oh. You're a natural at this." Hannah concentrated on the work as he helped smooth her move by placing his hands on her elbows. "Great job."

She giggled nervously, never taking her eyes off the glass. "Well, I want it to be special, just like the snow globe always was."

Katie could see how important it was to Hannah. Not just a prop, but tradition. She felt bad for making light of the snow globe now. She hadn't been fair to Ben.

It was telling that since the snow globe broke there had been no less than a dozen people trying to help put all the pieces back together, be it by consoling Hannah for breaking it or the crafters trying to do the repairs. Actual magic or not, that snow globe meant something to this town, and really, wasn't that what all magic started with, anyway? Believing?

She regretted her snarky remarks to Ben. Sometimes sarcasm got her into trouble. She hadn't meant to be mean, but she hadn't been understanding of his ties to his hometown, either.

Elliott blew the glass, and Hannah spun the pipe to keep it moving at a nice, steady pace to keep the fiery mass round.

Elliott and Hannah both glanced up as Megan measured the clear glass bubble that had formed at the end and then said, "We're right where we need to be."

"Ready?" Hannah looked up expectantly.

"Yes." Megan suited up in big, heavy gloves to help them through the last steps. Then with one well-placed tap, the new globe dropped into Megan's gloved hands. "Now, we just let it cool, and then sand down the bottom." Megan put the globe on the cooling rack, then walked over to the finishing area and lifted two boxes of completed Christmas ornaments into the air. "Word around town is Daisy's Country Store could use some help with their tree this morning. Who else wants to help?"

"We'll help," Elliott answered for himself and Hannah.

Katie slapped her notebook closed. "Yeah, let's go!"

As the sun set, others who'd joined in to help decorate the balsam fir in front of Daisy's Country Store had left, leaving Katie with Lisa to finish the job. It was a delightful surprise for Katie when six o'clock rolled around and all at once the white lights came on, outlining every single building in town for as far as she could see.

Lisa raised her hand in the air. "And this is just one more reason I love this town so much."

"It is..." She stopped short of saying "magical." What was the right word?

"Surprising. Right?"

"Yes," Katie agreed. At every turn, Evergreen was most surely surprising. She felt like a kid again, excited and anticipating something special. "You're so good at this," she remarked.

Lisa laughed, then realized Katie wasn't joking. "You didn't know?"

"Know what?"

"Before I bought the store, I used to stage stores for a living. Christmas was our specialty. Our business was based in Boston, but we traveled all over."

"Well, no wonder. It's like you know exactly where to put everything to make it go from good to amazing."

Lisa moved one of the big poinsettias. "Ah, well, I'll share a little secret with you. You see, the trick is to place things just a bit off-kilter. It attracts attention that way. If you ask me, symmetry is just lazy design."

"Oh. Well, that's good to know. I've been doing it all wrong."

"Now you know."

"How about I stick to putting the hangers on the ornaments and let you do the magic?"

"Works for me." Lisa moved a couple of orna-ments, then tucked a red one in the open spot before stepping back and giving the placement an appreciative glance.

"So you lived in Boston. We're kindred spirits. A couple of city girls."

Lisa nodded. "Yep. I lived here for a while, but then we moved away, and I always had such a sweet spot in my heart for this town. I came back, sort of expecting it to be nothing like I re-membered, but falling in love with it even more."

"So you weren't kidding when you said you came here on vacation and ended up staying for good."

"No. All true. Daisy's had been closed down for years and was in disrepair. Ezra had inherited it from his aunt but needed to sell it. I was here at the right time. I offered to help him put some lipstick on the old pig by staging it to help him get top dollar. In the process, I fell in love with the handyman. Realized my dream of owning my own store that I could stage every day was right in front of me. And here I am." She moved a strand of lights deeper between the branches. "Best decision I ever made."

"Really?" Katie couldn't imagine giving up the city for this...as charming as it was. "And you don't miss the city and that kind of life?"

"Sometimes, but to be honest with you, I had to learn how to be surprised. Like, for instance, I never thought in a million years that I'd be dating a guy who is essentially running a logging camp. Okay? Or that I'd own this incredible store. I love the charm of it, and the legacy I carry on for Daisy in this town. I mean, I'd dreamed of owning a store, but more of a city high-end kind of thing. Then, when I stumbled into this place... It was just perfect." She stepped back from the tree and smiled, then stooped down to pet the two foster dogs, Brutus and Max. "And look. Now I'm hanging out with these two dogs, which you know I'm probably most definitely going to end up adopting."

"Oh, yeah. No doubt."

"It's just one big surprise after the next."

"And that doesn't get exhausting?"

"Surprises?" Lisa looked surprised at that thought. "No. I mean, surprises are great. That's why we wrap gifts, right? We don't just hand them to people. Surprises are exciting. I don't know...maybe a little bit of magic." Lisa tossed a ball toward Katie.

Katie shrieked as the ornament came her way. With a bit of a klutzy juggle, she saved it before it hit the ground.

"Got your heart racing," Lisa remarked.

"It did. It really did."

"See? Surprises are good, and I think we're done with this tree. I love it." She picked up the nearly empty box of decorations. "Want to grab those leashes?"

"Got 'em." Katie followed her inside, imagining what it'd be like to live here. Have her own little dogs and a slew of surprises all year long. It seemed possible here. Maybe it was the pace. Or the attitude. She wasn't sure what it was, but for some reason, it seemed so much easier here than back in the city.

Chapter Eighteen

THAT AFTERNOON, BEN STRUNG THE lights on the Christmas tree in front of the library. The beauty soared every bit of ten feet tall. Maybe twelve. It was hard to tell outside. Either way, Henry had picked them a winner. The tree was so much larger than previous years that Ben had had to scrounge up a couple of extra strands of lights to do it justice. The brisk air became more comfortable the longer he worked. By the time he'd gotten all the lights strung, he'd had to come out of his scarf and jacket.

In years past, they'd decorated the tree outside with old glass ornaments Nan had collected over the years. They'd seen better days, and several had broken. Worried someone might get hurt, Nan had purchased new ornaments made from plastic at the end of the season last year. When they'd arrived, they were huge. Ben had teased Nan, saying they looked more like playground balls than ornaments.

He owed her an apology now, though, because

those big four-, six- and eight-inch balls worked great on a tree this size, easily filling in the bare spots. It hadn't taken nearly as long to decorate, either.

With the brilliant glass Moravian star on top, the tree was quite grand. Ben admired his handiwork, then stepped back and took a picture with his phone to post on the library social media page.

The tree dazzled in the sunshine, but he couldn't wait for Nan to see it all lit up tonight with all the extra lights he'd used this time.

Ben carried the empty boxes inside to store them in the attic.

This year, the holiday was turning out to be even more amazing than usual with the discovery of the time capsule, and now the daily advent calendar celebrations. He could hardly blame Katie for being a little skeptical under the circumstances.

He didn't want to be mad at her, and sour moods were no fun either. Part of his frustration was that he wasn't sure why he was really mad at her. She was entitled to her opinion. He didn't even know her. She surely didn't owe him anything. But there was something about her that kept his attention in a weird push-pull kind of way.

Evergreen was a small town, and she was a guest. He'd have to make nice with her. It was the right thing to do.

More cheerful after having accomplished a few things this morning and the decision to make up with Katie, Ben went back downstairs, whistling "Up on the Housetop." On his way out the front door, he noticed a red box with a green bow sitting on the desk. People were always leaving little thank-you gifts for Nan.

Curious, he stopped and picked it up. The box was as light as air. Tucked beneath the bow, a makeshift card from a folded piece of wrapping paper peeked out. It read, *"Ben, Winter Sports Attempt at the Skating Pond? 7 p.m.?"*

That light little box and note carried some weight. *Katie?*

A smile spread across his face. One so big he could feel it in his cheeks.

He lifted the top of the box and peeked inside. A glass star ornament edged in gold lay nestled atop a plush bed of cotton. He picked it up by the gold cord. *I know exactly what I'd wish for on this star.* To spend more time with Katie. Sharing a few smiles. Making her believe, like a real Evergreenian. Tucking the ornament back into the box, he was glad his afternoon was going to be busy with helping out at the pond to get things ready for the first night of ice skating. Otherwise, it'd feel like one long day.

He tucked his skates under one of the benches, then went over to the skate rental building to help them unpack the boxes donated by the Stralls.

The fire department posted their safety approval, and then everyone pitched in to get the holiday light tunnel set up where people would enter and exit the ice. Ben had been a part of this transformation since he was in high school, but still it surprised him how different everything looked decorated for the holidays.

By dinner time, Ben and Nick had already handed out a good many scarves. At six o'clock, the lights on the bridge automatically came on, only tonight there were other decorations too. He must've checked his watch more than a dozen times from that point, anxious for seven o'clock and to see Katie.

Thank goodness handing out scarves didn't require much attention, because he was squarely focused on the bridge that went over the skating pond.

Following the excitement from today's time capsule box, tonight had to be a record-breaking attendance for the first skating night. Everyone wore the colorful scarves. It looked like a kaleidoscope of colors with everyone skating and spinning on the ice. Smoky puffs from the warmth of the skaters' breaths in the frigid air disappeared as quickly as they expelled them. He sucked in a lungful of air. It smelled like snow to him. That fresh, clean air that seemed almost too thin to breathe sometimes.

Finally, he caught a glimpse of Katie walking across the bridge. She'd stopped and leaned over the railing, watching the skaters below. He grabbed the scarf he'd set aside for her. Technically, she wasn't a resident, but she'd been a big part of uncovering the mystery behind the time capsule, so it seemed only fitting she should get to partake in the gifts too.

"I've got to run," Ben said to Nick.

Nick followed his line of sight and smiled. "Yes, you do. I've got this. You go enjoy your evening," he said with a wink. "She's a special young lady."

"I think so too." Ben patted the old man on the back. "Thanks." He ran up the path toward the bridge, slowing to a walk to catch his breath, going over in his head what he should say.

Standing there holding Nan's skates, Katie looked beautiful.

"Hey," he said.

She turned with a smile. "I'm glad you came. Ben, I never meant to—"

"Thank you." He caught her elbow with his hand. He didn't want her to feel like she had to apologize. He smiled and lifted the soft scarf he'd been holding. "I brought you one of the scarves from the time capsule."

She took it into her hands. "I love it. Thank you."

"Thank you for the ornament."

"It reminded me of that star cookie you made at Megan's. The falling star." She mimicked his gesture from that night, his fingers waggling as he'd soared that cookie through the air.

"It's great." That had been such a silly antic, but it was so easy to be playful with her. "Are you ready to give this a try?"

"I got Nan's skates. I hope they bring me some luck." She spun around. "I'm telling you. No matter how many dance classes, gymnastics, even hours of vigorous Pilates practice I've done...I'm going to fall down."

"That's okay." He leaned against the railing next to her. "I'll be there to help you back up."

She pushed her hands into her pockets, staring out over the pond. "The view from up here is breathtaking, and this bridge...the heavy timbers. I can't imagine how it was built."

"It was built by beavers, y'know."

"The bridge?"

"No. The pond. Before anyone even lived in this area. I come out here in the summer to watch them work."

"And then in winter, they huddle into their little beaver shacks and...drink beaver eggnog?"

"Can any of us really know for sure?" He loved how she got his sense of humor. That had to mean something. Was that enough to build something on? They could play, but could they compromise and forgive?

She turned to face him, her back to the railing. "I was a little tough on you before."

"I was tough on you too. And I'm sorry about

that. They were your notes. I had no right to read them, or judge you by them."

"No, I get it. You really love this place. I get why you'd be protective of it."

"Well, and I also get how it'd look to someone not from around here. And I don't believe that all people living in a city are..."

"Cynical?"

"Yeah."

"Cold?" Katie teased.

"No. Not cold either, or maybe they are when it's freezing out, but you know what I mean." He knew she was teasing. "You know, I used to live in Chicago. Five years. I loved living in the city, actually."

"Really?" She folded her arms across her chest. "So then why did you leave?"

He liked her. If he was even remotely considering pursuing her, she deserved to know about his past. He hoped it wouldn't make a difference that he'd been married before. He wasn't sure how to share that.

Before he could respond, Michelle walked up with her skates draped over her right shoulder. "Hey, guys. Are you two heading down to the ice?"

"Yes. About to face my worst fears," Katie responded. "I see you are too."

"Yeah, and I had to bring David his hat. He's always forgetting it." She lifted the red toboggan, straightening it sweetly in her hand. "Thomas usually does this, but with him gone, I'm filling in."

Ben noticed the longing in her mannerisms. She was really missing Thomas, and she was such a natural with David. It was hard to believe they'd only been dating a year.

"Michelle!" The voice came from below on the ice rink. There, in the middle of the ice with dozens of people skating around him, Thomas stood on ice skates with his arms flung out wide into a hug.

"Thomas!" Michelle raced to the railing as if proving to herself she wasn't dreaming. "Thomas! It's you! You're early." She turned to Katie with her mouth and eyes wide. "I can't believe this!" She turned back, waving madly.

"I wanted to surprise you." He spread his arms again. "Surprise!"

"All right! Oh goodness. Thomas!" Michelle could barely contain her excitement. "You wait right there. I'm coming down!" She clenched her fists and set off down the bridge to catch up to him. "Oh, my gosh. I can't believe this. Excuse me."

"That is so romantic." Katie held her hand to her heart. Thomas wasn't waiting; he was already moving across the ice at a high speed toward Michelle.

"Shall we?" Ben asked, nodding toward the couple.

"Yeah. Let's."

He grabbed Katie's hand. They took the stairs like two athletes racing bleachers to the pond level to catch up with Michelle for the reunion.

Michelle raced across the snow to meet Thomas, who was skating through the decorated arches to the edge of the pond. She ran right into his arms, and they kissed.

Ben and Katie stood nearby. He wrapped an arm around Katie's waist as they looked on. She relaxed against him. He took in the scent of her hair as they watched on together.

"I was worried you wouldn't make it." Michelle reached for Thomas's cheek.

"I almost didn't. I got through just before they closed the roads. It was pummeling the place. I hope Kevin made it out too."

"Dad!" David sped across the ice as fast as an Olympic speed skater, ramming to a stop right into Thomas, bear-hugging him around the waist.

"Hey, look at you. You're even taller than when I saw you a few weeks ago." Thomas clapped an arm around his son's shoulder. "It's so good to see you both."

"We've been good, but we're glad you're back." David hugged Michelle.

"Who's ready for hot chocolate?" Michelle asked.

Both guys pointed to themselves. "Me!"

"Quite the reunion," Ben said as he and Katie watched nearby.

"They make such a beautiful family," she said. "How long have they been married?"

"They're not. But I think that's just a matter of time. They met last year during the Christmas festival. Thomas is Hannah's brother."

"Right, because David is Hannah's nephew. I got it." She glanced over again, a sweet look falling across her lips. "They look like they've been together forever." Her voice was soft, almost longing.

He felt the same way when he watched those two together. "I know, and she's so great with David." Ben took Katie's hand. "Come on. I'll get you a hot chocolate too."

"That does sound good."

Across the pond, Joe had the kiosk he often used in Kringle Alley set up rink-side. Only now, it was dressed up with a wreath and Christmas garland. There was no cash register, only a big glass pickle jar, which was already filling up with coins and dollars. The price of hot chocolate... just a donation.

Ben stepped up and ordered two. "Peppermint, please."

Katie grinned. "It smells so good." She took a deep breath in.

Joe filled green holiday cups to the very top, added a little peppermint, and then whirred them with a frother.

"Two peppermint cocoas." Carol dropped peppermint sticks into them and handed them to Ben.

He dropped a five-dollar bill into the jar. They stood there, sipping down the sweet drinks. "My favorite."

"I always just had it with marshmallows, but now I'm a big fan of the peppermint. What a treat. I'm going to miss this."

Stick around, then. "You can always visit to get your fix."

"Truly."

"Come on." He walked over to one of the benches near the pond. They sat together, clutching the warm cocoa. She leaned closer, bumping her shoulder to his. "It's nice out here."

"Not a ploy. Not marketing. Just locals getting together for ice skating."

"And not even a price on the cocoa. Can't get more real than that, can you?"

"Nope." He lifted a hand in the air, then dropped it on top of hers. "We've stalled about as long as we can. Are you really going to skate with me?"

"I am." She put the skates on the ground in front of her. "I wasn't lugging these around for nothing."

"Awesome. My skates are over there under that bench. I'm going to go get them. I'll be right back."

By the time he got back, Katie had laced up Nan's fancy skates. "I hope you're a good skater, because I'm going to need someone to hold on to."

He kind of liked the sound of that. "Nan taught me how to skate when I was just a boy. She was kind of known for her elegant ice dancing, but I'll tell you, that little woman was a kick-butt goalie too. She taught me everything I know about ice hockey."

"No way."

"Truth." Ben took both of her hands in his and helped her stand. Warmth spread from his fingertips right to his chest. For a moment, it was as if he were in some kind of dream. They edged their way through the grass to the edge of the pond. He stepped out on the ice first and then helped her.

Her feet scissored, but he steadied her.

"I told you I'm not good at this."

"Nobody is," he said, trying to get her to relax.

Several very good skaters whipped past them.

"They're good," she said, pointing at a couple holding hands skating gracefully. At that moment they parted and spun so fast they were almost a blur. "And they're great at it."

"Yeah. They're pretty good."

With her arms out for balance, she was a little clunky, but she was getting steadier. "So, you left Chicago because...?"

She never let up with the questions. He admired her tenacity. This was his chance to come clean. "I needed a change. I was at a job I didn't love, and I'd just gotten divorced."

"Wow." Compassion etched her face. "Breaking news," she said quietly.

"Right?" Ben had known he had to tell her about his divorce eventually. "So, I came home to visit, and while I was here, Nan broke her foot."

"Oh, no."

"Yeah, and I stuck around to help her out, and to figure out what was next for me after having my marriage end."

"I see. And did you figure out what's next?"

"I did. But after a few months, I fell back in love with the library, and then those few months turned into a year, and then five."

"So, five years go by, and you're staying in Evergreen forever? You don't miss the work?"

Ben confessed, "I do miss it, actually. I still sometimes scan job postings. Even in New York. But...Nan. I think Nan needs me here. So, this is where my life is now."

"Which begs the question. What's the dating scene like in Evergreen? Is there a magical snow globe that comes out at Valentine's Day too?"

"Are you kidding me? We're still singing Christmas carols at Valentine's. And we don't even take our trees down until Easter." But it was a legit question. He looked down, wishing she was part of this dating scene. "Our dating scene is small, which is a shame." He lifted his gaze, smiling as she hung on his words. "Because it's...it's fairly romantic."

"Yeah." She lowered her lashes as if she was dreaming of something romantic right now.

He could picture something like that so easily too.

"It would be a nice place to build a snowman with someone. Sit by the fire after." She lifted her gaze to meet his.

Ben wanted to kiss her, but he stopped himself. She'd be going back to the city. His life was here in Evergreen. Why complicate it? A snowflake landed on her eyelashes. He reached to brush it away as it fell to her cheek. "Sorry, you have a—"

"Oh?" She ran her glove across her cheek. "Thanks."

"It was just a snowflake."

Katie hesitated, her mouth slightly parted. He wished he'd kissed her just then.

"Hey, Ben." Thomas walked over. "I thought that was you. Good to see you."

"Hi. Welcome back."

"This is a new face," he said, noticing Katie. "Hi. I'm Thomas."

She extended her hand. "Nice to meet you. I'm Katie. Have to admit I just saw your reunion with the town mayor. Very romantic to surprise her like that."

"I try." His voice was as deep as he was tall, and happiness etched every line in his face.

Michelle and David walked over. "I see you've met."

He grinned. "I have a logging operation up in Maine. I'm setting up headquarters here, but I had to take care of things there until we shut down. It's taken a lot longer than I'd planned. It's worth it, though."

"Because of Michelle," David said.

The woman blushed. "Well, not really. It just—"

"No." Thomas stopped her. "David's right. Michelle is a big part of why I chose to settle here in Evergreen. My sister, Hannah, is here too, but it's Michelle. This beautiful woman in front me. She makes this town feel like home."

Michelle looked taken aback. "Thank you, Thomas."

"It's all true," he said, with a prideful tilt of his chin.

Ben longed for that same feeling Thomas had written all over his face right now.

Chapter Nineteen

*L*AST NIGHT, KATIE HAD USED muscles she hadn't used in a long time. Her legs ached from the ice skating, but it'd turned out to be a fun night after all. And she hadn't fallen but once, and even then, Ben had been right there to catch her before she'd hit the ground.

She carried a cup of coffee from Kringle Kitchen over to where Hannah was leading the choir members in a lovely version of "Angels We Have Heard on High." The locals slowly gathered around the advent calendar in preparation for opening the next box at the top of the hour.

The choir filled the square with a joyful noise, their voices lovely even with no musical accompaniment. It lifted Katie's spirits when everyone else joined in with the choir for those Glorias, the harmony rising to the heavens.

She sat down on the curb to write down everything that was happening and how she was feeling at this moment in her notebook while she waited.

"Still at it, huh?" Ben asked.

Her heart leaped at the sound of his voice. Had he been standing there long? "Hey, Ben. I am still at it. I was just going over all of my notes. I've interviewed a few more people. I didn't know the story about Lisa re-opening Daisy's General Store until I was helping her decorate the tree."

"Yeah. She came down from Boston for a visit."

"So I hear. And then never left."

"That's right. Happens all the time." His eyes searched her for something. Did he know that she was, in a way, wishing it might happen to her? Even though she knew she couldn't... wouldn't...make a life here in Evergreen, it was certainly alluring.

She tucked the notebook under her arm. "I also heard a great story about twin sisters who live on a farm called Two Pine Farms. I can't wait to interview them. They were there with Nan and Nick during the big blizzard."

"So you feel good about your story."

"I'm still working on it. I decided to try to talk about Evergreen in this article in a way that would make most of my jaded city friends want to come here for Christmas."

"It's a good angle," he said.

"Well, I'm really not sure it will work for the magazine. But luckily, Mom's been looking for other projects, so maybe she'll find a better article for the magazine and I'll be off the hook. Either way, I'm sticking around for a while to enjoy the festivities."

"Good." A wide grin spread across his face, and that made her day.

She stood. "Let's go get a good spot so we can see what's in the next box of the time capsule."

"After you." He swung an arm wide then walked with her past the choir to a spot right in front of the mural.

Michelle was right on their heels. She stepped in front of the advent calendar. "Good morning, Evergreenians. We'll be opening the next box here shortly, so grab your friends, and we'll get started in about five minutes."

"Just in time," Katie said to Ben.

Michelle walked over to Hannah. "Thanks for bringing the choir together for this. What a great idea."

"It makes it even more special," Katie added.

"Thanks. I thought we'd multitask. We all want to see what's in the daily box, and we need the practice. A win-win for the Christmas Festival."

"Ah, the Christmas Festival always ends up being just fine. I'm not worried about that."

Hannah stopped and looked at Michelle. "Is this my same friend who almost had a total breakdown over decorations at the last festival? Honestly, I don't think I've ever seen you this calm about anything." Hannah glanced over at Katie. "Seriously. One year we almost had to have her breathe into a paper bag to keep her from hyperventilating."

"Wow." Katie couldn't even picture it.

"True, but not anymore." Michelle popped a hand onto her hip. "Everybody's going to have to stop saying that. The Christmas season is upon us—we get to bundle up in scarves and eat pie for breakfast. What's to stress over?"

"I don't know...something is different this year. You seem very happy. And you have for a while now. Happy and relaxed."

"Is it the pie?" Katie asked. "If that's all it takes to be happy and relaxed, I'll take a double serving."

"Pie helps, but I can promise you that's not it." Michelle blushed. "I think that's what love does to a girl."

A high-pitched squeal escaped from Hannah as she wrapped her arms around Michelle. "I'm so glad you said that. He's so in love with you too. And thank you for not being mad with me about the snow globe."

"I'll be honest. I think the old me might have gone a little cuckoo when that snow globe broke. It's definitely a town draw, but I was more worried for you. You were the one who convinced me to wish again. When I wished on that snow globe last year, I had no idea that Thomas would be my answer."

"You?" Katie looked at Michelle, then to Hannah. "Your wish came true?"

Michelle nodded.

"It does grant wishes. We've seen it happen." Hannah squeezed Michelle's hand, then wrinkled her nose. "But now...I don't know. I think my wish needs updating."

"To what?" Michelle and Katie said at the same time.

"I'll let you both know *if* the snow globe is fixed." She crossed her fingers. "We're very close to having it all done."

Ezra showed up with the top hat for Michelle to draw the next person to open a box, and the town began applauding, anxious for the next big reveal.

Michelle walked over and addressed everyone. "Okay, everyone, let's open another advent calendar box, shall we?"

Katie looked out across the people of Evergreen bundled up with their rosy-cheeked neighbors, all anticipating the possibilities.

Michelle reached into the hat and pulled out a name, then read it. "Henry Miller!"

"Hooray!" Henry jumped in the air and jogged over. "I can't believe it." He rubbed his hands together, then moved the ladder to where he could climb up and pull out the next box.

A garland of Christmas trees represented an assignment for that night. The whole town was to get together for a tree lighting at seven o'clock. Forming a large circle around the tree, holding hands, the whole town was to sing "O Christmas

Tree." It was really the perfect box for him to open.

There was no way Michelle could've rigged that.

Magic? Have I gone crazy to even entertain that might be a plausible answer?

She stood there, trying to make some logical sense out of it all. There was no other explanation.

As if Ben knew exactly what was rolling through her mind, when she looked up and caught him staring at her, he winked. "I'm headed over to the library if you want to come with me."

"I do." She didn't hesitate, keeping in step with him the whole way over. Barely an inch between them as they walked.

Nan was already inside, tidying things up.

"I'm going to do a little research this morning if you don't mind." Katie took off her coat and hung it on the rack near the door.

"No problem," Nan said. "What are you looking for?"

"Articles about the blizzard fifty years ago."

"Not a problem. I've got all those old newspapers on microfiche. Do you know how to use one of those machines?"

"Sure do."

"Follow me." Nan led her to the room and got her set up with the films from that year.

Katie sat there for hours, reading the articles

and jotting down names, hoping to uncover more nuggets that would be interesting reading.

Her meeting later that afternoon with the twins over at the farm was delightful, but not very informative. They weren't sharing many details. They did, however, elude to having a special box in the advent calendar and left her with a *wait and see for yourself.* Maybe her investigative reporting skills weren't as sharp as she thought.

Then again, she didn't really want to be a reporter. She wanted to write fiction, and boy, did this place spark those ideas. Her notebook was now full of ideas for a book filled with tradition in a community that embraced the holidays and put friends and family first over anything else. She'd checked out a few holiday novels and had devoured them one a day for the last few days. Did the world really need one more Christmas novel?

Every time she read The End, she was convinced it did.

She wished she hadn't felt inclined to accept the challenge to write an article for the magazine, because if she'd been free to cut loose and work on a novel while she was here, she knew she'd have thousands of words on the page by now. Instead, she kept writing and rewriting the same fifteen hundred words, and it was a decent article, but it wasn't what she really wanted to be working on.

The next few days, she worried less about

that article and concentrated on just enjoying her time in Evergreen and getting to know the people. Each morning, she rushed to get dressed to go see what the advent calendar would behold. She'd be lying if she didn't admit that meeting up with Ben there was a big part of the draw. He dropped more Evergreen trivia on her daily, which set her day off to a good start.

And even though the contents of the advent boxes differed, they still all carried a thoughtful message that set the theme for the day, and with that she got to know Ben a little better. It was nice that she'd been able to extend her trip when they uncovered the time capsule. She would have hated to miss all of this. But now her time was quickly dwindling, and she worried she might be a little too interested in this small town man. As much as she loved this town and these people, she knew she couldn't live here. She looked over at him. He'd said he loved Chicago. Was there any way he might fall in love with New York City? Maybe even consider a move? A girl can dream.

On the fourteenth day, Michelle pulled the name out of the hat. "Day fourteen is Ben Baxter!"

Katie and Ben hugged in the excitement, and then he opened up the box. He pulled out a string of giant cookie cutters made from copper. "I think this means it's time for another night of baking cookies at Barbara's Country Inn. Who wants to help?" His eyes went straight to Katie.

Her heart fluttered at being considered one of the gang. "Count me in." She couldn't wait to get in the kitchen with him again. Shoulder to shoulder.

"We'll make a night of it," Megan said. "And whoever bakes cookies and wants to participate in a cookie swap, come to the inn Saturday at noon with however many you want to swap. It'll be a fun way to get a wide variety of goodies with a whole lot less work and mess."

That night, Ben came over to the inn with a bag full of groceries and a laminated recipe card.

When they walked into the kitchen, Megan was putting together a goody basket for new guests arriving. "You two make yourself at home in here."

"You're not going to help us?" Katie asked.

"No, I've got plenty of other things to do. Have fun."

Katie would be lying if she said she wished Megan had stayed. It was kind of nice being in the kitchen with Ben without half the town around. Just the two of them. Would it be like this in their own kitchen? She tried to picture him at home in her condo.

Ben unpacked the groceries and set them on the island.

"Laminated. This must be one special recipe." She reached for it.

"Yeah. Nan's grandmother's shortbread cookies. I think you'll really like them." He snagged the card from the table. "Of course, I'll have to swear you to secrecy. It *is* a family recipe, after all."

She zipped her lips. "My lips are sealed."

"Excellent."

"So, let's get started. What do we need to set the oven to?"

"Three hundred," he answered from memory.

"Are you sure? I don't think I've ever baked anything in my oven at less than three twenty-five."

"Trust me."

"Okay!" She set the temperature on the oven then went back over to the island. There were only three ingredients on the paper. Sugar, butter and flour. "Is this all there is to the whole recipe? Three ingredients?"

"Yeah."

"I can't believe you have a laminated recipe card for a three-ingredient recipe. It can't possibly be this simple."

"Believe it." He turned, then slowly, softly, said, "You know, the best things in life don't have to be all that complex."

She turned toward him to respond, just as he stepped forward. "Oh!" She stumbled, nearly falling into his arms, but he caught her by the waist, his hand grazing her lower back. Her breath hitched. "I believe that."

He pushed her hair back from her face. "Good."

The oven started beeping, indicating it'd reached the desired temperature. She touched her forehead and turned around to get a glass of ice water.

Before the night was over, they'd made sixty shortbread cookies using the cookie cutters from the time capsule. The stars were her favorite.

The next afternoon, she was working on her article when Ben walked in.

"How's it going?"

"Okay. Added the thing about Eisenhower being credited with inventing the Christmas advent calendar, and that gave me an opening to talk about the time capsule. I like that. I also mentioned that in addition to tourism growth, there's been population growth. I think—"

"You're done?"

Katie shook her head and leaned forward on her elbows. "No. I mean, maybe. It's gotten hard to write. It's a business magazine, so while I know what they want, more and more I feel like I'm missing something. The word count is there, and it's due tomorrow, but something about it isn't…quite…"

"What? Are you afraid they're not going to like it?"

"No. Not really. I love freelancing. And I've been able to do it for a while now, but that's not what I want to do. I think I'm more worried they will."

"Them liking it is a bad thing?"

"I want to write my second novel. It's harder. Takes longer. And there are no guarantees."

"Well, when are you going to start working on that?"

"I guess as soon as I turn this in." She looked at the stack of paper she'd accumulated about this town over the past couple of weeks. "So many people have told me so many wonderful stories about this town. I just want it to be wonderful."

"It will be. And hey, look at it this way. You're probably now more of an expert on Evergreen than any of us who live here are."

She wadded up a piece of paper and tossed it at him.

He ducked playfully.

"So, I guess I'll just have to do a final pass on it in the morning on the train."

"Tomorrow?"

"That's the plan, yeah." But she wasn't ready to leave. She looked at him. *Say something. Ask me to stay.*

But he didn't; he simply nodded with no clear expression on his face. This was it. Was this all there was meant to be for her in Evergreen?

"So, I guess I should go. I've got to get packed and—" Katie caught Nan from the corner of her eye as she came down the stairs, dressed in a forest-green wool coat and a beautiful scarf. "Wow, look at this."

Nan walked into the room. "Well, this was

my mother's caroling scarf, and her angel pin." She ran her fingers over the lovely red-and-green plaid. Gold threads woven into the design picked up on the shiny gold of the pin fastened to her left shoulder. The pride of tradition showed in Nan's eyes. "The Christmas calendar has everyone so excited about our old traditions, we've even fired up a few from long ago."

"Really? Like what?" Katie asked.

Ben looked on, and although Nan wasn't his mother, Katie could feel the special bond between them.

"Caroling tonight."

"Well, you look—and that sounds—amazing. All of it." Katie scanned the room. She would definitely miss Evergreen. "I should get back to the inn."

"Oh, we're about to go caroling out that way. Why don't you come and join us?"

Ben lit up. "You should come! It really is a lot of fun. I bring my guitar."

"You play the guitar?"

"I do."

Smart, creative and musical too? "I can't miss that. I mean, that does sound fun. Okay, yes. Do I need to know all the words or—"

"No, we know all the words very well. You can even just hum along," Nan said.

In a whoosh of excitement, Katie swept all of her research materials into one stack. "Great,

I'll meet you two outside in just a minute. I just need to re-shelve these."

As Katie eased the books back on the shelves in their respective spots, she overheard Nan talking to Ben. "I almost forgot. You know how finicky that old printer is. I found this jammed inside. I wanted to make sure you had it."

He took the page and looked at it. "It's just a job posting in New York. Yeah, that wasn't anything."

Katie heard the paper crumple, and the balled-up dream hit the trash can just before the door opened and they walked outside.

What would it be like if Ben worked in the city? Maybe meeting up for lunch occasionally? They could catch the train down here to Evergreen at the holidays. She could see herself spending more time with him.

She grabbed her coat and went out to meet up with them for her first time caroling.

Chapter Twenty

HANNAH HAD DRESSED IN HER caroling attire, a green sweater, before going to meet Elliott. She was due to catch up with the others in front Daisy's Country Store here shortly.

She leaned over the counter in the Tinker Shop, watching Elliott fill the new glass globe with liquid. He looked so handsome dressed in a button-down shirt tonight. He was wearing a fun Christmas tie, kind of out of character for him, but she liked this side of him.

Shivering in anticipation, she said, "It's really going to be okay, isn't it?"

"Oh, yes." Elliott kept his hands and eyes focused on his work. "This snow globe will be as good as new."

"I sure hope it still has the old magic."

"That...I have no control of." He gave her a playful grin. "It takes just the right mixture of water and oil." He picked up a sterling silver decanter that looked like a genie lamp, then tipped the tiny spout into the globe slowly to add the glycerin.

She couldn't take her eyes off him. The way he worked, so slow, methodical and patient. He was the most patient person she'd ever known.

He let one more drop fall into the globe. "I think this looks just about right. Oh yeah, we'll need glitter for the snow."

"White glitter," she corrected.

"I saw some somewhere around here. It was in a glass jar. It was in all the stuff that was already here. Would you mind looking in the bottom cabinet over there?"

"Sure." She tore herself away from him and rummaged through a few of the lower cabinets behind the counter. It seemed like old times, poking around back here where she'd spent so many years as a kid. "Oh, gosh. Some of this stuff has to be decades old."

"Wait. Do we think glitter goes bad?" Elliott asked.

"Ha-ha. No." She dug around a little more, kneeling on the floor to get a better look into the back of the cabinet. She popped up from behind the counter. "Here it is." She carried a vintage canning jar with a bail lid over to him. "My mom used to store everything in these jars."

"When I took over the place, I definitely kept a lot of the supplies. It's kind of fun to think that this glitter that we're getting ready to use, you might have used years ago on some project."

"I know. Right?" It was so sweet how he cared about her history with the Tinker Shop. Almost to the point of embarrassing that he seemed to think he needed to keep that tie. It was his shop now. He could do what he wanted. She also knew Elliott well enough to know that he'd make it a success in his way. "It's kind of crazy. My mom used to use the glitter for snow on the Christmas Village. Every year she'd add a new building. It was really quite elaborate. I have no idea whatever happened to all of that." Hannah opened the jar and dipped her fingers into the glitter. She sprinkled a little into the globe.

"Yeah. That looks good." Elliott took the wooden end of a paint brush and gave it a swirl.

"Right. We want it to look like a real storm, not a light dusting. It's so peaceful to watch."

"Nice. I think just a little bit more. Don't you?"

"I do." Hannah reached into the jar again, but her fingers hit a clump. Assuming something wet had once gotten into the container, she twisted it between her fingers but realized it wasn't just glitter. "Elliot?" She pulled her hand out of the jar and tipped her fingers up slowly. "Whoa. Look." Between her fingers and thumb, a ring covered in shiny glitter sparkled. She blew the glitter from the gem with a hefty puff.

Elliott looked up, momentarily confused. "Wait. Whoa."

"We just found my mother's wedding ring. It must have been lost in this jar all those years ago! Oh my gosh, oh wow, I can't believe it!" She clutched the ring with both hands. "We just found my mother's wedding ring. I can't believe it!"

Swept up at the moment, she threw herself into Elliott's arms, hugging him close and feeling closer to her mother at this moment than she had in so long. She squealed and held him tight.

He wrapped his arms around her.

"I have to go tell my brother about this. I—" She hugged him again, this time his arms drawing comfort, and she took a breath and relaxed into the safety, the feeling of him so close. Not wanting it to end, her hands softly grazed his shoulders as she came off tiptoes to a stand in front of him. Her forehead tipped toward his, her lashes lowered, and for a moment she thought he was going to kiss her. Their faces were just inches apart, but he didn't move.

As if in slow motion, she pulled her hands back, looking into his face. "Well, I..." Unsure of all the feelings rushing through her...was it the ring? Or was it Elliott? "I've got to go." She shook her head, not really wanting to, but so wrapped up, swept away by the excitement of finding the long-lost treasure.

He wrapped his arms around her, pressing his chin to the nape of her neck.

"I..." Then, Hannah quickly looked at her watch. "I've got to go lead the caroling."

"What?"

"The caroling. I'm late. You should come with me."

"No. Oh, you don't want to hear me sing."

"Please come." But she did want to hear him sing, to feel him close. "That's all right. It's just for fun and Christmas, and all this time I've spent with you again, I've—"

Elliott hesitated only a moment. "I'll come."

"Good!" She danced in place. "Come on. Get your coat." She pulled hers on. "It'll be fun."

"Wait a second. Let me see the ring."

She opened her hand, still full of glitter.

He took the ring to his workbench, sprayed it with canned air and swept the remaining resistant pieces of glitter from the white gold, then shined it with a soft cloth. "Here." He handed it back to her. "Put it on."

"You think I should?"

"Why not?"

She slid it on her finger and smiled, then balled her hand into a fist and pulled it to her heart.

He grabbed his coat and opened the door, waiting for her. He locked up behind them, reaching for her hand. They took the stairs and walked around the corner to meet the others in front of Daisy's Country Store.

Everyone was dressed in red and green, Katie and Ben included. Michelle was rounding everyone up and doing a head count.

"I'm here," Hannah called out. "Everyone warmed up?"

"I was getting worried about you! You're never late for caroling. I'm so glad you brought Elliott. The more, the merrier. We are warmed up, and we even practiced that song about wassailing, yes."

"My favorite!" Hannah squeezed Elliott's hand. "Come on, everyone!"

Michelle swept a white-gloved hand in the air above her head. "First stop, the retirement center, and the last, Barbara's Country Inn. Let's go!"

"Dashing," Hannah called out, and every voice, soprano, bass, on pitch, off-key, belted a hearty *dashing through the snow* as they began walking down Main Street, and it sounded as merry as if they'd been classically trained.

Some old timers didn't bother singing at all, choosing to ring leather straps of jingle bells at just the right moments instead, and of course there was always Henry, who brought his kazoo. Every year without fail, and although it was a running joke in the town, it wouldn't be the same if he didn't.

Folks on Main Street came out of the shops and watched, applauding as they walked by, some abandoning their last-minute Christmas shopping to join in the fun.

Chapter Twenty-One

THEY'D CAROLED THE RETIREMENT CENTER, Main Street, the gazebo, three houses where people couldn't get out of the house, and now stood in front of Barbara's Country Inn.

Ben leaned in to Katie. "We're the surprise guests tonight."

She clapped her gloved hands. "Fun."

Ben loved how Katie had enthusiastically jumped right in like she'd been an Evergreenian forever. He'd miss her when she left. Things would be a little lackluster once she moved on, and he wasn't ready for that.

They all gathered at the bottom of the front steps of the inn.

Fanned out around the front porch area, Hannah stepped in front of them and gave them a note, then raised her hands in the air as ever so softly they began singing "Silent Night," taking it louder with each round. Hannah's hand motions led them until finally the heavy wooden door of the inn opened.

Megan stood there, wearing a shiny green dress. Couples held glass cups of punch and moved toward the commotion. "Everyone! Come in and get warm!" Megan gave them room to enter. She already had treats and a hot chocolate bar all set up for them.

The carolers flowed into the inn, still singing, with Ben playing his guitar and leading them inside. They switched gears into a fast-paced "Up on the Housetop," and everyone joined in.

With songbooks in hand, the carolers sang with heart and animation that was contagious. Even people who'd already retired to their rooms were coming downstairs to see what was going on and ended up joining in from the steps in their pjs.

Megan jumped in between songs. "I have the new firepit out there putting off a toasty warmth, and all the fixins for Christmas s'mores!"

Katie and Ben looked at each other. "S'mores?"

"Oh, heck yeah." He put his hand on the small of her back and followed closely behind her to the firepit. And that was it for the caroling that night.

Snow fell sizzling against the firepit, and Christmas lights twinkled behind them.

Katie and Ben sipped cocoa by the firepit, laughing. "I'm so glad you came with us tonight," he said.

"Me too. I've never been caroling before."

"You did great."

"And you are quite talented with that guitar, I must say."

"Thanks. Ha, would you look at those two?" He pointed over to Elliot, who was feeding Hannah a perfectly brown toasted marshmallow.

"They are so great together," Katie mused. She patted her hand to her heart. "Sweet."

It was, and he could almost picture himself in that situation with Katie. Something he hadn't really given much thought to after the divorce. Those wounds were old. Sure, he was over it now, but it didn't mean he wasn't a little anxious about being in that situation again.

Thomas didn't mind being in charge of making the marshmallows for anyone who was game. "You want yours crispy?" he asked Michelle.

"That one looks perfect."

He pulled it from the fire and slid a marshmallow onto her plate.

Katie held her hot cocoa with both hands. "So many people I interviewed said the same thing. They came here for Christmas, and Evergreen captured their hearts."

"Wait. That didn't happen to you?" Ben teased.

"Are you kidding?" Katie made a face, but there was that playful edge again.

She was capturing his heart. Was that possible? "Really. If not, maybe you should stay a day or two longer," he said. "You could stick around too, ya know."

"I'm looking forward to Christmas with my mom. It's our tradition, and if we start skipping them, do they then become less special?"

Family was important to her too. He felt the same way about tradition. "Not as long as you keep some of them alive. The ones you really love."

"Our traditions are simple, but amazing. Just me and her. You know, we watch the old Christmas movies. We have these blueberry pancakes from this restaurant in town. They're amazing. We have them all season long. They're so good." She sat quiet, thoughtful. "Back when I lived at home, we used to get a tree at the lot on Seventh Avenue. We haven't done that in years. Now that we both live in apartments, we can only have fake ones."

"Oh, I remember walking through the city and smelling the trees being sold."

"Yes! It's so great!"

"Because it's out of place, I think. It always reminded me of home."

"I can see how that would remind you of this place."

Ben felt the time slipping away. He wanted to know more about her. Hear her get excited about the mystery of things. "Do you want to know a secret?"

"Of course."

"That day on the train when we met, I was coming back from a job interview. I had applied on a whim, and then..."

"How'd it go?"

"Awful," he admitted. "All my bylines were too old. I don't have recent publications."

"So, are you going to try again?"

"I don't know. I'm out of practice. It's not easy going back."

Hannah screamed "fire" as her marshmallow turned into an inferno. Elliott grabbed the stick, and they both blew on it. Unfortunately, the charred mess fell off and plopped right into the dirt, leaving the two of them gooey and laughing as they tried to rescue the mess before someone stepped into it.

The buttery, sugary, smoky aroma of the toasted marshmallows added to the enchantment of the evening.

Michelle hugged Thomas's well-muscled arm. The two hadn't been apart since they'd reunited at the rink the other night. "The other day I was walking by the library," she said. "And the town tree was up, and it was snowing a little, and I'd just heard "Do You Hear What I Hear?" Which, you know, is my favorite song. And I thought to myself...why am I so happy?" She looked into his eyes.

The smile on his face told its own story.

"And then I saw you in my mind. It hit me." Michelle grasped Thomas's hand, lacing her fingers through his. "I realize I've fallen completely head over heels in love with you. I think I fell in love with you the moment I saw you. I am so happy that I met you, and that you and David are in my life."

Ben watched Thomas and Michelle nuzzle closer. He knew that feeling of wonderment over being so happy. The source of his happiness recently stood in front of him. Katie. The fire made her hair appear as shiny as spun gold. He was tempted to lean in closer and whisper into her ear, but he didn't take the chance. "You could stay?" Ben wished she would. "I mean, like, a day. You know. Figure out what's missing from your article. Or just have some fun?"

"Stay in Evergreen another day?" Katie glanced over at the other carolers, all of them so in love, even if they didn't realize what she could so easily see already. The snow fell around her. The fire snapped and crackled. It all felt so perfect. "Yeah. I can do that."

Ben smiled at her, and the snow fell heavier.

The others gathered their things and headed indoors.

Katie stood, and Ben faced her, taking both of her hands in his. "Thanks for coming tonight. For staying one more day."

Chapter Twenty-Two

STAYING ANOTHER DAY IN EVERGREEN meant Katie could get one more visit in over at the Kringle Kitchen, which seemed to be the heartbeat of this town. When she walked inside, it was comforting to recognize others in the diner this morning, including Nick, who sat at his usual table over by the front counter. She waved and walked over to an empty table. Carol brought her a cup of coffee and then went to greet newcomers.

Every story Katie heard, every person she met, every special event ever planned in this town, seemed to somehow always lead back to this diner.

Even the time capsule had a connection to this place, and the magic snow globe and...

She laughed out loud. Truth was stranger than fiction. No one would ever believe all of this was true.

As she reached for her nearly empty cup of

coffee again, Carol appeared at her side. "Warm-up?"

"Absolutely. Thank you." She tapped her hand on her blue notebook, which remained closed on the table next to her as she daydreamed about all she'd learned and witnessed here in this town. Her phone rang. Mom again. It was the second time in an hour. She was most definitely checking up on that article.

Katie casually ignored the call and turned her attention back to her coffee. "That's plenty," she said. "Thanks."

"No breakfast this morning? Or maybe a kringle or something sweet?"

"No, thank you. I ate at the inn." She placed a hand over her tummy. "I'm almost afraid to step on the scale when I get back home. I've eaten more the last couple of weeks than I should have."

Carol set the decanter on the table and took a seat across from her. "Did you get your article done?"

"Technically? Yes. I wrote what I thought would work, but I'm hoping for a few more fresh ideas today to help finish up."

"If we can help, just let us know. It'd be our pleasure. Joe and I could talk about this place twenty-four seven."

"It truly is your life's work, isn't it?"

Carol's serene smile was answer enough. "Yeah. Yes, it is. It may seem like just a job, and not a fancy one at that, but we love being a part of these people's lives. Sure, the food brings them back in, but the relationships we've built are special. I wish everyone had the chance to live the life I get to live. Who knew Dad's recipes would still work like magic all these years later? It's so simple when you break it down, but it all works together so perfectly. Just enough, in just the right time."

"And now you have his recipe book, thanks to the time capsule. I had no idea that kringles were even a thing. I just thought it was a recipe named after this restaurant."

She clutched her heart. "I still can't believe I've got that recipe book. Kringles go way back. A Scandinavian pastry with all sorts of fillings. Dad didn't invent them, but he sure did perfect them."

Katie scribbled feverishly in her notebook. "What's your favorite?"

"Hmm. Not fair. That's like picking a favorite child. Probably the maple almond, because we use ingredients from the locals. There's a new flavor in the recipe book we haven't even tried yet."

"One more reason for me to come back for a visit."

Carol seemed to drift off for a moment. "I'd looked and looked for Dad's recipes over the years. All along, it was there waiting for me. For just the right time. You know, I always wanted to make our kringles taste just like his, but I could never quite get it right." She turned her attention back as if for that second, she'd forgotten Katie was there. "You won't believe what I was missing."

"What was the missing ingredient?"

"Right there in his recipe, in all capital letters, it says to make simple syrup with melted snow instead of water."

Katie tried to be polite about it, but really? "That can't be real."

"It must have been important to him to have included it in the recipe." Carol smiled. "Okay, we were skeptical too, but we tried it anyway. And I have to say, by changing that one thing, it really did make a difference."

Katie pushed her hair back over her shoulder. "I'm not sure you'd have come up with that on your own. Who would have ever guessed? I never thought I would learn so much about kringles, but I'm glad I did."

"And we're glad you showed up here. We're all going to really miss you. I hate that you're leaving already." Carol's words came over Katie as sincere. "I just know you and my Allie would have been fast friends."

She was sad to be leaving already too. "I have a feeling I'll be back. This place has a way of getting into your heart. And now that you've got me addicted to peppermint cocoa and kringles, I have to come back." She closed her notebook. "You can't just get those anywhere."

"Well, good. Then I've done my job." She

placed a hand on Katie's arm. "Don't be a stranger." She glanced down at her watch. "Oh, look at that. It's almost time to open another calendar box. I'd better get Joe."

Chapter Twenty-Three

THE SLEIGH BELLS ON THE door of the Kringle Kitchen jingled, and in walked Hannah with Elliott close at her heels. He carried the box, the one with the red and white poinsettias on it, that had held all those broken pieces of the magic snow globe not that long ago. That had been a heartbreaking day.

Hannah, all smiles, sang out a joyful imitation of a trumpet celebration and flung her arms out in a V. "Da, da-da, daaaaaaah."

Elliott removed the top of the box, and Hannah carefully lifted the now-repaired snow globe into view.

"Oh my gosh. It's perfect!" Carol ran toward the door. "How did you ever repair it? This can't be the same snow globe."

Joe and Katie joined them.

Hannah held it in her hands. "It's the same one. It was all Elliott. He's amazing. You can't see a single crack unless you're really, really looking for it, and I'm not going to tell you where to look."

"You are quite the fix-it man," Joe said as he looked over the piece. "It looks better than new."

"I did my best." He blushed.

"Thank you," said Carol. "Look at that! Oh, it's wonderful!"

Hannah's smile was as wide as her sigh was long. "Whew. I can't believe we were able to fix it. I couldn't have done it without this guy." Elliott's smile was genuine, but he hadn't taken his eyes off her. She was beginning to wonder if he was worried she might drop it again.

That made Hannah a little nervous. She put it back where it belonged in its place of honor on the stand, with the fake snow right there next to the cash register.

No sooner had she set it down than Elliott picked up the snow globe with an intent look on his face. He held it arm's length away, then shook it in rapid succession, sending all that carefully placed glitter into the biggest snowstorm of all time. He squeezed his eyes tight and made a wish.

"Wow, that was determined," Carol said, looking a little surprised.

Elliott raised a brow as he returned the snow globe back to the counter. "Can't help knowing what it is I want, I guess." A look of panic crossed his face, as if he hadn't realized he'd just said that out loud. "Um, I'll talk to you later." He hurried out the door.

Hannah wondered why he made such a hasty

exit. She turned back to the others, still riding high. "This has been a Christmas full of surprises."

"Oh, I wish Allie was here," Carol said. "She would have loved all of this. She called from Paris yesterday, and I told her all about the time capsule, but it's just not the same as being here a part of all of it."

"She's having the time of her life," Joe said, giving Carol a hug. "So is Zoe. She's already speaking a few words of French."

"That's so exciting," Hannah said.

Ben opened the door, coming to an abrupt stop behind the group of them huddled at the counter. "Hey!" When his gaze landed on Katie, he smiled even wider. "Everybody ready to open another calendar box?"

"Yes!"

"Good. Everyone get their coats. Let's go."

Katie, Joe and Carol grabbed their coats.

As Ben turned, he noticed the snow globe on the counter behind Hannah. "Oh wow. Good as new."

"Yes. Thank goodness." Hannah eyed the snow globe as everyone ran out to Kringle Alley for the daily calendar box opening.

Ben led Carol, Katie and Joe outside. Hannah hung back. Her fingers twitched as she went to grab the snow globe, but didn't. Nick watched from a table nearby.

Guilt filled Hannah. Would she ever be able to

pick it up without people being afraid she might drop it again? *Surely that's my imagination. Nick would never be like that.*

She wanted to make another wish. She knew exactly what it would be. Stepping toward the door, she caught the look on Nick's face.

He gave her a brief nod. Was he encouraging her to make a wish?

Why had she worked so hard to fix it if not for folks to still be able to make wishes? And she had one wish she needed to make.

She picked up the snow globe, holding it tight between her two cupped hands. She stared into the glass globe at the tiny church that looked just like the one here in town. "Okay, you," Hannah whispered. "I've made a few wishes in the past, and they've all come sort-of true. And then they kept not working out. So, this year, just... surprise me." Hannah shook the snow globe. Excitement rushed through her. When she opened her eyes and looked up, Nick was staring right at her, smiling. She set down the snow globe and raced outside to catch up to the others. *Please let the magic still be there. Let the surprise be a good one.*

Michelle had just pulled the name out of the top hat as Hannah got there. She crossed her fingers, hoping her name would be the one called to open today's calendar box.

"Katie!" Michelle called out, scanning the group of locals in front of her.

Ben nudged Katie, not looking surprised at all.

"What?" Katie's hands flew to her face. "I didn't even put my name in!"

"Someone did," Michelle said. "That's the name that came out."

"Go get 'em," Ben said.

"Okay!" Katie still clung to her notebook when she stepped next to Michelle in front of the giant advent calendar. "Lucky fifteen." She turned and slipped her hand into the arch at the top of the box, slowly sliding it forward while trying to sneak a peek. Everyone clapped as she presented the red envelope from the box. Sliding her finger beneath the flap, she slid the sheet of paper out and read from the letter.

"Dear Evergreenians." Katie spoke loud enough for everyone to hear. "One of the best gifts of building this calendar was how nice it was to spend time together. And so, today's gift is a little bit different." She straightened, seeming intrigued to find out what was special today. Her face twisted a bit as she scanned ahead silently. She smiled and read on. "Whoever opens today's box should name the Christmas activity they love the most but do the least. It's our humble request that the entire town spend a few hours together doing that activity."

Everyone seemed excited by that announcement.

Katie shook her head. "Okay, that's a lot of pressure." She looked to Ben, and then Michelle.

"I don't know. That red-letter envelope does feel legally binding," Ben said with a tone of authority. "I think you have to do it."

Katie turned and faced everyone. "Okay, well, there is one thing I really love doing, and definitely not often enough…"

"What is it?" Hannah screamed from the back as she worked her way to the front to lead the carols to follow.

"Snowmen. I love building a snowman."

Michelle raised her hands in the air. "Okay. You heard the lady. We'll all, as a town, be building snowmen together for a few hours. Let's gather supplies and meet back in the clearing next to the gazebo in an hour. There'll be plenty of room for a whole snow family, cousins and all."

Everyone clapped, then disbursed to get ready to satisfy the Day 15 challenge.

Hannah made a quick change to the scheduled song. "Under the circumstances, I believe a little 'Frosty the Snowman' is in order." And so the choir started, but the whole town joined in singing about that happy, jolly soul who came to life one day.

Chapter Twenty-Four

KATIE TWIRLED IN THE DEEP snow to clear a nice circular outline for them to build a snowman. Since fresh snow had fallen just last night, there was plenty of the white stuff piled up in the park. Some drifts rose a few feet against buildings and fence lines. It couldn't be a more perfect day to bring everyone together for her favorite Christmas activity.

Groups of people had staked out their little piece of the park and had started building snowmen, while others cheered them on as they frolicked in the snow. One family built a giant target, and they were already throwing pitches at it, trying for a bullseye.

Across the way next to the gas station, two men worked on a truck with a snow blade on the front. They'd probably be using that a lot this winter.

Katie teamed up with Ben, Nan and Michelle to build their snowman together. They worked great together. With barely a word, they had the base in place. Ben and David quickly rolled a hefty midsection and lifted it onto the base. Katie steadied it, and let Michelle check for position, until she finally gave them a thumbs up.

Thank goodness it's easier to level a snowman middle than a banner across Main Street.

"Katie, I have to hand it to you, building snowmen as a whole town is a great way to spend a morning," Michelle said. "We might have to make this an annual part of our celebration schedule."

"Fine by me. Can you name it after me? How about Katie's Snowman Day? Or better yet, we could make it non-gender specific and call it Snowbody's Perfect Day."

"We might have to vote on that," Michelle teased.

"I can't believe it's been so long since I've built a snowman. I used to love rushing out to Prospect Park to make a snowman during the first snowfall," Katie said. "It's been years since I've done it, though."

David stuck a long branch into the body of the snowman to make an arm. "It's fun."

"Hey, David, want to help me roll the head?" Katie waved him over.

"Definitely." He ran to catch up to her near a big drift of snow piled by the trees.

Nearby Hannah, Ezra and Thomas scooched a whopper of a snowball into place for a sturdy foundation, followed by a nice, round belly.

"Look at that." Ezra, bundled up in a black

ski jacket and heavy knitted scarf, lifted his cheeks to the sky, letting the sunshine wash over him. "Whew. Despite the chill, it has turned into a beautiful day, huh?"

"Ezra, I've never seen you like this." Hannah patted the snowman's midsection. "It's like you're floating."

"I am actually very happy! One day Lisa introduces me to someone, and wham, I'm moving to Boston. You just never know where you'll find the right person who will change your life. Now, when I move up there, my romance will be two blocks away, and only because I took a little risk."

David rolled the head for their snowman across the park slowly, building it bigger and bigger until he made it all the way over to where the others were.

"That's just the right size." Ben picked it up and plopped it right on top. Now Mr. Snowman was nearly as tall as him.

"Do you ever wonder how much risk is too much?" Hannah asked.

"What's too much? Even if you're unsure what it will be at the end, isn't it always worth a try?"

Katie overheard Hannah's conversation and wondered if she wasn't talking more about herself and Elliott than Ezra and his situation. Katie would bet the advance on her next novel that there was very little risk in that area. Those two were meant to be.

Yearning a bit for that magic Hannah and Elliott so clearly had, an emptiness fell over her. Time had gone by so quickly, and she'd be leaving all of this behind. She watched Ben. Her stomach filled with tingly wonder. If only.

She could easily picture being with him. Walking hand in hand, silly inside jokes, snuggling up to his shoulder as he played his guitar by a firepit on a cold night. Even ice skating and laughing until she couldn't breathe every time she fell. But as much as she cherished every single moment here in Evergreen and every person she'd met, she knew deep inside she could never live in this town. She loved the city. It was where she was meant to be.

Across the way, Michelle and Ben put buttons on the front of their snowman.

Thomas took in a big swig of winter air as he watched Michelle and his son working together.

"You two okay?" Katie asked.

"Yeah, sure," Hannah said. "Katie, you can keep a secret, right?"

"Of course. Besides, I'm getting ready to leave town. Pretty much any secret would be safe with me at this point."

"I'm going to miss you. We all will," Hannah said. "But while Michelle is busy, Thomas, I have something I have to give you." She turned back to Katie. "Don't tell anyone."

"I promise." Katie leaned in, now even more curious about what it was.

"Merry Christmas. I have a present for you."

Thomas tilted his head. "It's pretty early for a Christmas present, don't you think?"

Hannah pulled an old leather ring box from her coat pocket. "This is too special to wait. Merry Christmas." Flipping the box across the snow, Thomas caught it midair.

Puzzled, he opened it. "What's this?"

"I found it," she whispered. "It's Mom's wedding ring. I know it is. It was in the Tinker Shop in a vintage bail jar full of glitter. Remember how Mom used to keep things in those jars?"

"I do." His mouth dropped wide, realization spreading across his face.

"This one was filled with white glitter, and it had been pushed all the way back under one of the bottom cabinets."

The words came out in a rush. "I can't believe you found it."

Katie couldn't imagine what Hannah and Thomas must be feeling. Finding the ring after all of this time. Her romantic heart fluttered.

Hannah touched her brother's hand. "I think Mom would have wanted you to have it."

Katie pulled her hands over her mouth. How precious!

Thomas turned the ring over in his hand. "It's just like I remember it. I always thought the design on the sides looked like rope, the way it twisted. This is it." He lifted it closer, then looked into Hannah's eyes. "Wow, and lost all this time."

"You should have it," Hannah said, stepping in front of him and focusing on Michelle across the way. "Just in case you were thinking about doing something, I don't know, something where a ring would come in handy."

His smile grew as he watched Michelle and David interact. "I've been doing a lot of thinking about something like that lately. How did you know?"

"I'm your sister. I know these things."

Thomas glanced over at Katie.

Katie raised her right hand. "I'm just the secret-keeper, but I think that's a wonderful idea. You already make such a beautiful family. You should make it official." She'd never felt so excited for someone else. Evergreen certainly had more magic than its fair share.

"Mom's ring." Thomas tucked the box into his pocket. "I can't believe the timing."

"I'm going to leave y'all to this." Katie took a giant step back, practically bouncing with excitement. "I need to help my team build the best snowman before I have to catch my train so I can leave my mark on this town."

"Second-best snowman," Thomas and Hannah yelled to her.

Katie bolted back over to help her team. The excitement of Thomas's secret was difficult to hide. So romantic. How would she ever keep a straight face with Michelle? She was dying to run over and hug her right now.

Thank goodness Katie came across Nan first.

"Does anyone have an extra carrot?" Nan wandered from team to team in search of supplies for her and Nick's snowman.

"I don't." Katie patted her pockets.

Nan's lips pursed so tight she looked like a kissing gourami. "Nick wants to use a pinecone for the nose. That's just not right."

Michelle pulled a carrot from her pocket. "I happen to have an extra. I always come prepared."

"I should've known you would, Ms. Mayor," Nan said.

"Hey, do you have an extra one of those for us too?" Thomas yelled over to Michelle.

"For you?" She grinned with a flirty lift to the edge of her smile, then handed another to David with a nod.

"Of course we do." David ran it over to his dad.

Katie clapped her hands. Of course Michelle would share with Thomas. She'd never let him down.

Nan trudged through the deep snow where Nick had started their snowman. Three snowballs stacked, their project wasn't much over three foot tall, but he had all the personality of an elf with pointy ears and even shoes that rolled up to a point at the end. Nan jabbed the carrot into the snowman's icy face and struck a satisfied pose.

Katie leaned into Ben's shoulder as she enjoyed the moment until she realized the intimacy of that move. "Oh, sorry." She straightened.

"No, don't be." Delight danced in his eyes. "Are you glad you stayed?"

"Yeah. So glad." She gulped the emotion back. "Doesn't make it any easier to leave, though." She checked her watch. "It's almost time."

Did Ben just catch his breath?

Hannah and her team interrupted the moment when they walked over. "Wow, that looks great."

Thomas stepped behind Michelle and wrapped his arms around her. Katie was pretty sure that was a tear he just swept from the corner of his eye. He has to be so excited.

Michelle must have noticed too, because she asked him if he was okay.

Covering his emotion, Thomas said, "Yeah. Absolutely. Just cold out."

Hannah and Katie both sighed at the same time, then shared a panicked look. Trying to recover, Hannah quickly said, "Katie, thank you so much for choosing this activity."

"No, thank you. All of you." Katie would miss them all. "For everything. You really know how to make a girl feel at home. As much as I would love to miss my train, I've really got to go home now."

"Merry Christmas, Katie."

She and Ben went to pick up her luggage from Barbara's and go to the train station.

The Evergreen train depot was crowded with families welcoming their arriving guests from the city for the holiday. Only a few people stood by, ready to load up and head back that night.

Katie walked alongside Ben on the walkway next to the red-and-gold train, wishing the ramp was about a mile longer, because she wasn't ready for this to end.

"Well..." Ben was moving at a snail's pace too. "I guess this is it."

"Right." The time had gone so fast, and honestly, she wasn't ready for it to end, either. If only the one more day she'd stayed was still one more day away. Would he come to visit? She looked up, wishing she could read his mind. "If you get to the city, maybe we can—"

"Yeah. Definitely." Ben licked his lips. "Or if you're ever back in Evergreen and decide to spend a Christmas here—"

"Don't I have to come back for the snowman-building event next year?" Katie stopped near the stairs. *This is really goodbye.*

"Yes. You do." He looked like he had more to say.

She could barely breathe. *Please ask me to stay. Or promise me you'll call.* She folded her fingers into tight little fists; silence hung between them. He's not feeling it. Her eyes darted past him to the town. Maybe what she was feeling had been temporary Evergreen magic, not the real thing after all. She glanced back over to him. But it felt so real.

"We..." It came out almost a breathless stammer. He swallowed visibly hard. "If we weren't in such different places in our lives, and such different actual locations...maybe we'd be—"

Her heart fell into a thousand tiny icy fragments. She'd envisioned it. "Sitting by a fire after making a snowman?" She nodded with complete resolution. This was goodbye.

The conductor took her bag.

"Thank you." She stepped up backward on the first tread, eye-to-eye with Ben. "Merry Christmas, Ben."

"Merry Christmas, Katie."

She leaned forward, placing her left hand on his shoulder, kissing him softly on the cheek. She paused long enough to breathe in his scent one more time, then stepped away and turned to board the train.

Ben stood there as she boarded.

By the time she got to her seat, he'd begun walking back toward town. Her heart hung heavy in her chest, making it hard to breathe. She didn't want this to be goodbye.

As if by magic, Ben must've felt it too, because he stopped midstride and turned to look, then waved.

The announcement echoed throughout the station: "All Aboard for New York Penn Station!"

Following one long whistle, the train eased out of the station. Katie watched from the window as they pulled away. With each mile, she longed for Evergreen. Or maybe it was just for Ben.

She recognized the red bridge that led into town, the only way in and out of Evergreen.

Somehow, the beautiful countryside, although still just as picturesque as it'd been the first time she'd seen it, had lost its amazement. It lacked the sparkle without the people she'd met in Evergreen. More than just people. Friends.

Katie's phone rang. She looked down, her heart doing a little giddy-up hoping it was Ben, but it wasn't. "Hi, Mom."

"Hi. Just checking in, is the article—"

"Mom, I'm not sure I'm going to be able to turn this in."

"What do you mean?" She sounded disappointed.

"I mean, I wrote an article about a town for Christmas. And I thought I might be able to make it work for the magazine. I think I wrote... something else. I might need a little longer to—"

"Katie. You've never missed a deadline."

"I know. And I'm sorry. I know you were counting on me."

"Send me what you have. You're always so hard on yourself. I bet it's wonderful."

"Mom, I—"

"I am not asking as your mother. I am speaking as your editor."

Too tired to argue, she turned on the hotspot on her phone. "Right. I'll email it now."

She pressed send, then rested her head on the window as the train chugged along.

Chapter Twenty-Five

ANNAH ARRIVED AT THE CHURCH to get things set up for choir rehearsal. She cherished her time alone in this church where she'd grown up. Normally, she was the only one here this early, but when she walked inside the vestibule, she was met with an unexpected surprise.

She opened the door to the sanctuary, and beautiful music washed over her so loud that she closed her eyes to take it in.

A nimble flurry of piano chords, as gentle and unpredictable as rain drops, filled the space. She let the gentle vibrations of the piano strings hang like delicate ornaments among the Christmas lights that filled the tiny church. The candles on the piano were lit, casting a heavenly glow over the instrument.

She drifted in slowly, not wanting it to stop.

Was she imagining this? Elliott sat on the worn bench at the piano. Sure, they'd played songs side by side as kids on that very piano, but she had no idea he'd continued to practice over the years, or had become so accomplished.

Everything seemed to pull in around her, tugging her further into the sanctuary. He wasn't that little boy anymore.

The weight of his hands on the keys sent pure notes feathering into her heart, so clearly that even though she didn't recognize the song yet, she hummed along.

He hadn't heard her come in. He looked relaxed, at peace, his long fingers moving across the keys. Overwhelmed by the music, she followed it further inside past the first couple of pews, standing there taking it in until Elliott looked up and saw her.

He stopped immediately.

"Don't." The abandoned song hung between them.

He stood up, his cheeks red with embarrassment. "You heard all of that? Sorry. I was just..."

"Just amazing." Hannah raised her hands and clapped slowly. "It was beautiful." She walked toward him in awe. "I had no idea you could play so well." And she'd thought she knew everything about him.

"You spend so much time over at the Arts Center. I thought..." He shrugged. "Maybe I should help you out with the choir." He played a couple of notes.

She shook her head, her heart pounding. "You're incredible."

He looked down, but he was smiling.

She felt so brave right now. And surer than ever about her feelings.

"Hey, do you remember this one?" He started playing "O Christmas Tree."

"Do I? Oh, yeah. Hang on." She twisted out of her coat and laid it on a pew as he continued to play. "Oh my gosh. We must've played that five thousand times together as kids." And like that, the romantic notion had turned playful, and she'd let it pass. She hopped onto the bench next to him, picking up the high notes.

He played the low ones, and they laughed as they made their way through the notes until the very end, when Hannah reached across him to hit that last note. When she did, she was so close she could feel his breath on her cheek as they both laughed.

And the laughter felt like the old days, but the warmth of his body so close to her and his smile as he looked into her eyes was not childlike at all. Had her true love always been right here in the neighborhood?

She faced forward, letting out a long sigh. Fear raced through her mind. If he didn't feel the same way, she could ruin the best friendship of her life. But if she didn't...

"Elliot, I don't know how to say this...so I'm just going to say it." She pulled her hands into her lap, pressing them together. Wanting to be brave, but afraid to make eye contact. "I like you." She looked up, and he was already looking at her. She swallowed past the lump that had formed in the back of her throat. "I like you a lot. You are on my mind all the time—"

"I like you too, Hannah." He hitched closer. "I've been wanting to tell you that for such a long time."

She gulped a breath of air. "Really?" Tears tickled her eyelashes. *Thank you.*

"Yes. I just didn't know how."

The candles on the piano flickered, and there was something soothing, almost confirming, about that.

The fear fell away. You know what I'm feeling. "This is...so hard. You're my best friend." She shook her head. "I'm so afraid. Elliott, I would never want to lose our friendship. What if it doesn't work out?"

He shook his head emphatically. "What if it does?" His eyebrow shot up. "I'm more afraid of what happens if we don't try. Because I feel the same way, Hannah."

She nodded. Taking in the whole moment, still a little shaken by the fact they'd missed the signs for so long.

His voice was light and joyful. "Where should we begin?"

It didn't have to be fancy. Some of their most special moments were like this. Unplanned and simple, but so true. "How about we start with some hot cocoa?"

"It's a date," he said with a wink.

Hannah covered her face with her hands. "I can't believe you just said that. I said that to you, didn't I?" She lolled her head back. This was only the kind of thing you could laugh about with a real friend. *I'm the luckiest girl. Thank you, snow globe.*

He joined in the laughter. Not at her, but with her. He placed his hand gently on hers. "You did. I thought it was sweet."

"I was hoping you hadn't noticed. Oh my gosh, I'm so embarrassed." She rubbed her brow with her fingers.

"It was beautiful." He stood from the piano. "And now it's really happening. Let's get that choir rehearsal going so we can get done and go on our first date."

Chapter Twenty-Six

THE TAXI RACED DOWN THE busy streets, swerving in and out of traffic, honking impatiently. Katie held on to the door handle. She used to be so at ease in a cab; now she missed those meandering rides in the old red truck. Outside, the snow here in the city was wet and slushy, almost gray. Nothing like the puffy mounds along the streets of Evergreen.

People moved with purpose down the street, their faces tucked into the collars of their coats against the cold.

Not a single wave or smile.

The taxi turned onto her street.

She'd always loved the sleek warehouse style of the condos that lined her block. The tall walk-ups looked strong. A red building next to an orange one, next to a yellow, next to a blue...like a box of felt-tip markers.

Today, the metal and glass seemed stark and lonely.

Honk. Honk.

And loud.

The taxi driver swerved over to the corner and popped the trunk.

It'd be quiet, with nary an ornament or light, and not even a Christmas card lying around. For a moment she considered getting back in the cab and taking a detour to Rockefeller Center to see the lights on the tree first.

But the taxi driver already had her bag on the curb.

She got out and paid him, then rolled her suitcase up the walk to the front of her building. It felt less like home today, but there was her name on the intercom, CONNELL ~ 501. She'd worked so hard to buy this place. Her dream home.

She carried her bag up the steps, through the lobby. On the elevator, a flyer had been tacked to the corkboard next to the floor button panel. She read it as she pressed the button for her floor. There was a holiday mixer tonight. She'd never gone to even one of the many gatherings people planned in this complex. For a moment she tossed the idea around of going. It could be fun, like the caroling or cookie baking in Evergreen. But she dismissed the thought just as quickly. It wouldn't be the same as Evergreen. Nothing would ever be the same. Her heart hung heavy, and she wondered what Ben was doing right now.

When the elevator stopped with a jolt, the

doors opened, and she stepped off. Her suitcase rolled smoothly across the high-gloss floor in the hall. She punched in her code in the high-tech lock, and the mechanisms disengaged. She walked inside and kicked off her shoes at the door.

To her surprise, not only was every light in the apartment on, but there was garland hanging in her kitchen. Not the real stuff. There wasn't even the faintest hint of pine or spruce or fir in the air. White lights twinkled from her fake fig tree and plastic philodendron.

In the living room, a Christmas tree—fake, of course—rose to at least seven feet tall.

"Mom?"

"Hi. I came to talk to you about your article."

She rubbed her hand along her arm. A little groan escaped. "As my editor or as my mother?"

"Little of both." She held out her arms. "Hi, honey. Welcome home. Merry Christmas."

Katie hugged her. "You bought me a tree?"

"I did. I remembered all you had was that little three-foot-tall one you used to put on the table in front of the window."

"It's cute."

"If you like Charlie Brown trees, maybe." She stepped back. "You look good. I've missed you."

"Thanks, Mom. I missed you too."

"I wanted to surprise you with a little Christmas decor."

"You sure did."

Pam picked up a box of ornaments off the couch. "And have a look at these ornaments. These have been tucked away in my storage unit for years."

Katie recognized a lot of them. "You saved all these?"

"I did. Some are from when I was little; some I've collected. Some you made when you were little." She held up a red stocking with white rick-rack on it. "And this. You made in second grade."

"Isn't that cute?"

"You made it for me, and inside you'd made a Santa's list with my name on the nice side. I still remember crying when I saw it." Pam handed Katie a snowman ornament to hang.

Katie walked it over to the tree, looking for the right spot or, as Lisa had advised, the slightly wrong spot to hang it. The tree was pretty, even if it had no smell. *No terpenes. No snow.*

Pam hung an ornament on the other side.

"I'm really sorry I didn't make the deadline. I keep trying to think how to turn this story into something I can print, but—"

"You should publish it," her mom said. "As-is. Just not in my magazine." She stepped back, admiring the tree.

"What are you saying?" Katie waited, trying to understand.

"Honey, those characters! The town vet who stayed because she found love, the woman who moved there to run the general store, those competing anxious mayors."

"I know, but it wasn't meant to be about—"

"I know. And don't you worry. I have my eyes out for another article."

Katie breathed a sigh.

"The point is, I know you were looking for some inspiration for your next novel, and honey, I think you found it."

This was the first time she'd really heard Mom encourage her to work on the novel. Katie thought about the story she'd sent to her. It hadn't been right for the magazine. She'd known that all along, but there was something special about it. The people of the town, the age-old traditions. Mom's encouragement tonight just might make this her best Christmas in a long, long time.

Mom looked over at her, waiting for a response. As her editor, and as her mom, Katie knew she was in good hands.

Katie had taken her mom's support a little for granted. Like those people in Evergreen who cherished their traditions, she loved and cherished her time with Mom over the holidays, and there was room for them to do more. She hung another ornament from one of the higher boughs. "So, Mom, is the invitation still open to come to your office Christmas party?"

Pam's eyebrows shot up, and her mouth opened wide. "It is!"

Mom had wanted her to come for years, and she'd never given in. The happiness on her face was unmistakable. *I've been really selfish about this. It's time to change that.*

"Good," Katie said. "'Cuz you know I'm coming."

"I'd love that so much. That's great."

"And I will write that book."

"I know you will, and it's going to be wonderful."

Katie and her mom decorated the tree with little conversation, just enjoying their time together.

When her mom left, Katie sat in the living room on her couch in the dark, staring at the tree by only the illumination from the Christmas tree lights, wishing there was some way the two worlds, her life here and her friends in Evergreen, mostly Ben, could be one.

Chapter Twenty-Seven

THE FOLLOWING MONDAY MORNING AFTER the town revealed the contents of the daily calendar, Ben and Nan walked back to the library together to start their day.

While Nan went inside, Ben collected the books from the night drop out front and carried them inside for processing. His phone rang. The New York City number took him by surprise, and he didn't hesitate one second before answering.

When he finished the call, he walked inside.

Nan stood behind the desk, checking in the books left over from the weekend, pulling the cards from the pockets and stamping the date the old-fashioned way before placing them on the cart to be shelved.

Ben adjusted his glasses and picked up the other stamper to help. Stamp...stamp...stamp. They were in perfect time. "The strangest thing happened this morning."

"Oh, what was that?"

He stamped the next book, watching Nan for

a reaction. "I just got an interview request for that job in New York."

Nan opened the next book. "For the one that was on the printer a couple of weeks ago?"

"Yeah. The strange thing is, I never actually applied for it."

"My. That is strange." She stamped another book and never looked up. Didn't congratulate him. Just kept her eye on the task. So unlike her.

"Nan?" His tone had come out more like that of a schoolteacher getting ready to put the naughty kid in the corner. He hadn't meant for it to, but it wasn't so far from the circumstance.

"Hmm?" If it hadn't been for her averted gaze and the tight grip of the book in her hand, he might have even believed the innocent sound of the response.

Ben closed the last book and turned to her. "Did you send that application in?"

"Your application?" Her eyebrows shot straight up, but then she relaxed with a sheepish grin. "Yes." She removed her glasses, and pulled her shoulders back, looking him straight in the eye. "Yes. It was me. I saw it on the computer. It was almost completely filled out. I simply checked a couple of boxes and clicked send."

Ben already knew she had to have been the one to submit it, but her admitting to it still kind of blew him away. "But I'm not prepared. I haven't written anything serious in a long time."

She stood proud and pointed a finger to his

chest. "Well, Ben, then I suppose you'd better dust some old stories off and get started." Nan stepped even closer and looked him square on. "Ben, this library is *my* dream. It's something I've wanted to do for everyone my entire life. I love it."

"I know you do." And he loved that about her. The friends of the library were truly her friends, and she treated them like extended family.

"And you get it from me," she said.

"I get what from you?"

"The part inside you that makes you want to stay here and help me. But Ben, the only thing you owe me is to live your life as you want it lived."

"Nan. If I even think about leaving, who will watch over the library?"

"Me! I'll watch over the place." She smiled proudly. "And no, I know I can't do it all by my-self. But this is Evergreen. I'm quite certain we can find someone who'd like to help. Now go get started. You've got work to do."

Ben let out a breath, trying to make room to take in another. He loved being here for Nan, but the possibility of more sent his heart zooming as if it were on rails. He hugged her tight. "You've always been so good to me."

"I've let you stay here helping me for too long." She patted his back as they hugged.

He took a step back. "I'll never be far away." It was a promise he meant to keep.

"Wherever your dreams and desires take you is fine by me."

Yes, writing was a dream, but there was a bigger dream. He could picture Katie so clearly. He'd never been happier than while she'd been here. Her blue eyes twinkling, and the way she pulled her lips together and kind of squinted just a teensy bit when she was getting ready to give him a hard time. It was so cute.

I should never have let her go.

"Thank you, Nan." He hugged her again. A million thoughts raced through his mind. He'd have to look over his old portfolio of work for inspiration. That interview was only a week away. *If I land that job, I'll be closer to Katie. The sooner, the better. Please let there be a second chance with her. Can I really do this?*

Nan had continued stamping books when the front door opened, and in walked Ezra with a box of books.

"A donation," he said. "My apartment in the city is much smaller. I had to winnow down my collection." He plunked the box down on the corner of the desk. "You ordered most of these for me over the years."

"You've always had wonderful taste in literature," Nan said. "I'm sure these books will be well-loved on my shelves."

"I'm really going to miss this town."

"And we'll all miss you, Ezra, but you've made your mark. You won't soon be forgotten." She smiled sweetly. "You won't be a stranger, will you?"

"No, ma'am."

Ben enjoyed seeing Nan's special way touch the heart of others. He went into his office and sat down in front of his computer. He laced his fingers, stretching his hands. It'd been a while since he'd actually sat down with the intent to write something for publication.

Write what you know.

As good a place to start as any.

Once he started typing, the words came so easily. He resisted the urge to edit. Although he wrote pretty clean anyway, he focused on just letting the words pour out onto the page.

Nan eased open the door. "I don't mean to disturb you, but I brought you a little snack."

"Thanks." He looked at his watch. He'd typed nonstop for well over an hour.

"How's it going?" She set down a steaming mug of tea. The little plate sitting on top of the mug to allow the tea to steep held a giant shortbread cookie in the shape of a star. "I thought you might enjoy one of those. It's one of the cookies you and Katie made from my old recipe."

"I see that." He'd recognized the shape from the big copper cookie cutter immediately. A smile spread across his face. There was nothing subtle about his grandmother. He'd remember the fun they'd had making cookies together forever.

"Thank you, Nan. You really do always think of everything."

"You get that from me too." She patted the desk. "Chase that dream."

He wasn't entirely sure if she meant the job interview or Katie, but he had every intention of putting all of his attention on both.

For the next three days, he spent his time working on articles. He interviewed Ezra before he left for Boston, and Thomas about his logging camps and what had made him decide to set up shop in Evergreen for his headquarters. After choir practice, he accidentally ended up interviewing Hannah, who, thank goodness, didn't seem upset by the unscheduled intrusion.

"You know," Hannah said to Ben. "You bring up Katie quite a bit. I don't mind at all, but I thought I might point it out. You know, in case you hadn't noticed."

He rolled his eyes. "I'm that transparent, huh?"

"Oh, yeah. Don't let her get away. She's the real deal." Hannah clapped her hands together, then pushed them to her knees. "I'm so in love, I can't wait for everyone in the world to feel it too."

"On that note, I think I have all I need from you. Thanks for letting me interview you for my article. You're the best." Ben got up and marked her off his list of interviews for the day. Next stop, Daisy's Country Store.

He spent the rest of the afternoon stocking

shelves with Lisa at Daisy's Country Store and hearing her tell of her fancy Boston business and buying trips to faraway places, followed by her transition to Evergreen.

He and Carol spent a whole day alongside Joe in Kringle Kitchen, making those ever-famous kringles and shipping them out to customers who couldn't make it through the holiday without one, even though their plans wouldn't allow another holiday vacation to Evergreen.

And Michelle, the first woman mayor, not only had an interesting story to share about how she'd transitioned from being a kid who'd grown up here and come back after college, but also one about her big transition from education to public service.

He knew the stories, but hearing them retold from their own perspectives, their point of view, brought new facts to light, and as he was going through his notes, the angle for the story he wanted to tell about Evergreen became perfectly clear.

He worked on the article until he'd polished it to perfection. Then read it out loud and made a final pass of tweaks. Finally satisfied, he hand-delivered it to the editor and owner of the Evergreen Mirror, who read it on the spot.

The editor nodded as he read the pages, then stood and paced, even laughing once. He shook his head, rubbed his chin, then sat back down behind his desk. "I'm running this on the front page," he said.

All of Ben's nervous energy came out in a laugh. "Really?"

"Absolutely, and your timing couldn't be more perfect. It'll be in tomorrow's paper."

That was a stroke of luck, because Ben hadn't even considered that the local paper only came out every other week. "Wow."

"I wondered when you'd get back around to writing again. You were always such a talent. I'm glad you shared this with me first."

Ben couldn't believe how good it felt, and now he'd have something new to take along to that interview in the city.

He walked over to the skating rink. The heft and craftsmanship of this bridge had always been such a wonder to him. He'd have loved to have seen it constructed. There weren't many people on the ice this afternoon, just a couple of speed skaters racing around in circles, their scarves drifting in the wind behind them.

The last time he'd stood here overlooking the ice, he'd been with Katie. He pulled out his phone and flipped through the pictures. They'd packed in quite a bit of fun in her visit.

Picture by picture, he relived their time to-gether. The silly antics between them...and to think it had all begun with a clumsy misstep on the Evergreen Express that had landed her practically in his lap. If it hadn't been for that one bump, they might never have met.

He typed her a text.

I'll be in the city tomorrow. Lunch?

The daunting dot-dot-dot in the little gray box below his text made him nervous.

It disappeared, then started again. What had changed her mind? How was she going to respond? Why had he sent it at all?

He put his phone back in his pocket. He was nervous enough about the interview. Why had he added a chance to meet with her while he was in the city on top of it all?

Chapter Twenty-Eight

KATIE SAT AT HER DESK. The sounds of the city filled the room, even from here inside her apartment. The honks, hollers, the rumbling diesel of a city bus, and a siren.

The other day, she'd moved her desk right into the living room in front of the windows overlooking the busy New York streets below. If she was going to be a full-time author, by golly, why not take over the biggest room in the place? It had the best view, and the best light.

The night she'd come back home from Evergreen, she'd found a new confidence from her mother's words as they'd decorated the Christmas tree together. It'd been the first time Katie had heard her mother really sound like she was excited about Katie working on another novel. That had been empowering.

While in Evergreen, Katie had been so focused on that assignment for the magazine that she'd completely missed that her new novel was already being mentally created, even though she hadn't started an outline or plotted the story.

And although Mom was crazy about the characters, as she called them, Katie knew those people as friends, and they wouldn't be the heroes and heroines in her novel. No doubt some quirks and experiences would sneak their way into the book, but what she'd gained through those experiences with them was so much bigger.

She now had a true appreciation for small-town community, and an understanding too about how the same problems in city life still happened in those little towns. There were different ways to handle problems, and at the end of it all, each person was on their own special journey.

The people still loved, lost and fought for what they believed in. They told stories of triumph over tragedy. Second chances. New love found its way into old friends' hearts. The simplest things all around us every day went unnoticed, then redis-covered at just the right time. Those things would inspire others.

She felt armed with the experience to write such stories now.

She'd tucked a copy of the article she'd turned in for the magazine into a file folder. It had a purpose. A single step on her journey, and every single one, even the ones that felt like stumbles, held importance. The folder sat right next to the inch-thick stack of rejections she'd received on her first book when she'd sent it out on submission. She'd printed every single one of those heartbreaking emails to remind her. Humbling, yes. But a necessary step in the process.

Mom had been an engaged listener as Katie had shared every detail about her trip. They'd had afternoon breakfast at their favorite restaurant, the one with the pancakes, and while shopping, Mom had purchased an advent calendar for her as a joke.

Katie poked the cardboard perforated edge of the window number twenty and withdrew the tiny chocolate. There was no way for Mom to have known how perfect the snowman theme was after her stay in Evergreen. *This little cardboard advent calendar might be my favorite present of the year. A new tradition.*

Mom had meant it to be a substitute for missing the rest of the advent calendar in Evergreen, and the thought had landed sweetly on Katie's heart.

She tucked the piece of overpriced chocolate into her mouth, letting it melt on her tongue. Suddenly, she wished that chocolate was between two graham crackers with an ooey-gooey overheated marshmallow around the fire pit at Barbara's Country Inn with someone special. *Ben.*

As had become her writing ritual since she'd come back, she lit the candle at the corner of her desk. She'd had to sniff about a dozen holiday-scented candles before she'd finally found the one that smelled just like the trees at Henry's Christmas Tree Farm. It smelled so close. If it snowed in her apartment from the terpenes, she wouldn't even mind.

She settled in at her keyboard, opening the file to her as-yet-untitled Christmas novel and began typing, and she didn't stop, not even for a sip of her now-lukewarm coffee, until her phone chirped, pulling her out of her zone.

She picked up her phone and swiped the screen. She took in a quick breath at the words on the screen. Ben will be in town tomorrow. Excitement raced through her, but at the same time the goodbyes were so hard. As perfect as he seemed for her, she just couldn't picture herself in Evergreen year-round. She looked out the window at the traffic below. This city inspired her. She wished they'd met in New York, instead.

But they hadn't, and even if they couldn't be a couple, she wouldn't trade the chance to catch up and spend time with him for anything. Away from Evergreen, things would probably feel more real. Just relax and enjoy it. No pressure.

Chapter Twenty-Nine

BEN WATCHED THE NEW YORK City traffic out the window. The incessant honking and people pushing past one another on the sidewalk in the snow made him a little anxious. But in all fairness, it'd been a hectic day between the train ride, the interview and now this.

He sat at the table in the restaurant, waiting for Katie, sipping on his second glass of ice water to keep himself from sweating in his navy suit. This, meeting Katie here today, was much more stressful than the job interview.

When she walked through the restaurant door, she took his breath away.

The maître d' took her coat, and her smile could've lit up the room. She wore a pretty green dress with a short jacket over it, and Ben couldn't take his eyes off of her.

His heart stammered as she weaved through the tables in his direction, her eyes dancing when she finally laid eyes on him. Her steps quickened as she got closer. "Wow. Look at you."

Her surprise threw him for a moment, but then, she'd never really seen him dressed up. He stood up to pull out her chair, but she hugged him first. "Hi, Ben. It's really good to see you."

She felt so good in his arms. "You look beautiful," he said, stepping back to get a good look at her. It was hard to believe he was really here. With her. "The city suits you."

"Well, you too." She sat down and placed her napkin in her lap.

He'd worn his nicest suit for the interview, but also for her. He'd meant to impress her, but the comment still made him flush a bit. "So this is it." Ben leaned back in his chair, spreading his arms out. "The famous ramping-up-for-the-Christmas-holiday restaurant that serves blueberry pancakes all day long."

"Yes, and I highly recommend you try them."

Was it just his nerves, or was she acting a little too reserved? He'd counted on her being as excited as he was about tonight. "Well, I might be one step ahead of you."

As if on cue, the waitress carried two plates of pancakes out and set them in front of the two of them. Perfect golden blueberry pancakes, garnished with fresh, plump blueberries and whipped cream with a light dusting of confectioners' sugar.

Katie lit up. "Aww. You didn't."

That was the excitement he'd wanted to see. "I did, and would you look at that?" He put his napkin in his lap and took his fork in his hand. "This looks amazing."

"That's what I'm saying." She seemed nervous, a little giddy. "So. How was your interview?"

"I think it went pretty great."

"Of course it did," she said.

"Well, to be fair, this friend of mine had a pretty good freelancing career going. I might have been a little inspired by her." He meant to flatter her, but the banter felt a little forced, or maybe it was just his nerves.

Katie blushed and changed the subject. "How's the Christmas calendar? What have I missed?"

He felt her distancing again, keeping him at arm's length, and he wasn't sure how to fix it. He tried to stay focused on the conversation. "It's good. I've actually kept a list of every day."

"We're so much alike."

"I'll have to share it with you. There've been so many neat things, and facts about the town none of us knew or remembered."

She set down her fork and raised her hands. "I just love that whole concept." Her eyes brightened, and she leaned in.

He was drawn by her interest. "One day there were cards with receipts from each of the merchants in town at that time. Each receipt had the price of something on it. They handed them all out and challenged everyone to donate the price difference between then and now to the food bank. I thought that was a pretty good idea."

"It was."

"There's three days left, and people are still pretty pumped. Oh yeah, you met the Cooper twins. They performed a duet and have started giving free piano lessons."

"Wow." She looked like she really missed Evergreen, but had she missed him? He wanted to know.

"How about you?" he asked. "Is Christmas in the city everything you wanted it to be?"

Katie hesitated, and he gave her the time to answer even though the silence hung. "I don't know," she finally admitted. "Something about this Christmas feels...different."

"Anything I can do?"

She took a bite of her pancake and looked up with a sly grin. "Actually, there might be. What time is your train?"

"Right after this. I wanted to see you."

"Could you take a later one? Come to a thing with me?"

He leaned in. "What kind of a thing?" She sparkled, just as he'd remembered.

"Just say yes. You'll see."

He sat back in his chair. She'd taken a later train for him before. The least he could do was the same. "Okay. Yes."

They finished their pancakes, then headed to

the *thing,* which she was still keeping close to the chest.

The streets of New York bustled. People moved with purpose, balancing glossy shopping bags and gift-wrapped boxes. As in Chicago, there was that hum of life in the streets. He'd forgotten how much he loved that. The store windows were decorated for the season, and there was a line for Santa that wrapped around the street corner in front of the famous toy store.

At the next corner, Katie stopped in front of a glass door. "We're here," she announced.

He looked up at the tall office building. *We're not in Evergreen anymore.*

A doorman opened the door for them, and Ben placed his hand on the small of her back as they walked inside. Katie led the way and signed in with the guard, who checked in their coats, then led them to a private elevator that took them straight to the top floor.

When they stepped out of the elevator, live music played loudly, and well-dressed people mingled in the large space. In a corner, a few people dressed like Santa's elves filled big red bags with toys and canned goods, that were then stacked in bigger boxes near the freight elevator.

Ben looked out the window. "Would you look at this view? Amazing."

"Wow. It is."

"You've never been up here at night?"

"Never been up here at all. Mom's office is on

the eleventh floor. That's as far as I've been. This is the first time I've ever come to the Christmas party."

"Well, thanks for bringing me."

"Thank you for coming."

Inside, long tables made up an assembly line; some people wore Santa hats as they boxed food donations. Next to that, others wrapped presents.

Across the room, a buffet stretched for what had to be thirty or forty feet. Troughs of seafood were iced down, and shiny silver trays held warm dishes. A photographer made the rounds, capturing memories.

"So, office Christmas party?" Ben followed closely. "A big one." There had to be a couple hundred people here.

"Yes. Not mine. My mom's. For the magazine. First, we do some good by helping with the gift and food donations, then we have eggnog and eat—"

"After all those pancakes?" Ben shook his head. "I don't think so."

"Or dance if you're up to it."

"This is definitely a *thing*."

"It is." She squeezed his hand. "Thanks for coming with me."

Her hand fit right into his hand, small and delicate. He wouldn't want to be anywhere else tonight. "You're welcome. I'm glad we got to spend a little m—"

"There she is." A red-headed woman ran over to Katie. "You're here. You did make it."

"Hi, Mom. Ben, this is my mother, Pam."

"Hello." He extended his hand. "Very nice to meet you."

She nodded, kind of giving him the once-over. "Ben? Hi, nice to meet you too. It's Ben from Vermont, right? I have heard a lot about you."

"Okay. Wait. Not a lot. I mean, I mentioned you, but..." With a blush, Katie tried to soften the statement, but it made him happy to know she'd missed him enough to at least mention him to her mom.

"Your office party is also a charity event? That's some real Christmas spirit," he said.

"Yes. It's evolved over the years."

"It really is amazing, Mom." Pride poured from Katie in a way that made him want to make her proud of him, too.

"I told you it would be fun." Pam sailed off to help someone with something.

Katie turned and shrugged. "She's always busy."

"Shall we do our part wrapping a few presents?" he suggested. "I'm pretty good at it."

"Why am I not surprised?" She pulled her hands to her hips. "I'm pretty good at wrapping myself."

"May the best one win." He put his hand out, and she shook it.

"You're on."

He followed Katie to chairs at the very end of a long table. They wrapped games meant to be family gifts and topped them off with shiny bows. They each wrapped three, which turned into a bit of a contest, then they moved on.

As they walked around, skipping the buffet, he guided her to where it was a little quieter. "Can I ask you something?"

"Sure."

He'd been waiting all night for just the right time to share his article with her, but if he didn't do it soon, it'd be time to go. "You know, all that time you spent writing that article, I never got to read it. I was hoping you'd sneak me an early copy."

She slowed down and faced him.

"When does it come out?"

"It's not coming out," she said wistfully. "Turned out it wasn't right after all, but I'm working on something else now."

"I'd love to read it," he said. "Um. Maybe we swap?"

Her questioning eyes told him she hadn't picked up on the hint. He reached into his coat pocket and pulled out an extra copy of the front page of the Evergreen Mirror.

She looked a little confused at first, and then stammered, echoing the headline. "Evergreen's Magic: The Women Behind the Town." She looked up, her mouth open. "You did it."

His insides swirled, and nervous laughter

came out with his words. "I figured, what the heck, give it a try. I did some interviews, talked with some people. Wrote this."

She took the newsprint from him, then punched him playfully in the arm. "This is such a great angle."

"Yeah. It worked." He was happy with the article. It'd turned out better than he'd even hoped, lifting his confidence. Just a little proof he hadn't entirely lost his writing chops.

"Totally works. It's an entire town run by female business owners. I'm sort of bummed I didn't think of it myself." She stopped and silently read through the article.

He stood there, watching for her response. He'd looked up her articles. She was talented, and that made him a little nervous. He wanted her to enjoy the story, and hopefully he'd tickle a few of her awesome Evergreen memories. It was hard to stand there as she read it right in front of him. His jaw pulsed as he waited for her response.

"This is great," she said. "Really well-written. You know, you should run this at your new job."

He kind of wished he hadn't told her he'd been in town for the interview now. "Actually, they emailed me. I saw it on my phone about a half hour ago. I didn't get the job." He shook his head. There'd be another opportunity. He was sure of it. He wondered if she'd been imagining them together in the city like he had. Was another opportunity going to open the possibility of more for him and Katie? Or was this fate telling him to move on?

"I'm sorry." Her expression lost its zeal. "Oh, Ben. I'm sorry. But there're more jobs out there. Probably even better ones. This town is full of opportunity."

"Yeah. I'll try again. After the new year." That felt so far off, though. That little voice in his head was chanting at him, Tell her you want a chance.

Katie's smile had faded too.

He'd let her down. He could see her disappointment. He just wanted to get back home to Evergreen. "I should probably get going. The train."

"Yeah. I'll walk you." She slid her hand under his arm. "We can swing by my favorite enormous Christmas tree. It's right on the way." Her hand was wrapped tightly around his arm, her chin grazing the arm of his jacket as they walked.

"Sounds good."

They stopped on the sidewalk directly across the street from the giant Christmas tree in Rockefeller Center.

"Okay. You win. This tree is bigger than the one at the library."

"But I hear you have a certain flair with the lights. In fact, I was quite impressed by your work."

"I am the light guy."

"I know." She pressed her face into his jacket.

He ran his hand through her hair. "You were right. That tree has a lot of lights." He was happy to be standing here in front of this tree with her. It was a greeting-card moment of beauty.

"I hear it's decorated with, like, five miles of lights," she said.

He let out a long whistle. "Glad I'm not the light guy for this one."

"That would be a job. It's one of my favorite parts of living here." Katie smiled. Neither of them said anything else.

I could imagine living here. With Katie. He rubbed his hand on her back. There was that little voice again. Tell her. He wished the night didn't have to end. "Well, here we are again, about to say goodbye, outside a train station."

"Yeah. Should we say some confusing things about our feelings before we walk away again?"

Ben closed his eyes. That last goodbye had been so awkward. "Sorry about that. I was caught up in enjoying my time with you."

"It's okay. Me too. I guess, in a lot of ways, no matter where you are, some people just feel like—"

"Home." He moved just as she did.

She reached up and kissed him.

Her lips were soft and warm against the chill of the night. Her hair silky in his hands. In that moment the noise of the city fell away, and it was as if it was just the two of them kissing in front of a huge Christmas tree with a ten-foot star. He'd never felt so off balance. So in love. He looked into her eyes, wishing this night could continue. "Are you sure you won't come back with me?"

"I can't leave my mom for Christmas." But the tone was apologetic. She was feeling it too. Besides, he knew how much she loved the city. She'd made no secret of that. Her words softly tickled his cheek. "Are you sure you don't want to stay?"

Oh, I want to. I want to so much. But he had people counting on him back in Evergreen. He knew he had to go back tonight. He understood the disappointment in her eyes. "As much as I can see myself here, I haven't missed a Christmas in Evergreen yet."

Katie kissed him again, and by the time she pulled away, it was hard to let her go. Flummoxed, Ben backed away with his pulse still racing. Breathing in her scent, every moment they'd racked up in their brief time together felt like more than some couples enjoyed in a lifetime together.

Her smile said one thing, that she wanted to be with him. He wanted that too, but neither of them could. *Another time. Another place.* His heart ached.

Katie backed up, the braver of the two. "Merry Christmas, Ben." She turned and walked away as powdery snowflakes began to fall.

He cleared his throat. At least it wasn't goodbye this time. "Merry Christmas, Katie."

His heart hung heavy in his chest as she walked away. Her long blond hair bounced against the back of her coat, and with each step away from him, he felt lonelier.

Ben boarded his train. He sat in the same seat he'd been sitting in when he'd met her the first time. Ahead of him, the seat where she'd sat remained empty.

Come back, Katie. Just walk right through that door.

But no one else boarded. The train conductor announced, "All Aboard for Evergreen," and the train pulled from the station.

Chapter Thirty

ON THE MORNING OF CHRISTMAS Eve, it was pretty clear no one had tired of the new tradition of the advent calendar. People lined up four and five deep to see what was going on.

Booths were already in place for all the crafts and games for the festival, and the food vendors were already starting to cook, sending a mix of salty and sweet into the air. Later, the choir would sing from the gazebo, and local performers would take their turn entertaining everyone.

Ben crossed the square as the biggest crowd yet gathered around for the opening of the Christmas Eve box. The last one on the calendar. The choir singers, dressed in their burgundy Christmas Eve robes, sang "The Twelve Days of Christmas."

He mused about how they'd all sung that while at Barbara's Country Inn baking cookies.

"And a partridge in a pear tree." The choir sang loud and clear and held that final note all the way to the release, when Hannah swung her hands in a circular motion and pinched her finger and thumb together.

Everyone applauded wildly.

Michelle took the microphone. "Thank you for joining us this morning. It's hard to imagine this is our fiftieth Annual Christmas Festival here in the town of Evergreen. With all the tradition, and this time capsule, I don't know how we'll ever top this."

Heads bobbed, and people clapped.

"But we'll try, right?"

Cheers filled town square.

"We'll figure it out together." Michelle picked up the snowman's hat and reached in to pick the name of who'd have the honors to open the Christmas eve box. She laughed as she turned the slip of paper around to prove she wasn't making it up, then read the name. "Well, it's only fitting that our Christmas Eve pick should be... Hannah."

"Yes!" Elliott threw a fist in the air. "Yay, Hannah!"

Hannah blushed, probably excited about being picked and by Elliott's public display too.

Ben liked those two together. They seemed happy, and it'd been no surprise to anyone around here. There'd been that little something in their relationship that had seemed like more than friends for years. Funny it had taken them so long to realize it. Their joy touched him. He hoped he'd have that and more with Katie. They'd met and matched so quickly. Like it'd been in the works for years. How often did that really happen?

He missed her like crazy. He had a stack of possible jobs to apply for, even a couple in New Jersey, within commuting distance from the city. Anything to get him closer to Katie. He wished she was here to see this today.

Hannah stepped up to the calendar. "Well, is everyone ready?" She turned and opened the box marked twenty-four. Like the others, there was a red envelope, but instead of a crafty whimsical holiday something or other, Hannah struggled to lift the heavy metal box from the drawer. "What could this be? I might need some help. This thing weighs a ton." But she managed to get it out of the drawer and onto the table. "It's heavy." The sturdy gray box had a bright red ribbon tied around it, with another envelope tucked beneath the bow. Only this envelope wasn't red like all the others. It was green.

People whispered among themselves in anticipation of what might be in a box that looked more like a fireproof safe than a present.

Hannah opened the envelope and read, "Dear Evergreen. As the Mayor of Evergreen, I..." She stopped, glancing over at Michelle, who knew exactly what she was thinking. Hannah scanned the group in front of her, then directed her comment to the outgoing mayor. "Ezra, would you like to read this?"

"Me?" He looked up, excited to still be included.

"It seems only right that you do."

"I don't know." He fumbled with the edges of his scarf.

Michelle marched right over and dragged him from the crowd. "Come on."

Hannah handed him the letter.

"Written by the mayor?" Ezra's eyebrows rose. "From fifty years ago?" He lowered the letter. "My grandfather was the mayor then! It must have been very cool to be the mayor throughout that blizzard and the creation of this time capsule." He cleared his throat, taking the position in front of the time capsule with pride. "Ahem. As the mayor of Evergreen, I have been granted the honor of bestowing both of today's gifts. In this box you will find savings bonds"—he gasped, his mouth open—"hopefully having now matured these fifty years."

"Fifty years? That would add up to a lot," Thomas said from the crowd.

Hannah opened the metal box and handed the stack of notes to Michelle. "Oh my gosh!"

"How much is there?" someone asked.

"It's hard to say." Michelle shook away her surprise. "But it looks like the town budget just went up considerably."

Nan's eyes lit up, her hand squeezing tighter around Ben's arm.

Ben wondered if this too had been an act. He leaned down and whispered, "Nan? Did you know that about this?"

"I most certainly did not."

Ezra read on even more enthusiastically. "Help the needy. Increase education. Keep the roads clear. Help our small businesses thrive. Welcome all travelers to Evergreen. As the old saying goes, when you have so much, you build a bigger table." He leaned over to Michelle and stage whispered to her, "Maybe even build more than one road in and out of town. That's what I'd do."

Michelle saluted him. "Definitely!"

A cheer went up as the town enjoyed this last part of the time capsule.

Nan looked up at Ben and leaned against his shoulder. "Isn't this wonderful?"

"It truly is." This town had amazed him repeatedly. He was proud to have lived here. To have grown up with these values, and with a community that still came together through the good and the bad.

"Hold on, everyone. There's more!" Ezra danced around, which only excited the crowd further. He waited for people to quiet down before he continued. "While I'm sure you've enjoyed opening these boxes, we want to be sure you all get to spend Christmas morning with your families. And so, we have officially started a Christmas Festival to be held on Christmas Eve each year."

"We've kept up that tradition every year, no matter what tried to get in the way," Michelle said.

"Tonight," Ezra continued, "on what we hope will be the fiftieth anniversary of that festival, you are to open the final green envelope with as much of the town present as you can muster. As a town. As a family. As Evergreen."

Hannah raised her hands in the air and, on the count of three, the choir sang "Jingle Bells." The joyful noise filled the air as folks sang along.

Ben stopped in at the Kringle Kitchen for breakfast, and Nan went back to wrap a few gifts and meet a few folks she'd ordered books for. He watched as children deposited their last-minute wishes into the Letters for Santa mailbox. How old had he been when he'd finally given up writing to Santa? For the life of him, he couldn't remember. Nan had always instilled in him that "if you don't believe, you don't receive," so he'd carried on the charade for many years.

He laughed as he lifted a forkful of Carol's incredible apple dumpling to his mouth. Maybe he should drop a note to Santa this year. There was only one thing on his list.

Nick and Hannah walked over and sat down at the table with him.

"Merry Christmas! How was your trip to New York?" Nick asked.

"It was good. The job didn't work out, and I'll be honest, I'd kind of hoped Katie might want to come back. That didn't happen." His heart sank. The connection had felt so real, but it had been fast. These two probably would think he was a little crazy to be pining away for her. Tourists came and went. Everyone knew that. "But I still made a good friend, and it was good to see her in her environment."

"Well, sometimes that's how it starts." Nick looked at Ben and then over at Hannah.

Ben wondered if Nick was talking about Hannah and Elliott or people in general. Could he be thinking of Ben and Katie, or was that just wishful thinking? Ben had hoped Katie would be in touch, but it'd been radio silence since he'd left. Even on the ride home, on the train, he'd had to keep himself from texting her. He missed her already.

"I made a wish on the snow globe," Hannah admitted to Nick.

Nick danced a jig. "Something good, I hope."

"Definitely. Funniest thing. Having to repair it, we saw the key underneath the sleigh. And that led to finding the mural and the calendar—well, the time capsule. And breaking the snow globe brought Elliott and I together to fix it. I see him in a whole new light. And all because I dropped it that day with you, Nick."

Nick nodded ever so slowly. His eyes twinkled and the air of mischief hung above him like mistletoe. "Some things...just take a little push." He stood before either of them could say a word. "I'm late for something very important." And just like that, he took off into a jog across the square.

"Did he just allude to making me drop the snow globe?" She wasn't asking Ben so much as making an observation.

Ben watched Nick dash away. "I'm not sure what just happened."

Chapter Thirty-One

THE SUN HAD SET, AND kids were getting sleepy-eyed despite their excitement about Santa Claus coming tonight. Later, they'd line up for the candlelight processional. Such a beautiful tradition, with the hand-crafted candles, the church bells and a cappella carols lifting glory to the heavens. The true reason for the season.

Ben went over to the library to see if he could help Nan with story time tonight. When he walked inside, Nan and Nick stood side by side, looking a little suspect.

Nan seemed to be explaining the business to Nick. "And of course, if they're willing to shelve a few books sometimes, we like to waive overdue fees."

"Makes sense to me," Nick said.

Ben approached the desk. "Hi. What are you two doing?"

"Ah, Ben," Nan said. "You're just in time to meet our new part-time employee."

"Nick?" Ben shook the man's hand. "Welcome aboard. But—"

Nick bounced on his toes as he spoke. "When I heard the town was putting dollars in the budget for a part-time employee here at the library, I thought it would be great to spend more time here." He looked over at Nan with more than business in those twinkling blue eyes.

Does he like Nan? They'd been friends forever. When Nick had been talking about Hannah and Elliott, had there been a little personal experience in that truth too? "At the library?" Ben waited for confirmation.

Nick made a slight head nod toward Nan.

That wasn't very subtle. How had Ben not noticed that before? Nick and Nan. Sure, they'd been running around together like school kids over the advent calendar, but how long had that really been going on? How about that? Nan thought she was cramping his style, when all along Ben might've been the one holding her back from other things.

Ben enjoyed the broad smile on Nan's face. "So there's no story hour tonight?"

"Actually, there is." She raised a finger in the air. "But my new employee and I decided that since it's Christmas Eve, it would be best to do story hour in front of the new town mural."

"But who's doing the reading?"

Nan and Nick responded together. "Go see."

Why do I feel like I'm being set up?

Were those two becoming an item? For all the years he'd lived with Nan, he'd never even considered she might've wanted to find someone to share her life with. Her life was so full of friends and the library. But something was definitely underway between them, and he couldn't believe he hadn't noticed it before.

Ben walked over to Kringle Alley. Maybe David was doing the reading. That kid could do anything. It'd be a good thing for him to do, although Ben had to admit the storytime readings had always been the favorite part of his day. He was a little sad they hadn't asked him to do it.

There was a huge crowd. So many people that he couldn't even hear the story being told. Was it "The Night Before Christmas"? Maybe "The Gift of the Magi," or something fun like "Rudolph the Red-Nosed Reindeer." All crowd favorites.

He politely pressed his way through the crowd. Someone had moved Henry's antique sleigh here, and adults and children alike were gathered around it.

There, sitting on the velvet seat, Katie read from Louisa May Alcott's book.

He blinked. How had Nan pulled this off? He stepped closer, trying to wrap his head around what was happening right in front of him. Her voice was full of life; she had her own array of wonderful inflection that added to the tale. Her hands moved gracefully as her gaze met each child, tempting them deeper into the story.

"And Effie fell asleep with a happy smile on her lips, her one humble gift still in her hand..." Katie's voice carried over the tiny heads filling him with so much pride, happiness, joy. It was so good to see her. The best Christmas present he could ever ask for.

Ben took great delight in the fact that everyone enjoyed her reading so much. He wanted to shout a hello or wave, anything to grab her attention, but he stood there, holding on to each of her words.

She lifted her gaze, and their eyes met. She sucked in a quick breath but kept reading, but a smile tugged at the edge of her lips. "...and a new love for Christmas in her heart that never changed through a long life spent in doing good. The end." Katie closed the book between her hands.

Kids jumped up and clapped. Families moved toward the games and booths.

"Hi, Mr. Ben," one of the boys said, raising his hand in the air for a high five. "Merry Christmas."

"Hi, guys." Ben waved, recognizing lots of them.

She still sat in the sleigh, talking to one of the parents.

Ben walked over, trying to wait his turn. Finally, the woman wished Katie a Merry Christmas and left. "When did you—" He couldn't even string words together. "You look beautiful. What are you doing here?"

With a playful lift of her shoulder, she said, "Someone had to read Louisa May Alcott. Did you know she wrote a Christmas story, too? It's..." She lowered the book in front of her, and her tone became more serious. "I came for you, Ben."

Overwhelmed by her comment, almost afraid he may not have really heard what he thought he'd heard, he replayed it in his mind. He'd dreamed she might one day say those words.

"I kept writing about Evergreen." Her eyes held his gaze. "And the more I wrote, the more I fell in love with this place. More than that. I was falling in love, am in love...with you."

Emotion swirled through him. *Love. She loves me too.* Ben put his hands softly to her cheeks and pressed his lips to hers. There were no words that could say it better, and he was glad he was the one to start the kiss this time. Their lips lingered between smiles. "I'm so glad you're here," he said. "So. Are you staying here?"

"For Christmas, yes." She nodded, sucking a breath as she did. "But I'm a city girl. I always will be. At least, I think so. But I realized what it is about Evergreen that got me. I wanted to spend Christmas with my mom..." She pointed over her shoulder.

"Your mom!"

"And just...a ton of other people. And especially you."

"This is pretty special."

"It is. And, um, there's something else?" Katie's mom walked over, carrying three hot cocoas.

"You're right about this cocoa, Katie," her mom said. "It's incredible." She handed a cup to her daughter.

"Thanks, Mom."

It was nice to see Katie and her mom together here in Evergreen. That it was special enough that Katie wanted to share it with her thrilled him. "Hello, Pam. Nice to see you again."

"Ben, I enjoyed your article on Evergreen female-owned businesses." She handed him one of the other cups of cocoa. "I read it on the train, and while I have a few notes, I'd like to run it in the magazine, if you wouldn't mind."

Today just kept getting better and better. "Um. Wow." He could barely get the words out. "Yes. Of course. This is very unexpected."

"That's not all." She glanced over at Katie with a grin. "I'd also like you to come interview at the magazine after the holiday."

He looked over at Katie. She most certainly had had something to do with this chain of events. She wanted it as badly as he did. "What do I even say to that?"

"Yes!" Katie gave him the of-course look. "Say yes!"

"Yes. Thank you, Pam."

Katie spun around, an enormous grin on her face. "Isn't this an amazing place, Mom?"

"It is. You know, your brother would love it.

Maybe next year, all of us could spend a few days here."

"A new tradition?" Katie's mouth dropped, and she stepped closer to Ben. "I kind of like the sound of that."

"I love the sound of that." He took her hand and squeezed it.

Later that night before the midnight processional, a small group of them had gathered at the Tinker Shop. Elliott handed out candles he'd had the kids work on for the event. Each one had been hand-poured, then when they were done, the real work had begun: decorating small discs that slipped over the tapers.

"Like little pieces of artwork. I'm totally keeping mine." Carol lovingly admired the painted protective ring at the base of the candle. "Not only will it keep the wax from dripping, but it's so pretty."

"I helped make some of them too," David said.

"He did, and guided the younger kids. He was a big help," Elliott added.

Michelle and Thomas looked on. Michelle spoke as she picked up two candles, handing one to Thomas. "We met when Thomas was helping me look for candles last year for this. Remember?"

"I do," he said. "Like it was yesterday. They

were on the top shelf in that back storage closet in Daisy's Country Store."

"Yep." She wrapped both of her arms around his bicep. "Best day ever."

Elliott walked over to Hannah. "I have a little something for you."

"A gift? I didn't get anything for you. We've never before—"

He caught her hand. "It's not like that. It's something I've been crafting for you."

She pressed her hands together. "Those are the very best gifts. You know me so well."

"I think you're really going to love this." He led her over to the counter, where a beautifully wrapped box sat there with a shimmering bow on top.

She moved toward it tentatively. "Should I open it now?"

"Yeah. Sure. It's Christmas Eve," Elliott encouraged her.

The others inched in, sensing something big about to happen.

Hannah didn't waste a second. She ripped through the paper and opened the box. "Elliott? You made this?" It was a perfect miniature replica of the time capsule Christmas advent calendar.

"I did." He tugged one of the small drawers, about the size of a ring box, open. "All the drawers open too. Next year, we can fill them with our own surprises."

"Next year? That sounds good." She leaped into his arms. "I adore it. And you. You are the best."

Elliott spun her around. "I'm so glad you like it. I hope to make you something special every Christmas, every year, of the rest of our lives."

"I'm going to have to step up my game," Hannah teased.

"No. You just keep being you. You're perfect just the way you are."

"Finally!" Katie said, followed by a playful laugh. "I thought you two would never figure it out. It was crystal clear to me the moment I saw you together."

Everyone in the room nodded. "About time."

"Now this is one Merry Christmas," Hannah whispered. "Thanks, snow globe."

Chapter Thirty-Two

MICHELLE LISTENED AS THE JOYOUS sounds lifted into the air. It was kind of sad to know that the last box on the advent calendar had already been opened. Tonight, the air was crisp, but the temperature had risen enough that it was bearable with just a coat—scarf optional. In fact, it seemed like perfect snow weather, and what could top a white Christmas morning?

She took a big sniff of the air. It even smelled like snow.

Michelle stepped in front of the large crowd. As mayor of this town, she was proud to be part of such a wonderful group of people. She felt emotional tonight. This town. Thomas and David. Her friends. *Life is good.*

Just about the whole town was gathered here. Everyone attended the midnight processional, so the timing for this one last act from the time capsule couldn't be more perfect. People filled the streets, kids on their parents' shoulders, and some even stood on the benches to see over the crowd.

Michelle used a microphone tonight. "Hi everyone. Merry Christmas. I'm so proud and humbled to be your new mayor. Thank you for being a part of these wonderful festivities and annual traditions. Staying involved helps our community remain strong."

Everyone cheered.

"Before we open this final gift, I'd like everyone to raise a glass of cocoa, or eggnog, or whatever you have handy, and join me in thanking Ezra Green for all his years of service as Mayor of Evergreen."

"To Ezra!"

Ezra couldn't even speak. He simply raised his hand in the air, waving as he turned in a circle. Overcome by emotion, tears ran down his cheeks, but he'd never looked happier as everyone toasted him.

Katie and Ben leaned against each other, as they toasted him as well, yelling a big thank-you above the crowd. Michelle saw Thomas whisper something to David.

Everyone finally quieted down, and Michelle raised the microphone again. "Since he helped us find the time capsule, we decided that the final box should be opened by David." Michelle called him up to the podium. "Come on up here, David." As they'd planned, she playfully put the

Evergreen Hat Company top hat on his head. "Okay, there. Fit okay?"

"Yes." He nodded and stepped away from her, but before he read the last gift, he stopped. "Oh, Michelle?"

"Yes?"

"We forgot to ask you…"

"Ask me what?" They'd already rehearsed all this earlier. This was not part of the plan. Had she forgotten something?

"Turn around." David pointed into the crowd.

Michelle turned around. So tall, Thomas stood out easily in the crowd, and even more so when he went down on one knee, with a wedding ring box in his hand. A scream escaped from her as the crowd slid back, leaving Thomas front and center.

With a smile as wide as a crescent moon, he said, "To ask you to marry me, Michelle."

"Oh, wow!" She covered her mouth. David beamed from across the way. He was such a good boy. She loved them both.

"You are, without a doubt, the most special and beautiful woman I have ever met. I knew you were the one the first day I laid eyes on you."

"Yes!" she squealed.

"I haven't asked you anything yet."

"I know. But yes."

"Michelle, will you marry me?"

"I really will, yes!" She ran into his arms.

Cheers rose from all around them. Whoops,

hoorays and applause veiled the Christmas song the choir had begun singing.

Tears in her eyes, they kissed, and David patted his dad on the shoulder in a gesture showing how much he approved of Thomas and Michelle together. That touched Michelle to the core.

"Wait." She tried to pull herself together. "David. Finish the—"

David reached into the last envelope tied to the time capsule and pulled out the letter.

"What does it say?"

"It says, 'Now refill the boxes, seal up the wall and send a Merry Christmas to Evergreen in fifty more years.' Which means we have a lot of work to do this year."

"We're going to seal up the wall?" someone asked.

There were mixed feelings about that among the crowd.

"I'll be like Nick and Nan in fifty years. One of the old people in town dropping hints so they know to open it," David sang out. "That is really cool."

"It is," Thomas said.

In the gazebo, Elliott kissed Hannah on the cheek. She skipped as if on wings to her spot. She lifted her hands gracefully in the air to lead the choir, Elliott included, in a quiet and appreciative carol.

Everyone sang along.

A little distance away, Lisa sang from the sidewalk with her two foster dogs on leashes, each wearing a brightly colored Christmas bandana from the store. She turned to look across the way and saw her boyfriend Kevin step from the crowd. She and the dogs ran to meet him halfway.

There was a noticeable spark between Nan and Nick walking closely behind Michelle and Thomas to lead the people of Evergreen through town square toward the church in their candle-light processional.

Katie and Ben held their candles, but more than just candles lit their way tonight.

Ben looked over at Katie. "I'm so glad you're here to share this tradition with me."

"Traditions." Her smile spoke volumes more. A promise there'd be more traditions between them.

A few days later, the Evergreen Express sounded the horn for passengers to board to return to the city. Those who'd been visiting for the holidays hugged teary goodbyes and well wishes. Others were bound for new adventures.

Nan and Nick stood with Ben near the train. Nan had tears in her eyes.

"It's only an interview," Ben said.

"I know." She kissed him on the cheek. "I want you to do the very best job that you can."

"Of course. I'll make you proud."

"You always have, Ben." She straightened his scarf around the collar of his jacket.

"Nick." Ben shook the man's hand, knowing Nan had someone new to watch her back and help out these days.

Katie's voice carried from the platform. "I'll see you on the train in a minute, Mom." She raced over to join Ben as her mom boarded. Breathless, she took Nan's hands. "Bye. Oh?" She wrapped her arms around Nan. "I miss you already. Who will help me with all my research?"

"You always have a spot in my office in the library. Come anytime."

"Thank you."

"You have an enjoyable train ride," Nan said.

Katie walked over to Nick. As much as she'd resisted the notion, she was almost convinced he was the true-to-life Santa Claus. "Bye, Nick." She leaned in and whispered, "I'm beginning to think you are behind all the magic in this town. The snow globe. All of it." She stepped away, and Nick didn't deny it. "Thank you all. Bye." Katie walked over and boarded the Evergreen Express with Ben right behind her.

Ezra stepped up on the train and waved.

Michelle clung to Thomas's hand. Ezra had been a wonderful mentor. Katie had no doubt that Michelle would be just fine without him there as a safety net.

Across the way, Nick and Nan stood along with other locals, all saying goodbyes to holiday guests. Hands lifted in the air, waving to the smiling faces in the windows as the train readied for departure. A blend of goodbyes, thank-yous and Christmas salutations filled the air. Michelle knew Evergreen would always be a special place where memories were made. She couldn't wait to help spread that joy throughout everything the town did all year long.

She watched Ezra take a seat in a row at the front of the train, ready for his new life in Boston. As excited as Michelle knew Ezra was, he looked a little nervous.

Katie's mom was busy typing on her computer, and Katie took an empty seat a couple of rows in front of her. She leaned toward the window, waving. Michelle waved back.

Ben boarded the train. Michelle had a pretty good idea they wouldn't be seeing as much of him from now on. She saw him pause at the seat where Katie was. Katie slipped over, allowing Ben to slide in close next to her. She laid her head against his shoulder.

Michelle pulled her hands to her heart. Friends, old and new, as they left Evergreen. But they'd all be back, if only for a visit.

Thomas wrapped his arm around her. His love warmed her to the core. She placed a loving hand on David's shoulder. Her ring caught the sunlight, sparkling, lighting her way. With her family. She pulled David and Thomas closer.

She had no idea how the three of them would

ever top her first Christmas as mayor of Evergreen, but she had no doubt that next year would be even more magical.

The people of Evergreen busied themselves all winter and well into the spring, planning the next time capsule for another exciting adventure on the one hundredth annual Christmas Festival. Each day of the advent had been assigned to the person who'd opened that box. Those who'd left Evergreen weren't forgotten. They were still part of the elaborate project. In true Evergreen style, it'd become a bit of a competition, raising the stakes to make the two hundredth year anniversary even more spectacular. Ezra, Katie and Ben would manage their teams through the wonderful tools in this age of technology, and Katie had already decided to make her box, the fifteenth day of December, a snowman-building challenge.

That spring, Ben officially moved to the city and began his job at the magazine. His fresh writing style engaged the readers, and although he missed the library and Nan, he found new inspiration in the bustling city with Katie and new friends.

Katie wrote a heartwarming novel of hope and second chances set in the town of Evergreen that involved a set of twins, a mystery and a couple planning a wedding in the small church the following summer. There were already whispers of a sequel.

No one could really say for certain that the snow globe had anything to do with Katie's success...or the love she felt for Ben, which grew stronger every day, and which he returned in full. But Katie mentioned to Ben the need for a visit back to Evergreen soon to make one more wish on the snow globe at the Kringle Kitchen, just in case.

The End

Cranberry Crostini

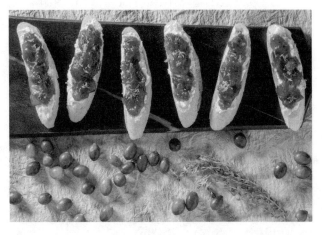

In *Christmas in Evergreen: Tidings of Joy,* the Meet and Mingle at Barbara's County Inn is a chance for the Evergreen community to share friendly conversation and holiday cheer over tasty hors d'oeuvres. Katie has two of the Cranberry Crostini before Ben arrives...and for Katie, his presence makes a great party even better. These delicious and pretty Cranberry Crostini are perfect for any holiday mingling.

Prep Time: 25 minutes
Cook Time: 15 minutes
Serves: 10

Ingredients

- 1 baguette, cut on the bias into 1-inch slices
- Olive oil, as needed
- Kosher salt, to taste
- Black pepper, to taste
- 12 oz. fresh cranberries (can substitute frozen)
- 1 orange, zested and juiced
- 1/2 teaspoon red pepper flakes
- 1 teaspoon thyme, fresh, chopped
- 1 to 2 tablespoons prepared orange marmalade
- 8 oz. goat cheese, softened

Preparation

1. Preheat oven to 350°F.

2. Place baguette slices on a baking sheet, generously brush with olive oil and season lightly with salt and pepper. Bake until lightly brown and crisp, about 15 minutes.

3. In a small sauce pan over medium heat, combine cranberries, sugar, vinegar, red pepper flakes, thyme, marmalade and a pinch of salt.

4. Bring to a simmer, stirring occasionally for about 5 minutes.

5. Reduce heat and continue cooking an-

other 10 minutes or until mixture begins to thicken.

6. Let cool.

7. To assemble crostini: top each crostini with a smear of goat cheese and a dollop of cranberry marmalade.

8. Garnish with fresh thyme leaves and orange zest, if desired.

Thanks so much for reading
*Christmas in Evergreen: Tidings of
Joy.* We hope you enjoyed it!

You might like these other books
from Hallmark Publishing:

Christmas in Evergreen
Christmas in Evergreen: Letters to Santa
The Secret Ingredient
Wrapped Up in Christmas
Wrapped Up in Christmas Joy
Christmas in Bayberry
Christmas Charms
A Timeless Christmas
An Unforgettable Christmas

For information about our new releases and
exclusive offers, sign up for our free newsletter at
hallmarkchannel.com/hallmark-
publishing-newsletter

You can also connect with us here:

Facebook.com/HallmarkPublishing

Twitter.com/HallmarkPublish

About The Author

USA Today bestselling author Nancy Naigle whips up small-town love stories with a whole lot of heart. She began her popular contemporary romance series Adams Grove while juggling a successful career in finance and life on a seventy-six-acre goat farm. Along with the *Christmas in Evergreen* books, she is the author of *The Secret Ingredient, Christmas Joy,* and *Hope at Christmas*, all made into Hallmark Channel Christmas movies. She's also the author of the Boot Creek Novels and the G Team Mysteries. Now happily retired from a career in the financial industry, she devotes her time to writing, horseback riding, and enjoying the occasional spa day. A Virginia girl at heart, Nancy now calls North Carolina home.

Turn the page for a sneak peek of

WRAPPED
UP IN
CHRISTMAS JOY

USA TODAY BESTSELLING AUTHOR
JANICE LYNN

Chapter One

"I'LL PAY SOMEBODY FIFTY BUCKS to take my place," Cole Aaron offered his fellow firefighters at the Pine Hill Fire Department.

What were the odds that he would be the one to pull the "winning" green candy cane from the fuzzy red stocking he and the guys had passed around? Not that he felt like he'd won anything. If anything, getting stuck in the role of Santa felt like a huge mistake. Did they really think it was a good fit for a former tough-guy Marine turned firefighter to dress up as Santa in the Pine Hill Christmas parade?

He didn't have any Christmas cheer whatsoever. Christmas generosity, perhaps, such as when he'd offered to pay for poinsettias for the nursing home residents—but trying to make up for all the bad things you'd done in life didn't suddenly make you qualified to be *Santa*.

"This one is all you...Saint Nick," Andrew snickered.

Of course, his best buddy Andrew would find humor in the idea of Cole donning a red suit, fake belly, white beard, and wig. Had the roles been reversed Cole would be cracking up, too. Only, Andrew hadn't gotten the short end of the stick, er...candy cane, in the "Who Gets to be Santa on the Rescue Truck for the Christmas Parade?" lottery. Cole knew they should have gone with rock, paper, scissors. He was good at that.

He turned to Ben, another of his close friends.

"Don't look at me," Ben advised, continuing to help Jules and another firefighter decorate a ten-foot tree to "give the fire station a festive spirit," as the chief had put it. The Christmas music blasting over the intercom system all week had also been Chief's idea. As if to taunt Cole, "Santa Claus is Coming to Town" came on.

The guys all snorted with laughter.

Cole groaned. "I look nothing like Santa."

"Which is what that's for." Andrew gestured to the red suit Chief had sat on the table where Cole had been doing a crossword puzzle just minutes before, trying to ignore how Christmas was taking over his beloved firehall. "Come on. You know red's your color."

Glaring at his best friend, Cole peeled the plastic wrapper off the offending green candy cane and stuck the end in his mouth. *Yuck.* He couldn't even determine if it was green apple, watermelon, spearmint, or some horrible combination of all three. It certainly didn't taste like peppermint or anything to do with Christmas.

"That bad, eh?" one of the other firemen asked, looking just as amused as Andrew and Ben. The entire crew found it funny that the new guy had to be Santa. Or maybe they were all just ecstatic they weren't the one stuck with having to put on the red suit and go around saying, "Ho, ho, ho. Merry Christmas."

Not Cole's idea of a good time, either.

Any of the other crew members would be more qualified than Cole to spark the magic of Christmas for the kids at the parade. He suspected most of the guys would even like playing Santa, but were enjoying ragging him too much to step in.

Cole hadn't even celebrated the holiday in years. How was he supposed to pull off being Santa to this full-of-Christmas-spirit small Kentucky town?

"Not nearly as bad as having to wear that." To prove it, he stuck the tip of the candy back into his mouth—and immediately regretted doing so. It should be against the law for candy canes to come in any flavor other than peppermint.

Or for guys with tainted souls to play the ultimate Christmas good guy.

"Come on, Cole. Model the suit for us," Jules said from where she stood on a stepladder placing an ornament of a Dalmatian in a fire helmet on the tree.

Ben handed another ornament up to Jules as he added, "You do need to make sure the costume fits."

Glaring at his coworkers, Cole bit off a piece of the candy and crunched the disgusting stuff between his teeth.

"Ben's right," Chief confirmed, his salt and pepper mustache curling upward as he rocked his six-five frame back on his heels. "Last year, the pants had to be hemmed for Bob. I suspect you'll have to have the extra length let back out."

"Or maybe Bob should just be Santa again this year," Cole mumbled, wondering how long the candy's bad taste would linger in his mouth.

"His daughter is expecting her first baby that week," Chief reminded, his brown eyes twinkling with humor, as well, beneath his bushy brows. "Bob will be in Connecticut to meet his grandchild."

There was that.

"I'll be in my office—I have a meeting in a few minutes." His gaze connected with Cole's. "But for the record, I couldn't have chosen anyone better to be the department's Santa. You'll do great."

Cole wasn't the type to argue with his boss, nor did he usually feel the desire to do so. But, for once, he longed to list all the reasons Chief was wrong.

Instead, he sighed.

Whether he wanted to or not, he was going to be Santa in the Pine Hill Christmas parade. Santa should be some happy, jovial fellow, not a former Marine who'd done things that still haunted Cole's dreams.

No one else at the firehall battled the demons Cole fought.

Thank God.

Cole was proud to have been a Marine, proud of the brotherhood he'd belonged to. He would die filled with love for the good ole US of A and pride that he'd served his country with all his heart. But when it came to the things he'd done...

There was no pride in himself, nor should there be.

"Put on the suit," Andrew repeated, barely able to contain his laughter as all the crew began chanting along with him.

"I've heard about taking advantage of the new guy, but this," he held up his putrid green candy cane, "is ridiculous."

"Hey, I think it's cool you get to be Santa," Ben said, and Cole had no doubt he meant it. Cole's friend would have jumped at the chance to take the role if he'd drawn the green candy cane. Ben always smiled, was friendly to everyone, and would make a great Santa.

"Just think, all the kids are going to love you," his friend continued.

Not one of Cole's life goals. Not that he wanted kids to dislike him—far from it. He just didn't think much about kids one way or the other. He certainly had no plans to ever have any of his own.

No way would he ruin a kid's life by giving him or her a dad as messed up in the head as he was.

Cole still marveled at the life he'd made in Kentucky, at how much he had changed from the civilian drifter he'd been when he'd signed up for firefighter school. Working as a firefighter had given him purpose, and coming to Pine Hill to move into the farmhouse his late uncle had left him had given him a home. The Marines had been his family for more than a decade, and now he belonged to a second family, too. But at times like these, he questioned the motives of his brother firefighters. They sure liked to push him out of his comfort zone, and if he didn't know better, he'd think they'd rigged the stocking draw.

Regardless, being Santa in the parade was what was expected of him. Cole would do his job, and he'd do it well. Never again would he be the weak link of his team.

"Fine. I'll put on the suit. But if I catch any of you with your cellphones out taking pictures, I refuse to be held responsible for my actions."

Andrew grinned. "Just be sure to say cheese when you come back out."

"Instead of 'ho, ho, ho'?" Cole shook his head. "Not happening. If I'm going to do this"—and it looked as if he had to—"then I'm going to do it right, so every one of you clowns better straighten up if you want to stay off the naughty list."

At six foot one, Cole was a good four inches taller than Bob, and the pant legs currently only came down mid-calf. The cuffs definitely needed to be let out, Cole thought miserably as he stared at himself in the mirror. His tall black boots mostly hid the poor fit except when Cole moved and they rode up, exposing his calves.

He noted the tilt of the red hat with its big fuzzy white ball on top, the fake belly that added girth to his middle but did nothing to fill out the sleeves and pants, as his muscular legs and arms were far more toned than Santa was meant to be. Additionally, his furry coat sleeves were also a bit too short, though he supposed they could be made to work with a pair of gloves that covered more of his wrists. The white wig and beard fit right, at least, and covered most of his face except for his eyes, nose, and the top of his cheekbones.

He eyed the furry white stick-on brows and shrugged. *Why not?* He removed the backing and pressed them over his own eyebrows.

With some adjustments and help with make-up from Jules—and a position up on top of the fire truck, where no one could see him all that closely—maybe none of the kids would notice what a terrible Santa he made.

"Here goes nothing," he muttered to his Santa

reflection, and then, sucking in a deep breath, he embraced his role.

Like true brothers, the other firefighters would just keep ribbing him about the being Santa if they thought it bugged him, so the best way to get through this would be to show how unbothered he was. As he reentered the break area, he slapped his round midsection and bellowed, "Ho, ho, ho. Merry Christmas. Who's first to sit on Santa's lap?"

"Hey, Cole, there's someone here to see you." Andrew's voice cut through where Ben sang along to the Christmas music still playing on the overhead speaker.

Looking over, Cole saw the pretty young woman standing next to his best bud, looking toward him with wide, surprised hazel eyes and her shiny hair—light brown streaked with gold—falling around her shoulders. She wore jeans, midcalf boots, and a red sweater with a big cartoonish reindeer face on it, and her jaw was hanging open as her gaze met his.

A hard punch landed deep in Cole's gut, making his breath whoosh out from between the white hair that surrounded his lips.

Sophie Grace Davis.

He almost took a step back from the impact of her expressive eyes. Which was saying a lot because Cole usually ran *into* the face of danger, not away from it. Always had, and he suspected he always would. And for some reason, meeting

Sophie's eyes felt exactly the same as all those times he'd seen danger straight ahead.

Not that Cole knew Sophie. Not really. They'd briefly met over the summer at Andrew's Grandma Ruby's Fourth of July picnic and had bumped into each other a few times around town in the months since then. All of which Cole could recount in vivid detail, even if he'd barely said two words to her.

Seeing Sophie always left him a bit discombobulated, uncomfortably aware that he was too stiff and awkward. But seeing her while wearing a furry red suit that didn't properly fit, with the wig and beard that mostly covered his face, and with his great entrance comment...yeah, could this day possibly get any worse?

Not in a million years had Sophie Davis expected to see Cole Aaron dressed up as Santa Claus. Why hadn't Chief warned her?

Of course, Sophie had instantly recognized Cole. As much as she'd tried, she'd not forgotten his pale, almost icy, blue eyes, or how ruggedly well-built he was—which even the costume couldn't fully disguise.

Nor had she forgotten how standoffish he'd been on the few occasions their paths had crossed. She'd taken the hint and avoided him the last few times she'd spotted him around town, and she was well aware he'd done the same.

"Here to give Santa your Christmas list?" Andrew teased, standing next to her with his arms crossed. Their families were friends, but Andrew was several years older than her, so they'd never been close. They just occasionally saw each other at family and town events.

Family friend or not, she felt like elbowing him at his teasing.

Taking a deep breath and forcing a smile, she kept her gaze locked with Cole's. "No, but I am here to return something of Cole's."

Had he even realized what he'd done? That he'd accidentally donated his journal for the church's Christmas fundraising rummage sale?

"Wouldn't happen to be eight reindeer and a sleigh, would it?" Barely smothering his laughter, Andrew rocked back on his heels.

"She kinda looks like one of Santa's reindeer herself," another teased. "Hey, Cole? You missing a cute reindeer to lead your sleigh?"

Heat rushing into her cheeks, Sophie glanced down at her bright red Christmas sweater with its big, flashing red nosed reindeer. It was one of her favorites, and this was her first time wearing it this Christmas season. Was it too soon to have turned on the battery-operated nose?

On the other hand, Cole was wearing a Santa suit, so what was a snazzy Christmas sweater in the grand scheme of feeling self-conscious? It wasn't as if she hadn't felt self-conscious every other time their paths had crossed, too.

She gave him a pleading look. "Is there somewhere private we could talk a few minutes?"

"Hey, Sophie. Santa Cole been threatening you with the naughty list, too? Doesn't he know your name is written in permanent ink at the top of Santa's nice list?"

At hearing the familiar, friendly voice, Sophie smiled at Ben Preston. How had she not noticed he was helping decorate the cutest fire department–themed Christmas tree ever?

Then again, Cole had always had a knack for capturing all her attention, and that was *before* she'd realized he was her wounded warrior.

"Hey, Ben." Sophie had always liked the good-natured man she'd known since high school. He'd been a couple of years ahead in her dear friend Sarah's class rather than Sophie's, but they'd all hung out together in their church's youth group. Ben's frequent smiles, sparkly dark eyes, and his love of God, had impressed Sophie. She'd crushed on him a bit in high school, but she'd missed the boat; the only time he'd shown interest, she'd had other obligations. Now, she could only see him as a friend.

"No, Cole...er, Santa Cole, hasn't threatened me with the naughty list."

Ben smiled and went to stand near Cole, who'd not taken a step or said a word since spotting her.

"Good to know he hasn't been bothering you."

Not unless one counted how his written words tore at her peace of mind and invaded her dreams. If those were factored in, then Cole had bothered her a great deal.

Cole studied her with an intensity that didn't at all match his white wig locks, bushy white brows, and thick fake mustache and beard. "There must be some mistake," he said. "How could you have something of mine?"

Not wanting to explain where everyone could overhear, she replied, "I promise I'll only take a few minutes of your time if you'll humor me a bit in private, please."

"See, that Santa suit is already bringing you good luck." Ben elbowed Cole's arm and earned a quick glare. "Go talk to the lady."

Ignoring Ben and looking puzzled, Cole's gaze held hers. "Okay if I go change first?"

Sophie nodded, because, really, what else could she do?

One of Sophie's favorite Christmas carols came on and she attempted to let the song ease her mounting nerves at just standing in the large, open area of the firehall where the men were gathered. Surely, thoughts of Santa being up on the housetop would calm her jitteriness.

But it wasn't working. Because Cole was now Santa in her head. A Santa in desperate need of a good seamstress, which she just so happened to be.

Sucking in a deep breath, which triggered a grin from Andrew who still stood next to her, Sophie ditched him to walk over to where Ben had returned to decorating the tree. "How's LaTonya doing?"

Ben smiled at the mention of his twin. "Living the lawyer high life in Louisville as she fights for justice for all." Visibly proud, Ben told of his latest phone conversation with his sister.

Sophie tried to keep her attention on him, but her mind kept straying to Cole. Maybe Ben wouldn't notice how many times she said *Mm-hmm* and *Oh, really?*

When Cole came back into the festively decorated firehall, he glanced around at the others who were watching them intently, then frowned. "We can go outside. It's not private, but it's better than being the main event in here for these jokers."

"Yes. Going outside sounds like a great idea."

Maybe she would be able to breathe better outdoors.

Sophie waved goodbye to Ben and Andrew, then smiled at Cole, grateful that she'd be able to give him the journal privately so he could tuck it away if he didn't want the others to see.

His coworkers might already know about his time in the military, but if not, he should be the one to decide who knew about the things he'd gone through. No one else.

Which made her feel a smidge guilty at having

read his journal in the first place, but there had been no name. She'd only meant to read enough to try to figure out whose diary it was, but once she'd started, the pages had beckoned to her with a call she hadn't been able to resist.

Even after reading it completely, she'd still not found a name. All she'd known was that the author was a male Marine who'd seen and endured too much, just as her father had. Not having a name or a face to assign to the journal meant that the connection between the two men had blurred.

For a week, the intense journal had haunted her. Nightly, she'd picked it up to reread passages that had left her chilled and aching for the man who'd written the heart-wrenching words. Who was he? Where was he? Had he pieced his life back together or...or had the darkness overtaken him as it had her father?

Only when she'd found the Christmas card tucked into a crossword puzzle book that had also been in the donated box had she realized the writer's identity. Discovering that the quiet, stoic man she'd briefly met at Ruby Jenkin's Fourth of July party was the wounded warrior monopolizing her every waking thought had been a surprise.

Apparently, Cole was full of surprises. She certainly wouldn't have expected to find the man whose journal she'd read wearing a Santa suit and teasing his coworkers.

Maybe she should have insisted that he keep wearing the suit. Talking to Santa Cole had to be easier than talking to Gorgeous Fireman with a Tormented Past Cole.

Her stomach was a fluttery tangle of nerves.

She shouldn't be nervous at all. Her palms shouldn't be clammy. Her heart shouldn't be racing. She snuck a glance toward Cole and gulped.

He made her feel giddy and feminine and a whole lot nervous. He'd had that effect on her even before she'd read his journal, and now that she'd read it, she wanted to help him.

Needed to help him.

Not that he looked as if he needed help. Now that he was out of his Santa suit, he looked tough, handsome—a bit dangerous, even, as if he could take on the world and win.

He wore the standard black uniform pants and a polo shirt with the firehall emblem over his heart and short sleeves that accentuated his muscles. His dark brown hair was cut in a no-nonsense short style. His eyes—a Siberian Husky pale blue with a darker, deep blue rim—flashed with intelligence, curiosity, and annoyance.

On the outside, Cole was a good-looking, well-put-together firefighter who had probably started more than a few fires in the hearts of Pine Hill's female population. Hadn't she noticed him at the picnic and every time their paths had crossed since?

But now, Sophie knew the heartache his handsome exterior hid.

Catching her not-so-sneaky peek in his direction, Cole's brow rose. "Did I misunderstand you a minute ago? Are you here to pick something up from me rather than give something back? I told the lady on the phone I'd drop the money for the poinsettias by the nursing home. Did they need the check right away?"

Poinsettias? He was the one who had donated the money to buy the poinsettias for the nursing home residents? She'd heard someone had, but—

Sophie half-tripped over her own feet and almost face-planted on the concrete firehall floor. She steadied herself in time that she didn't think he noticed her lapse as they stepped outside into the sunshine. Or if he did notice, he didn't let on.

A soft mid-November breeze blew, tickling her face with her hair.

"I'm not here about the poinsettias or money," she began, tucking the stray strands behind her ears in hopes of keeping them at bay. "And you didn't misunderstand me. I found something that belongs to you, and I'm here to return it."

She reached into her bag and pulled out his journal that had the Christmas card tucked inside it.

"This is yours, isn't it?"

Cole's gaze dropped to what Sophie held. A sucker punch rammed into his stomach, knocking his breath out of him and leaving him going-to-retch-his-insides-out nauseated.

He could stare down an enemy holding an AK-47 and not flinch, but the book that Sophie held made his knees weak.

"Where did you get that?" he growled, barely managing not to snatch the book from her hands to hurl it aside, like a grenade that needed to be thrown as far away as possible for everyone's safety.

For *his* safety.

Sophie winced. He felt a pang of regret over the harsh tone he'd used, but he couldn't formulate words to apologize. The beauty from the BBQ had his journal.

"I found it at Pine Hill Church in a box of books."

The sinking sickness pitched back and forth in his stomach, making him wish he'd forgone his protein shake that morning. His journal had been in the stuff he'd dropped off at the church?

"I, well, when I realized whose it was..." Her nervousness was palpable as she sank her teeth into her lower lip and looked up at him with hesitation. "I knew you'd want it back." She gave a little shrug of both shoulders. "So here I am."

"You were wrong." Bile rising in his throat, he gestured to the abomination she held. "I don't want that."

Further confusion darkened her eyes. "But..."

"Look." He ran his fingers through his hair,

still not completely used to having anything more than stubble after years of keeping his dark hair buzzed. "I'm sorry you wasted your time. You should've just thrown it out. That book's nothing but garbage."

Lots and lots of scribbled garbage a chaplain had suggested he get out of his head by pouring it into the journal the man had gifted to Cole. Not for the first time, Cole regretted giving in to that advice. Seeing everything written out just made him more disgusted with himself, causing the memories to hang even heavier on his shoulders.

Why hadn't he burned the book rather than packing it with the things he'd brought with him to Pine Hill? The mere act of destroying the journal might have gone further in annihilating his memories than putting them onto paper ever had.

"But," Sophie began again, her eyes wide and her voice a little trembly. "But it's…I mean, well, it's—"

"Garbage," he repeated, cramming his hands into his pants pockets and clenching his short nails into his palms as deeply as they'd go. He just wanted away from their conversation, away from the book that felt like his personal Achilles' heel—the weak spot in his defenses that could ruin everything good he'd patched his broken life with. "Throw it away."

"I…"

At her indecision, understanding dawned.

"You read it, didn't you?" Cole felt a fool for not immediately realizing. A new wave of nausea spread through him, popping sweat beads out over his skin despite the crisp November air.

Wide-eyed, her lips parted but no sound came out. No matter. She didn't need to say the words. The truth was written all over her face.

One of the things Cole most enjoyed about being in Pine Hill was that no one knew of his past. Chief had some idea, and the guys had picked up on a little thanks to Cole's occasional nightmares, but none of them were in on the nitty-gritty details.

In Pine Hill, he was seen as a man who volunteered his time and energy to everything the firehall was asked to participate in; a man who put his life on the line to save others.

If, while out battling those fires, he fought inner demons, trying to quench them the way he and his crew squelched nearly uncontrollable blazes from time to time, well, no one needed to know that but him.

Only, Sophie had read about his bleakest moments—and his biggest mistake. She knew the truth.

"I'm sorry," she said, looking truly remorseful that she'd pried between the pages of his private hell. "I opened it thinking I might find a name so I could return it, but there wasn't one." Grimacing, she continued. "And, well, the truth is that once I started reading, I couldn't stop."

She'd read it all. Of course, she'd read it all. She probably thought him a monster.

As much as he wanted to look away, he didn't. Jaw locked tight, he kept his gaze unyielding as it met hers. He could handle whatever judgement she placed on him.

Lord knew she couldn't judge him any more harshly than he judged himself.

"How did you figure out it was mine?"

"There was a Christmas card addressed to you inside a crossword puzzle book that came from the same box. I stuck the card there, inside your journal."

Without looking at the book, he knew the one she meant. Why had he kept the photo card his mother had sent?

"Toss it as well."

"But..." she paused, "You're sure?"

"Positive." He didn't want the sentimental reminder of the family he'd never felt a part of any more than he wanted the journal. His mother had her new life, as did his father, complete with new families. There wasn't a place for him in that picture—but at least they were happy. That was enough for Cole.

"I'm so sorry for what you went through," Sophie said softly, hugging the journal to her as if she was clinging to the book in effort to keep her hands to herself. As if she wanted to reach out to him.

He didn't need or want her pity. He'd rather

she screamed and yelled at him for his failures. Feeling sorry for him? That, he couldn't take. He wasn't some emotional charity case needing her Christmastime goodwill.

He was fine.

Frustration and anger that she'd read his journal burned, taking hold and quickly consuming him. The rational part of him knew it was his fault for not realizing the journal was in the donated box, but in this moment, rational thinking didn't matter. That book had never been meant for anyone to read, and especially not the bubbly, full-of-goodness woman he'd met over the summer. She never should have been exposed to the pure ugliness marring the pages. Marring him.

When he spoke again, he kept his voice low and steady. "I get that you didn't know who the journal belonged to, so you read it. Fine. Go back to your life-is-a-bed-of-roses existence and forget everything you read."

Wincing a little, she shook her head. "I can't do that."

Surprised at how her gaze hadn't wavered from his when he'd expected her to walk away and never waste another breath on him again, Cole frowned. "What's that supposed to mean?"

Her chock-full-of-emotion gaze studied his. "I won't forget what you wrote as long as I live."

"Then I'm the one who's sorry." No one should be subjected to his failings. Not in real life. Not in writing. "But that doesn't mean I want the book back. Thanks, but no thanks." He couldn't bring himself to look at the journal clutched to her chest, much less to touch the worn leather book.

"Do the world a favor and throw the thing in the trash. Or better yet, burn it." Even Superman has his Kryptonite, he reminded himself, determined he would not let this drag him down into a place he never wanted to return to. "I don't care so long as you get rid of it because I never want to see that book, or you, again."

Read the book!
Wrapped Up in Christmas Joy is available now!